ONE

Mid-May

The taxi slowed to a stop, the driver's eyes moving to the house on his left. Others he had passed as he drove into the area had told him that it took serious money to live here. He glanced at the dashboard clock: eleven fifty-six p.m. He yawned, blinked, listening for sounds of preparatory movements behind him, getting none. He eyed her in his rear-view mirror. She was just sitting there. He had sensed she was trouble within a couple of minutes of picking her up. He had to drag an address out of her. Once he had it, he realized it was beyond the city boundary. Things hadn't improved during the drive, and now she was making no move to get out. Tired, his general mood dipping lower, he gave a verbal nudge.

'This the house, love?'

Even in this area, it demanded you look at it. He did. Big didn't cover it. Distanced from other houses. Ultra-modern. A lot of glass. It felt as though it was looking down at him. He gave her another quick glance. She had to be worth some serious money. 'This the one?'

His irritation spiked, his double shift catching up with him. His initial view of her had suggested late forties or early fifties at a push. Attractive. Well dressed. The kind who could afford a hefty tip. His sole reason for diverting her to his taxi. Once she was inside it, having got an address out of her, she had sat there, silent to all conversational openers about the weather and whatever play she had just seen. Not that he cared. It had stayed that way for the whole journey, and she was still giving him the same routine. He felt a quick stab of resentment. A bit of civility cost nothing. Cab-driving was a hard enough game without passengers acting as if you didn't exist. He wanted to be rid of her.

He glanced at the house again. Anybody who could afford to live in a place like this had no right to be so bloody miserable. He checked his meter. £15.60.

'That'll be twenty-eight sixty.' Still she sat, not moving, staring at the house. He sent another verbal prod in her direction. 'I said, twenty-eight pounds—'

The passenger door opened. He watched her get out. If she had already paid him, he would be gone, leaving her to it. He frowned at the windscreen. Light, misting rain was falling now. He slid down the window closest to her.

'OK, love? Home now, yeah?'

She was still staring at the bloody house, but now she looked as though she was shaking. He had learned a lot from cabbing. You could mostly never tell from an initial glance at somebody that there was a problem. With this one, though, he was getting the mental health message loud and clear. If he was right, there was no way he was getting involved. He shoved open his door and got out. 'Listen, love, you're my last fare. I need to get back to Brum, so give me—'

'Come inside with me . . . *please.*'

There had been a time when those words would have been music. Or a way of passing the odd half hour. Depending on the woman, of course. And his own situation. Now, all he wanted was to be out of the sodding rain, inside his cab and away. He hesitated, his eyes moving slowly over the house. No sign of a CCTV set-up, but that didn't mean there wasn't one. He glanced at houses some distance away. If you lived here, it's what you would have fitted, pronto. Which was a problem. If he drove off right now and left her, and she *was* a headcase and had a funny turn, collapsed right there on her drive, there was a risk that he would be identified as her last known contact. He knew cabbies it had happened to.

'Sorry, love. Can't be done. Company policy, but I'll see you to the door, OK? Call it twenty quid and I'll be on my way.'

She opened her handbag, pulled out keys, then a purse, took out a wad of notes from it and held it towards him. He looked at it with a quick, practised eye, took it from her and walked her towards the house, hearing what sounded to him like a soft laugh. Edgy now, he looked up at the house. A shadow was moving slowly across one pale upstairs blind. Somebody was home. Pushing the wad of notes in his pocket, he rang the bell, left her standing at the front door, returned to his taxi and climbed inside, wanting to be done with her before she or whoever was waiting

REFLECTIONS OF DEVIANCE

A.J. Cross

**SEVERN
HOUSE**

First world edition published in Great Britain and the USA in 2023
by Severn House, an imprint of Canongate Books Ltd,
14 High Street, Edinburgh EH1 1TE.

Trade paperback edition first published in Great Britain and the USA in 2023
by Severn House, an imprint of Canongate Books Ltd.

severnhouse.com

British Library Cataloguing-in-Publication Data
A CIP catalogue record for this title is available from the British Library.

ISBN-13: 978-1-4483-0800-2 (cased)
ISBN-13: 978-1-4483-0802-6 (trade paper)
ISBN-13: 978-1-4483-0801-9 (e-book)

Typeset by Palimpsest Book Production Ltd.,
Falkirk, Stirlingshire, Scotland.

for her realized how much money she had given him. He pulled away without a backward glance, followed the curve of the road, then swore, a sudden urgency bringing him to a halt. He got out, headed for some nearby trees. After a minute or two, relieved and zipped, he walked back, giving the house a final look. The front door was open. She was going inside. He got back inside his cab, took the wad of notes from his pocket and checked it. Fifty quid.

Inside her house, Marion Cane was thinking about her car, a few walls away inside her garage. She would get it out. Drive back to the city. Find a hotel. It had been months since she had driven the Porsche. It took her several seconds to recall why. She had sold it. She went into the kitchen, filled a glass with ice-cold water, drank it, forcing herself to breathe, then to the huge sitting room, its ceiling so high that it had thrilled her when she first saw it. Now, it gave her vertigo. This house was to have been the start of her new life. Away from streets filled with siren screams and traders who knew the value of nothing. Until the bubble burst on a tidal wave of reality, wrecking everybody's dreams of a better tomorrow, London soon to be engulfed in a similar tsunami of chaos. She had finally traded the life she had loved for the peace and sanctuary of this house, a quiet way of being and living that she would relish in this idyll, separated by barely four miles of greenness and smooth tarmac from the nearest heavily populated Birmingham suburb, its name once synonymous with car production, now an opportunity wasteland. Yet this area thrived, clutching its silky hems and its prosperity to itself. Moving slowly to the Persian rug at the centre of the huge room, she gazed down at its intricate patterns woven in wools of rich yellows mixed with browns and blues, remembering the feel of it against her cheek. Heat swept over her face, her chest. Her mind often failed in its recall, but her body remembered. Her eyes moved slowly to the small, brown bottle on a low table, then up to her own reflection in the mirror and the small, brightly coloured squares of paper bearing words of comfort. The door behind her opened. Without turning, she watched him approach, open his arms and enfold her, his eyes on her, his face next to hers.

He whispered, 'You look tired.' He pointed to one of the

colourful squares. 'Have you read what I left for you? Even when I'm not here, you have my thoughts and my love.'

She stared at their reflected faces and knew she would never be free from him. The Devil was here to stay.

TWO

Wednesday, 13 November. 7.25 a.m.

The lightest touch of hand against skin, arms, legs entwined in the darkness, carrying them on a rushing wave. Two phones beeped in unison from their respective sides of the bed. She silenced hers and, on a quick roll, did the same to his, then looked down at him through her mass of blonde curls, lowered her face and kissed him on the mouth.

He held her. 'Where were we?' he whispered.

She took his hands in hers. 'I *think*, somewhere around . . . here.'

His phone beeped again. He reached for it. 'Hi, John. Tomorrow? I'm lecturing from eleven thirty until three p.m. How about half an hour after that?'

He ended the call.

'What does John Heritage want?'

'He didn't say. Probably a case he wants me to consult on.'

He smiled down at her, felt her hands move over his chest then down. Reaching for her hair, he kissed her face, her eyes, and pulled the duvet over them both, enclosing them in their private place.

9.40 a.m.

Detective Chief Inspector Bernard Watts was sitting opposite Superintendent John Heritage, his newly appointed boss. They were discussing Watts' most recent investigation which had resulted in a whole-life sentence for a man who had murdered two young women, its length attesting to the abominable cruelty he had inflicted on them. Three other women had met a similar end at his hands, but the court had not held him responsible for their destruction. All the indications were that they were dead, but Watts and his investigative team had failed to find any trace of them. He could recall a time, very early in his career, when evidence was almost routinely fabricated. He had never done it. He was a rule follower. Had long accepted that endings weren't always neat. He knew that he and his team had done all that it was possible to do within the law to gain justice. Yet, even now, months after, the case filled him with anger. He switched back to listening mode. Heritage was sounding upbeat.

'. . . that you fully accept the great result you and your officers achieved and that all of you recognize that accomplishment.'

'Sir.'

'Bernard, if there's any need for support via Human Resources for you or anyone else involved, I'll arrange it.'

It was widely known at headquarters that Watts wanted out of the job, but he was determined that it would be on his own terms. Which didn't include getting involved with HR and a likely referral for psychological evaluation. When he did retire, it would be without questions hanging over his emotional status or abilities.

'No, sir. All's fine.' He watched a number of A4 pages slide towards him.

'Good. There's something I want followed up. A death six months ago, just south-west of Birmingham. Newton Heights, to be exact. Do you know it?'

Watts reached for the A4s. 'No.'

'Marion Cane, aged fifty-nine, single woman.' He pointed. 'That death certificate indicates she died of heart disease.'

Watts absorbed details: *Some limited plaques within the blood vessels suggesting ischaemic heart disease* . . . 'On the young side, but it happens.' He looked at Heritage. 'Why are we interested?'

'Take a look at the sheet underneath.'

Watts did. A letter of sorts, addressed to headquarters. No date. Brief. Unsigned. A few handprinted words suggesting that Marion Cane's death required investigation.

'It arrived three days ago.'

Watts frowned. 'Six months is a long time to wait.'

'There's nothing on it to identify the sender. I want you in Newton Heights making a few subtle inquiries.'

In Watts' many years of experience, anonymous communications were rarely acted upon and then only when they gave something. There was nothing in what he had just read that provided any incentive to get involved. He said so.

'I agree,' said Heritage. 'I still want you taking a look at it. You know why.'

Watts did. A visit to the area in response to this unsigned letter would be recorded. A testament to the willingness of West Midlands Police to follow up on all available information. 'Marion Cane was a very wealthy woman. I want to be certain that that note is irrelevant, that there's nothing about her death that we should know. Your contact is the deceased's sister, a Mrs Janine Franklin. These are her details.' He pushed them across the desk, his hand still on them. 'How is PC Judd?' Heritage was back to the previous homicide investigation and Human Resources territory. Things had gone very wrong for Judd, but she had dealt with it. Was dealing with it.

'She's fine, sir.'

'Good. I want her on this with you. She needs to be kept busy. Make it sometime today.'

Getting a speculative look from Heritage, Watts guessed another question was on his mind. One Heritage had raised some months before, about Judd's promotion plans. Or, rather, the lack of them. Watts knew why. He knew Judd probably better than most at headquarters. He knew what others didn't, that she'd had a tough start in life. Parental neglect in her early years had led to her being taken into care at seven, which probably saved her. What it hadn't done was remove its legacy, part of which was a rampant fear of not measuring up. Judd feared failure. He gave Heritage a quick glance, hoping that he wasn't planning to question Judd directly. If he did, he would find out something else about her. She had no filter. What she did have was a capacity for expressive language, via which Heritage would receive her views on privacy and people she saw as overstepping. In the brief time since he had arrived here, he had shown himself to be a boss who expected a lot but was also reasonable and sympathetic. Yet even he had his limits. A mouthful from Judd would go way beyond them.

Picking up the A4s, Watts stood. 'I'll crack on with this, sir.'

Reaching Reception, he paused at the desk. 'Is Chloe Judd in?'

'Not due till eleven, sir.'

That 'sir' was inside Watts' head as he came into his office. Heritage, formerly of Oxford police, had been here three months. Consensus was that headquarters had landed on its feet when he took over from Brophy. The only change he had insisted on to date was that all officers be addressed by rank, in Watts' case as either 'Detective Chief Inspector', 'Sir' or the least favoured, 'Boss'. 'Sarge' was no longer acceptable. Watts' previous super-intendent had had no quarrel with it. Brophy's sole focus was investigative progress or lack of it, which invariably involved whipping his own and everybody else's tension to near breaking point. He had retired the previous June, returned to the Thames Valley area where, two months later and halfway through inflicting a third stripe on an already pristine lawn, he had collapsed. Dead before he hit the grass. It confirmed Watts' own view of life. He wanted out of the job while he still had one.

Inside his office, waiting for the kettle to heat up, he added a generous spoon of instant coffee to a mug, followed it with three equally generous sugars, plus dried milk. He poured boiling water, watched it billow and turn from black to a pleasing dark tan. A quick stir, sip and nod, and he took it to the table where he sat. A second glance at the death certificate and the anonymous note, a quick time-check, and he reached for his phone, tapped a number and waited. He got Judd's voice. There was an edge to it.

'Yeah, *what?*'

'If you're not in sight of this building, you're *late.*' He picked up faint metallic tapping sounds. 'And if that's the latest music you're into, I'd think again.'

'Sassy's escaped. I can't leave her outside. She's too little.'

There was a time, very early on, before he got to know her, that he might have considered it an apt description for Judd herself.

'Sassy? I thought you'd settled on Whoopsie?'

'It's a rethink. I don't want her self-concept wrecked by a few kitten errors.'

'I'm on my way to your place. Heritage has given us a job.'

Twelve minutes later, he was standing on decking, arms folded against damp cold, looking through mist as Judd searched small shrubs, calling the cat's name, clattering a fork against the inside of a tin. A sudden pounce and scoop, and she straightened, face flushed, the kitten pressed to her chest. She looked down at it. 'Remember what I said, Sass? *I* call. *You* come. Got it?' The kitten responded with a tiny headbutt against Judd's chin. She grinned, hugged it.

Inside the house, Watts watched her cross the kitchen and gently place the kitten in its basket with a furry toy, surrounded by newspaper, a pristine litter tray close by. She straightened. He caught her glance at the lower half of his face and sent her a repressive look. She ignored it.

'Still there, Sarge. When I saw you last Friday, it was coming off, cos I said it made you look older.'

'Wrong on both counts. This is protest hair, on account of I'm still working.' He sent a nod in the cat's direction. 'She looks like she's got all her mod cons. Let's get going.'

He drove, relishing the sweet lavender smell of the BMW X5's interior. He had had it deluxe-valeted inside and out the previous day. Frowning at moisture beads gathering on the windscreen, he switched on wipers, took a quick glance at Judd. During the three years that they had worked together, Judd's default position to anything work-related was to start a stream of questions. He'd tried to view it as keenness, but also found it distracting and irritating. He had had few questions from her since their last case. That wasn't the only change. He took another glance. Gone was the immovable blonde quiff upsweep with dark roots. It was now replaced by soft-looking blonde hair cut in a fringe, smooth sides curving around her face. A bob, according to his partner, headquarters' in-house pathologist, Connie Chong. There was a lot that was different about Judd. The investigation referred to earlier by Heritage had led Watts and his team to someone they had never considered capable of such purposeful cruelty. Not so, Will Traynor, criminologist. His know-how and logical approach had eventually led to the arrest. It had hit Judd the hardest. The arrested man was someone she thought she wanted in her life. Until she realized who and what he really was. He checked his mirror, changed lanes. 'We're on our way to a place in the Rednal area. Newton Heights.'

Her eyes stayed fixed on the scene flashing past her window. 'Sounds posh.'

'It's a village—'

'I hate villages. All that olde-worlde, cottagey-thatched crap where nothing ever happens.' She waited. 'What happened?' 'A woman died there.'

They continued on in silence, Watts eventually making a left turn on to a rural lane, over a small bridge, then slowing to enter a wide asphalt space. The car park of the local pub. He switched off the ignition, squinted up at the signage: The Running Man.

'We'll walk it from here. I want to get the feel of the place.'

They got out of the BMW's warmth into dull mist. He had checked out the area online. There was marshland somewhere around. You wouldn't catch him buying property close to anything like that. Just the thing if you wanted backache. Which he didn't. Hands thrust deep into the pockets of his heavy jacket, he started walking, his eyes narrowing on the phone Judd was now scrutinizing.

'Ready to be briefed?'

The phone disappeared.

'There's not much to tell. Six months ago, a woman named Marion Cane died here.'

'Of?' asked Judd, reverting very slightly to type.

'Heart disease.'

'So? Why are we—?'

'Because Heritage is the boss and it's what he wants. And because of this.' He pulled a transparent plastic wallet from his pocket, the anonymous note inside. She took it, read the few words. 'I'm still stuck on "So?" All this says is that this woman's death needs to be looked at. No reason given. Anything found on it?'

'Heritage hasn't bothered to test it.'

'Oh, yeah? That shows how relevant *he* thinks it is. You know what this is, don't you? *Busywork.* It's Heritage box-ticking.' They walked on in silence. 'Did he say anything about me? If he did, I want to know.'

'You didn't feature.' He gave her a sideways glance. 'I thought you liked him?'

'I do, but I'm no idiot. I know when we're being fobbed off with what looks like a job.' She waited, guessing he knew more than he was saying. 'Come on, Sarge. You've checked her out, this Cane woman, right?'

'There's plenty online about her. She was highly successful in the financial world. Jobs all over the place. London. New York.'

Judd the feminist arrived, her small fist raised. 'Yo!'

He knew she had a streak of ambition a mile wide. He wasn't about to tell her that Heritage was again querying her seeming lack of interest in promotion. He stuck with the business at hand. 'Cane returned from New York to the UK a few years back to do the same work in London. After some more years, she decides to chuck it all in.'

Judd's head shot up. 'Why, if she was that successful?'

He was about to respond that years of hard work and the success that went with it might have a downside, but knowing that it wouldn't fit with her philosophy, that she wouldn't get it, he said nothing. They walked on, Judd's head turning this way and that.

'Dead posh, Sarge, plus dead boring, if you want my opinion.' Her eyes settled on two well-dressed young women pushing expensive-looking buggies. 'At least not everybody living here is a hundred years old, but, after New York and London, why would Cane choose *this* place?'

'Marion Cane had one close relative, a married sister, Janine Franklin—'

'Who lives here. Got it.'

They continued, taking in more extensive, well-spaced homes. Watts pointed to a house still some distance away, backed by tall firs. 'That's where Marion Cane lived and where she died.'

Judd slowed, her eyes fixed on it. 'Holy f—!'

'Step on it. The Franklins are expecting us.'

They walked on, Judd sending backward glances to the house as they passed. They reached the wide frontage of a bungalow beyond an open five-bar gate, two cars parked on the drive, one a dark-blue Mercedes, the other a mint-green Volkswagen Beetle, both pristine.

Within five minutes, they were inside a warm conservatory overlooking a gentle sweep of open land, mist thick in some low-lying areas. Watts had introduced himself and Judd to Janine Franklin and her husband, John – he silent, she fretting and now verging on a tizz.

'I'm *sorry*, Detective Chief Inspector, but I *still* don't understand why you're *here*. Why would the police be *remotely* interested in my sister's death after all this *time*?'

Having anticipated the question, he said, 'It's not that unusual for us to make a few inquiries about a death from natural causes.'

Behind her professional face, Judd heard this as news but nodded confirmation to the Franklins.

Watts added, 'We'd appreciate knowing a bit more about your sister.'

Franklin glanced at her husband.

'We were both absolutely *shocked* by Marion's death, weren't we, John? It was so *sudden*. She was four years older than me, but fifty-nine isn't *old* these days, and Marion was *fit*. She walked *everywhere*, gardened, took *Pilates* classes.'

His scalp tightening at each emphasis, guessing that Franklin was the type who lived in italics, Watts asked, 'Did she mention any health concerns to you?'

'*No, none*. She talked about feeling *stressed* sometimes, but who *isn't*, and that was only in passing.'

Watts studied her. 'You were surprised at what happened?'

She sent him a look. 'If you mean her dying, that's exactly what I'm *saying*. It was *totally* unexpected, wasn't it, John?'

Her husband's eyes went to the window and stayed there. 'Yes.'

'Did she tell you what she was stressed about?'

Franklin shook her head. 'My sister wasn't the kind to indulge in personal talk. She was a *very* independent person. *Very* clever. *Very* confident. She had to be, to do the job she did and be so *successful*.' She gazed at Watts. 'But she's been dead *six* months. I *still* don't understand why you're taking an interest *now*.'

'Just a routine thing, Mrs Franklin. There's a lot of that in police work. How long had your sister been living here in Newton Heights when she died?'

'Marion quit her job in London and settled here a couple of years ago, didn't she, John? She told me that she had had enough of the work she was doing. *Nobody* makes the sort of money my sister earned unless the job they're doing is *highly* demanding. She had only herself to please; she was wealthy, *free* to make her own choices, which she *did*, and she retired.'

'Why did she choose Newton Heights?' asked Watts, already knowing the answer. Franklin shrugged. 'I was her only close family and she liked the area. She stayed with us a couple of times when she was on leave from her New York job, *didn't* she, John?'

Fed up of the italics and now ready to leave, Watts asked, 'Where did her death occur?'

'At her *house*. It's some distance along the road from here.'

'She was alone at the time?'

Franklin sent him a frown. 'I'd have thought that my earlier comments would have indicated that Marion lived alone. It was her cleaner who found her.'

'Do you know the cleaner's name?'

'Theresa Yates. I believe she goes by the name *Terry*. That's all I know about her, but the landlord of the local pub can probably tell you more. She also works there.'

'So, your sister's death was a shock, yet one you accepted?'

'Of *course*. John travels a lot for his work, which is similar to Marion's, so he wasn't here, but when I got the death certificate stating that it was due to natural causes with some reference to her heart, it suddenly made *sense*, given her years of work in the financial world. A *very* high-stress environment, apparently.'

'Did your sister ever refer to a health problem?'

'Marion was a *very* private person, even with me, but she did mention going to see her GP. I need to think about what she said – something about dizziness, rapid heartbeat, difficulty concentrating, that sort of thing. She didn't sound at all worried about it.' She looked at her husband. 'Can *you* remember me telling you anything else, John?'

'No.'

'Is your sister's house on the market?'

'No, but it *should* be. The estate agents have all they need – details and photos – but we're *still* waiting for the probate process to finalize. Her house is just as she left it. I suppose I should have her belongings removed but the house has a security system fitted, so I haven't got around to it. She had a will, of course. *Very* organized, my sister. She left everything to *me*, but we're in no hurry in regard to the house, are we, John?' She looked at Watts, then Judd. 'Would you like to see some photographs of her?'

Her husband frowned. 'I doubt the police are interested in the kind of photos we have.'

Watts nodded. 'If it's no trouble.'

Giving her husband a triumphant look, Janine Franklin left the room. They waited in silence. She returned within a couple of minutes, holding a small box which she placed on the low table between them. She removed the lid and picked up the topmost photograph. 'There aren't *that* many, actually. Mostly ones she sent me.' She passed the photograph to Watts. He and Judd looked down at a shapely blonde woman wearing a white sweater beneath black salopettes, mirrored sunglasses shielding her eyes, even white teeth displayed in a wide smile.

'*That* was taken in Colorado when she was on holiday. Let me see, she would have been in her early fifties or thereabouts when *that* was taken, but she didn't change much from then to when she died.'

'Who took the photograph?' asked Judd.

Franklin shrugged. 'I've no idea.'

She removed more photographs, laid them in front of them, pointing at one. '*That's* her house here.'

Watts and Judd looked down at the house they had seen earlier. To Watts' eye, it was an odd mix of the ultra-modern and the traditional, with its extensive glass and red-tiled, gabled roof, the mix suggesting it couldn't make up its mind about itself. Franklin reached for the photograph and shook her head.

'To me, it *never* looked like a home, but Marion *adored* it.'

She glanced at her husband who was looking at his watch, then back to Watts and Judd. 'Actually, we have a couple of *friends* arriving in half an hour. Here, take the photos with you.' She returned them to the box, replaced the lid and slid it across the table. Watts reached for it. 'We appreciate your help, Mrs Franklin.'

'Not at *all*.'

'We'll let you have them back in a day or so.'

They retraced their steps to the pub, Watts murmuring, 'I'd have developed a tic if I'd had to listen to that for another minute.'

Judd's voice drifted to him on the chill air. 'Not too bothered about her sister's death, is she?'

He glanced down at her. 'She's had six months to get used to it. Fancy a hot drink?'

'Like, you need to ask? Cappuccino. It might stop me getting pneumonia.'

He tapped the box he was carrying. 'If it's not crowded in that pub where we parked, we'll take a look at these.'

'What are we looking for?'

'I want to know who Marion Cane was, this high-flyer, big earner and big spender if her house is anything to go by, because I didn't get much else from her sister or brother-in-law.'

'We got *zilch* from *him.*'

'Don't you start with the italics.'

They passed by what had been Marion Cane's house without comment. Coming inside The Running Man, they found it deserted except for an elderly man, a small dog snoozing at his feet.

Judd chose a distant table and Watts went to the bar. The young woman behind it was dressed mostly in black, with heavy, black eyeliner, dark lipstick, her long hair also black, except for one vivid pink stripe, all of it in a mass around her face. He ordered the coffees, got a sullen look and headed to where Judd was sitting. He removed his coat and sat down. At least the place was warm. After a few minutes, their drinks arrived on the table with some force. Watts frowned at the young woman's back as she returned to the bar, then poured the spilt coffee from his saucer back into the cup.

Judd reached for hers. 'Looks like you didn't get a biscuit. Want this one?'

He looked at it, small and cellophane covered. 'No, thanks. Any observations?'

Judd crunched, pointing with the half-biscuit at the photographs. 'Most of them look like they were taken in America. These three here might be more recent, probably taken in London, judging by some of the buildings.'

Watts said nothing. They drank coffee.

'No offence, Sarge – *sir* – but how much time are we expected to waste on this? We've done what Heritage asked us to do – talked to the bereaved relatives. Well, one.'

He reached for the photographs, his eyes moving over them, aware of Judd getting to her feet.

'Back in a minute.'

Watts glanced up from the photographs. The elderly man they had passed earlier was also on his feet, zipping up his bulky Barbour jacket, pulling gently on his dog's lead and heading for the exit close to where Watts was sitting. He reached Watts and paused.

'You're here about Marion Cane.'

Watts stood. 'Sir, if you knew her, I'd appreciate a quick chat with you.'

The man shook his head, his voice low. 'I didn't, but I spend a lot of time walking around the area. I have some advice for you. Keep asking your questions.'

Before Watts could fully absorb the quiet words, man and dog were through one of the double doors and gone. Watts stared after him. He had to be local. It should be easy to get his name. Judd returned, reached for more photographs, gazed down at each of them, then passed them to him.

'I think some of these were taken inside the house we saw earlier. See? The windows are the same.' A short pause and she handed him another. 'Look at the furniture! That's what I call a lifestyle.'

She looked at another, this one of a dining table heavy with serving dishes, champagne bottles, a massive turkey. 'It looks like Cane liked to entertain. Has to be Christmas. If the Franklins were her only relatives, she must have invited friends and neighbours to help eat this lot.' She turned the photograph over, shook her head. 'Nope. It says here, *Thanksgiving 2000*. Obviously taken in America.' Watts gathered the photographs together, replaced them in the box.

'Come on.'

They left the pub and headed for Watts' vehicle, Watts scanning the area for the man and the dog. He didn't routinely keep information from Judd, yet the words said to him earlier barely warranted the description. He wanted to consider what the old chap had said and decide if there might be any value in it.

THREE

Same day. 3.30 p.m.

Heritage stood, extended his hand to the tall, fair-haired man coming into his office.

'Thank you for coming in, Will. Have a seat.' Heritage

also sat, looked down at his desk, straightening the files on it. 'I need to talk to you about some information I've received.'

Traynor nodded. 'You know I'm always glad to help whenever I can, John. It's good to see you again after all these years. Oxford's loss is definitely Birmingham's gain.'

Heritage took a deep breath. He had to ease into what he was about to say, beginning in safe territory. 'How is Jess?'

'She's very well, thanks.'

'And you?'

Traynor nodded. 'The same.'

'You did first-rate work for us on the most recent investigation.'

'It had its difficulties, but thanks to Bernard's team, we got the result.' He waited, his eyes on Heritage's face. 'What is it, John?' Memories of when he himself lived in Oxford came into Traynor's head, the many times he had gone to see John in Oxford after he himself had left the city, to suggest, sometimes demand, investigative ways forward in locating his missing wife.

'I have some news, Will.' He looked directly at Traynor. 'It's about Claire.' He watched the colour leave Traynor's face as he slowly stood. Heritage came quickly from behind his desk.

'Easy, Will. Sit down.'

Traynor slumped on to the chair, his hand quivering as he reached to wipe away perspiration on his forehead. Heritage leaned against the desk, his hand on Traynor's shoulder.

'I'm sorry. Oxford police rang yesterday to tell me that remains have been located. They confirmed early this morning that they belong to Claire.' A silence built between them.

'How . . . who . . .?'

'A man walking his dog on open land saw the dog taking a keen interest in a small area. He went to it and looked at what had got the dog's attention.'

Traynor closed his eyes, his face ashen.

'He reported what he saw to the police.'

'When was this?'

'Sunday.'

Traynor stared up at Heritage. 'She was found *three* days ago and no one—'

'They had to recover what was there, sample the DNA. It matches the DNA they already had for Claire.'

Traynor hung his head.

'I'm sorry I'm the one who's had to give you the news, Will. I know how hard and how long you searched for her, but at last you know where she's been for so many years.'

They stayed where they were, Heritage's hand still on Traynor's shoulder, his memory spooling back over those years: Traynor moving away from Oxford but returning often to ask about the investigation, demand that Heritage step it up. Eventually, that demand had changed to his wanting the investigation reopened, and all through that terrible time the signs of Traynor's post-traumatic stress had become increasingly evident.

Claire's disappearance had had an impact on Heritage himself, because he had known her, and because of his force's failure to find her. He recalled the many times he had reminded Traynor of what they both knew: that 'abduction' was a euphemism in relation to Claire's disappearance, given the significant blood evidence left in the family home. Now they both knew without doubt that Claire had died back then – ten, eleven years ago. Which left Traynor with another task. He would have to break the news to his daughter. Heritage tried to work out how old she might be now. Eighteen? He gazed down at Traynor, good looking, in his early forties, realizing for the first time that he and Claire had probably met at university. He took his hand from Traynor's shoulder and watched him stand, his face pale, his posture rigid.

'Thank you for telling me, John. Rather you than someone I don't know.'

Heritage nodded his understanding, gave him a close look. 'Don't leave just yet. Give yourself some time. Make sure you're OK to drive.'

They walked from his office to Reception, where Traynor turned to Heritage and shook his hand as Watts and Judd came inside, both stopped by the two men's facial expressions.

'You're sure you're OK to drive?' asked Heritage. 'I can get somebody—'

'No.'

They watched him leave, saw him get into the Aston Martin and, after a brief pause, drive slowly from the car park and away.

'What's going on?' asked Watts.

Heritage lowered his voice. 'I've just had to break the news that remains found a few days ago near Oxford are those of his wife, Claire.'

Heritage walked away, leaving Watts staring after him. With a sudden, pressing need to be somewhere, *anywhere* else, Watts headed back out to his vehicle, Judd watching him go.

It was colder than it had been when they were in Newton Heights earlier. He headed towards the pub, seeing a few more drinkers inside. Nobody behind the bar. He waited. After what felt like too long, he reached for a heavy glass and rapped it twice against the bar's wood. A door creaked open. The young woman who had served him earlier appeared, sulky as before, now with more than a touch of belligerence.

'I was just *coming*. What do you want?'

'A chat with Theresa Yates, your cleaner.'

Dark-rimmed eyes widened as she pantomimed a look at the large clock behind her, then back. 'At *this* time of day? You must be joking—'

'Got a phone number for her?'

'No.'

Thinking that he wouldn't get anything reliable or useful from her, he asked, 'Who runs this place?'

'My mum and her boyfriend.'

'I'll have a word with one or other of them.'

'You'll be lucky. He's hardly ever here. She's gone to the supermarket to do a big shop.'

Reaching deep for patience, he lowered his voice and pointed. 'There was a man in here earlier, sitting over there. I want to know who he is.'

'How would I know?'

Watts' irritation soared. 'There was nobody else here and you were serving, that's how!'

'What time?'

'Around one o'clock. He looked local.'

'What's "local" look like?'

Watts was back twenty-plus years, conversations with his daughter running inside his head. She'd been a pain-in-the-tail teenager, but never like this. He recalculated. This one ought to be at least eighteen to work here. 'Elderly man. One dog. Who is he?'

'You should have said about the dog. That would be Jack.'

'Jack who?'

'Dunno. He lives a mile or so out of the Heights along the Rednal Road. You want a drink?'

'No.'

He drove the 'mile or so' along the narrow, deserted road in fast-fading light, his window open, seeing no sign of a dwelling or anything else. Picking up a subtle smokiness, he slowed, pulled on to a small rise on his side of the road and stopped, his eyes fixed on a distant wisp of smoke now a few metres behind him. Somebody close by was using a domestic wood-burner. A quick U-turn and he guided the BMW's nearside wheels on to rough ground edging the road, the smoke now to his left. If this was where the old guy lived, how did he manage to walk from here to Newton Heights and back without paving of any description, in meagre to poor light on his return journey? It probably had no connection to him, but whoever lived here might know him, at least by name.

Pulling up his jacket collar, he got out, pushed his door quietly closed and started walking in the direction of the smoke. It led him into a thick press of bushes and trees and on to a hard-to-see pathway. Picking up the muffled sound of a couple of vehicles passing, he continued along the curving path, getting no visuals as to what might be ahead, his suede shoes sliding over soft earth and leaf drop. About to give it up in favour of a Google search inside his warm vehicle, the path suddenly widened into an open area. He stopped, his eyes on a small house – more a cabin – of wood construction with curtained windows either side of its front door. If this was where the old boy lived, he had need of a good fire. A quick reach into his pocket for ID and Watts approached shallow steps, covering them in a single stride, and tapped against the door. Straightening to his full six-three height, he listened, his eyes moving slowly, right to left, a subtle, a creeping sensation moving over his neck and shoulders, prompting a look back in the direction of the road, now entirely obscured by the thick screen of bushes and trees. He tapped the door again, harder this time, sending one or two birds rising, something else skittering. What had Ms Cordiality at the pub said was the old guy's name? He leaned towards the door.

'*Jack?* Open up, please. This is the police!' He waited. 'Come on, Jack! You spoke to me at the pub, remember? We need to talk some more.'

He looked down at the door handle, weighing his next action. He was on private property. He hadn't been summoned here, which meant he had no jurisdiction. If the old boy was sleeping and woke to find Watts inside his residence, there could be ructions. He gripped the door handle. Getting no resistance, he pushed the door open on a high-pitched creak and stood, feeling warmth on his face.

'Jack? If you're here, I need to know you're OK.' He waited. 'Can I come in?' Still nothing. 'I need to ask you about something you said to me. That's why I'm here.'

He pushed the door open further and stepped inside the big square room. The low glow from the fire was enough for him to see that the place was constructed entirely from wood. Watts' eyes moved over a single bed, its covers neat and uncreased, slippers side by side on the floor. He walked further inside, hearing nothing but his own breathing. To the right of the fireplace, a half-open door was showing a narrow slice of bathroom. His eyes moved to a large-screen television, an armchair facing it, and on to a table and chair. Watts went to the table, looked down at the unsliced loaf, ran his finger lightly over the cut side. Dry. His hand went to a teapot which felt cold, his eyes moving over a wedge of cheese, a knife and a mug. All the signs were that the old man's light tea had been interrupted. Watts frowned at his watch. It was getting on for seven o'clock. Something he hadn't noticed now claimed his attention. A dog basket. Wherever Jack was, his dog had gone with him. His eyes moved slowly upwards to something hanging from a hook screwed into the wall. A dog's lead.

'*Here*, boy! Where are you, eh? Come on.'

He moved quietly to the bathroom door and pushed. It resisted. Using his forearm, he pushed again. Senses now on high alert, he gripped the edge of the door in his big hands and pushed harder. It moved, enough for him to get his head and shoulders inside. He looked down at short grey-brown hair. Holding the door in place, he got out his phone. His call to Longbridge, the nearest station, was picked up. Identifying himself, he gave location details.

'I'm calling from the Rednal Road, the best part of two miles from the Newton Heights turnoff, on the other side of the road. You won't see the dwelling from the road – it's obscured by trees – but my vehicle is parked there.' He gave his registration, nodded. 'Yeah. Black BMW. Quick as you can. I'll be waiting.'

Tension surging across his shoulders, he cut the call, made another which got him the engaged signal, then listened again for the faint noise he had just picked up from outside. He moved quietly to one of the windows, moved the curtain a fraction, looked out, then did the same at the other window, seeing only low branches and bushes churning in the stiff wind. Letting the curtain fall back into place, he rang Connie again.

'Remember that old guy with the dog I told you about? I'm inside his house, which is like a cabin in the woods.'

'Sounds idyllic. Except it's November.'

'His dog is here. I think it's dead, and there's no sign of the old man. I'm waiting for a couple of Longbridge officers to arrive. I'm concerned because he's an old chap with no transport of his own and the temperature's dropping. I'll look around for anything that might indicate where he's gone and get back to you.'

Call ended, he walked across the room to an old bureau. Gloves on, he reached for the flap, lowered it, looked down at utility bills neatly clipped together, addressee Mr J. Beresford. There was also a hospital letter dated some weeks previously about a replacement hearing aid that would be posted to him. Watts closed the bureau, went to the door, cracked it open and looked out at darkness and steadily falling rain. He closed it.

Moving to the small single wardrobe in one corner, he pulled open the door, looking for something specific among the few shirts, a couple of pairs of trousers, one lightweight cardigan. He ran his hands over the pockets of the item now claiming his attention, a bulky black Barbour jacket. Wherever Jack had gone, he had left his winter coat. At a sharp knock on the door, he went and opened it. Two uniformed officers were standing there, neither of them looking a day over eighteen. He gave them a quick summary of what he knew.

'I want you here until officers from headquarters arrive.'

'Do we wait inside?' asked one, looking hopeful.

'No. Use the time to search outside for any sign of the elderly owner of this place.'

'We've got torches in the car, sir. I'll fetch 'em.' The young officer turned and headed back to the road. Watts called after him. 'Bring one or two evidence bags as well! Just in case.'

* * *

Jess was trying to concentrate on preparing dinner. Heritage had phoned her earlier to tell her what had happened. It was news she had both longed for and dreaded since she and Will had met three years before. She had owned a local newspaper back then and he had come to talk to her about a police investigation in which he was involved. She had quickly recognized his intelligence and sensitivity, also his deep sadness. She had also felt an instant, powerful attraction towards him. Much later, she had invited him to where she was living at the time to share Christmas with her. He had arrived, his manner edgy, bringing Boy, his newly adopted dog from the investigation. During the course of that day, she had come to realize that the edginess was in part his wanting her and also his guilt that he was forsaking his missing wife. It was the closest he had ever come to letting her see his grief.

She tensed on hearing the Aston Martin's unmistakable engine sound, then the front door opening. She went into the hall, watched as he came inside, put his keys and backpack down. He looked up at her, came slowly to her, kissed her cheek. Boy appeared from the kitchen, looking subdued. Traynor leaned down and stroked him, the dog responding with a whine and a tail wag.

'I'll take him out. I won't be long.'

After an hour of walking and avoidance, he had come home. They had eaten in silence. He had stacked the dishwasher. She had made coffee. In the low-lit sitting room, she glanced several times at him. He was staring at nothing, his index finger against his mouth. She understood. He would not, could not speak. Later, when they were in bed, he had said, 'Sorry,' and turned from her.

FOUR

Thursday, 14 November. 7.15 a.m.

Watts was on the phone, listening to Jack Beresford's elder son. He nodded.

'That's one of the reasons I'm ringing you this early, Mr Beresford. Given your father's age, we're very concerned for his wellbeing.' Having picked up worry in the son's voice, he held back for now on the dog and the old man's lack of warm clothing.

'I've got officers on standby at his house and I'm thinking that it might inform our search if you could describe your father's routines, his social contacts and so on.'

After fifteen minutes of note-taking interspersed with occasional queries, Watts ended the call and looked down at what he had been told. *Jack Beresford. Man of routine. Walk. Pub. Home. Television.* He made another call, relayed the information to the officers he had sent from headquarters to Jack's house. Hanging up, he made an internal call to confirm his plan for the imminent start of a search for ninety-two-year-old Jack. He checked his list. He had already rung Connie, who was making the necessary arrangements relevant to the dog.

His office door flew open and hit the wall. Judd walked in, her face stormy.

'I *can't* believe you went back there without *me*!'

Recalling the impact of Traynor's news and his own pressing need to get out of headquarters, he said, 'I thought I'd check the old guy out—'

'*No*, what *you* did was follow up an idea without telling me! We're a team, or that's what *I* thought.'

'Yes, and as your boss, I get to choose where I go and what I do!' He saw the surprise on her face at his tone. One he didn't use very often. 'I didn't know anything had happened to him. Just . . . settle *down*.'

She sat and he told her about Jack's small wooden house and what he had seen there. 'I've talked to one of the old boy's sons. Have a read.'

She took his neat notes, read them aloud as she routinely did. 'Jack Beresford. Ninety-two . . . some background blah . . . apprenticed as a builder. According to the elder son, his father chose building due to the destruction he saw as a very young lad.' She frowned up at Watts.

'Second World War. Eventually, he formed his own company. Two sons, Michael, fifty-two, and James, forty-nine, who now run the company. Both married. I asked them where Jack might have gone. They were unable to identify any friends. Michael described his father as a loner. Not a talker. More an observer of people . . .' She looked up. 'This is all you got from them? Not much help in finding him, is it?'

'There was something Michael told me about his younger brother that was interesting—'

'I get it.' She rubbed her hands together. 'He's the black sheep who spends money like water and—' She caught Watts' look. 'Carry on.'

'He said his brother built himself a house in Newton Heights, lived in it a couple of years, then sold it.'

She looked up at him. 'Where does it say this?'

'On the next page, which you haven't read yet.' Giving him a look, she flipped it, read it in silence, then looked up at him. '*No way!*'

'The very same: Marion Cane's house.' He checked the wall clock, got to his feet. 'But don't start knitting up any scenarios out of that. Yes, it's a link, but that's all. There's a meeting with Heritage—'

'I'm coming with you.'

'Did I say otherwise?'

Heritage listened as Watts outlined the previous day's developments and what had been learned from Beresford's son. When he'd finished, Heritage said, 'This is an extremely vulnerable man we're talking about. Any ideas as to his possible whereabouts?'

'Not yet, sir, but a search including a K9 team is underway at the area around his home. His sons weren't able to suggest any places Jack might have gone. It seems the old man leads a fairly solitary life, which at ninety-something shouldn't come as a surprise. I haven't released to the family anything about his lack of warm clothing or what's happened to the dog.' He flipped pages of his notebook. 'Longbridge has no SOCO availability – in fact, no SOCO full-stop, so I've sent three of ours to do a full forensic sweep of the house, after which they'll bring the dog's remains here. Doctor Chong has contacted a vet who's agreed to conduct a full forensic examination of it.' He waited, anticipating a demand as to when, which had always been Brophy's go-to position. It didn't come.

'Good. Have SOCOs found anything of interest at the residence?'

'Not when I last spoke to them at around half six this morning.'

'What took you to this Beresford's house?'

Judd gave Watts a sideways glance as he told Heritage about their visit to Newton Heights and The Running Man pub the previous day, repeating Beresford's words to him as he was leaving. 'I think he deliberately chose the exit near to where I was sitting.'

'You're saying that he purposely approached you?'

'That's how it looked to me. He stopped and spoke to me, kept his voice low. He knew we were there in connection with Marion Cane's death. There was something in his manner, in the way he said the words. It wasn't casual. More like something he didn't want anybody else hearing.' Heritage's eyes stayed on him. 'You sound like you trust what he said and that it might be relevant to what's happened to him.'

'I am, until I hear any different. My take on him is that he's very much on the ball, regardless of his age.'

Heritage nodded. 'Carry on with the Marion Cane aspect, but your main investigative focus is Beresford's disappearance. Keep me informed of both, please.'

They headed back to Watts' office, Judd looking aggrieved. 'You never told me that this old guy actually spoke to you at the pub.'

'Don't start. I've got enough to think about.'

As he walked into his office, a familiar, deep voice broke into his thinking. 'Good morning, Bernard.'

Watts stopped, did a double-take. Following an earlier, light-on-detail briefing to all headquarters staff from Heritage on Traynor's current situation, Traynor was the last person he had expected to see today. He went to him, his hand outstretched, seeing shadows in the criminologist's face and deep inside the miss-nothing blue eyes. He softened his voice.

'I wasn't expecting to see you, Will.' He stopped, searching for something else to say. 'How about some posh coffee, yeah? I'll get it going. Take a seat—'

'Not for me, thanks, I'm here to see John.' Having followed this brief exchange, Judd had something to say to him.

'Will . . . I . . .' She flushed. 'We know what's happening in Oxford and we're sorry if it's . . .'

The desk phone shrilled. Watts lifted it. 'Yes. I'll let him know.' And to Traynor, 'Heritage is waiting, Will.'

As Traynor left, Watts shook his head. 'Least said, the better, Judd.'

'One of us had to say something. We couldn't just totally ignore it.'

Inside his office, Heritage was looking across his desk to Traynor. He had no further news for him from Oxford. What he now had was an investigation which might provide Traynor with some limited distraction. What he actually wanted from Traynor was his doctoral skills as a criminologist on the investigation. He felt uncomfortable asking at this time, but it had to be done. 'How busy are you, Will?'

'If you mean my university work, I believe I'm about to be placed on a couple of weeks' compassionate leave.'

Heritage nodded. 'That's . . . good.'

'With plenty of time to think? I don't see it like that, John.'

Heritage selected his words carefully. 'Bernard has a new investigation. A missing person. There's what looks to be a possible side issue, the death of a woman in the same area, but Bernard can tell you about all of it. How do you feel about giving him some assistance? You don't necessarily have to get directly involved if you'd rather not. It could be done by email and phone.'

Traynor made no response.

'Sorry, Will. You have enough to deal with right now.'

Traynor stood. 'I'll think about it and let you know.'

Some hours later, Watts was in his office, he and Judd listening to Connie Chong deliver what she knew about her vet colleague's examination of Jack Beresford's dog.

'An external examination yielded no evidence of injury, so he did a full post-mortem.'

'And?'

'He found evidence of a slow-acting sedative.'

Watts thought about this.

'It looked docile when we saw it, but what else would you expect of a dog nudging a hundred, give or take? Is it possible a vet prescribed it?'

'I doubt it. It was given way too much.' She stood. 'I need to get back to the PM suite where a less-than-joyful Igor is waiting for me to start our next post.'

She leant towards Watts, running her fingers gently over the lines on his forehead, then glanced at Judd. 'You never saw that.'

'Saw what?'

As the door closed on the pathologist, Judd eyed Watts sitting back in his chair, arms folded, looking at nothing. 'You're worried about Will.'

'He doesn't need me worrying about him.'

'So, why the face?'

'One, Beresford is still missing. Two, he's over ninety with no coat and it's cold. Three, his dog, which was left behind, was full of a drug which probably killed it. Four, Beresford's words to me at that pub, and *don't* start on about that again. Whatever he meant by them, that's what I'll be doing. Asking a *lot* of questions.'

Judd thought this over. 'He might have heard local gossip about what happened to Cane and fancied turning detective. When you're that old, life must be dead boring.' She headed for the kettle, 'Want coffee?'

'No.'

She studied him, kettle in hand. 'If it was me saying all of what you've just said, you'd probably say I was "knitting together" isolated facts. What the old guy actually said to you – what if he's the only person in Newton Heights who welcomes strangers and he just wanted to talk? Take an interest. Be involved. Who have we met there so far? A moronic teenage goth at the pub, Marion Cane's sister giving us her view of her sister's *life*, which sounded *sanitized* and/or *superficial*, and her husband, an information dead loss.' She waited for a response, not getting one.

'The residents I've seen from a distance look to be a bunch of suited, booted idiots driving Range Rovers, with zero interest in anything going on in the place they live in or why we're there. I doubt we'll get much help from them. They probably get fired up only when they see an empty crisp packet blowing along the road, threatening their "property values".' She paused. 'Or it could be that Jack's words to you were intended to encourage us to follow up Cane's death because something's not right.'

'Finished?'

'In case you haven't noticed, I just switched sides. I'm with you on this.'

'Our investigative focus is Jack. Come on.'

'Where to?'

'Discounting Outer Mongolia, let's make it Newton Heights.'

FIVE

Same day. 10.36 a.m.

Judd peered through misting rain. Even the gazillion-pound houses looked depressing. They entered the pub car park. 'You want to see that stroppy girl who was behind the bar yesterday, right?'

Watts made no response. They left the BMW's warmth and headed for the pub. As they walked inside, the few customers there stopped talking and looked up at them. They went directly to the bar and the mature-looking woman behind it wiping up spills.

'Yes, sir. What can I get you?' She barely glanced at his ID. 'I already know.'

'Where's the young woman who was working here yesterday?'

The woman eyed him. 'In the back, washing up. Why?'

'She provided us with some minimal information. I want to hear what else she knows.'

'I'm her mother. I want to be there when you do.'

'Best give her a shout, then.'

They watched her leave the bar and waited. '*Solange!*' A pause. 'Come down here, *now*!'

Judd's brows shot up. 'I was expecting something along the lines of Sharon—' The woman reappeared. 'She's coming.'

After almost a minute, the young woman appeared, sullen as before. Reaching the bar, she leaned on it, not looking at them, her face a study in *Don't care*. Watts asked, 'What do you know about Jack Beresford?'

Sullenness morphed into a yawn. She blinked. 'Who?'

Her mother's tone was brisk. 'Come on, Solange. You know Jack.' She pointed across the room. 'The elderly man who usually sits over there with his dog. Tell the officer.'

Solange took a crisp from an open bag on her side of the bar. 'I already told you I'd seen him in here. That's it.' The crisp disappeared, quickly followed by another three. She chewed, her gaze insolent on Watts' face.

Repressing a quick urge to slap her, Judd said, 'You served him a drink yesterday.' Beneath the heavy black brows, the eyes edged by thick lashes moved slowly over Judd.

'Did I?'

'You were the only one serving here. Jack had a drink in front of him.'

Solange smirked. 'Ooh-er, Miss-Bloody-Marple—'

'*Solange!*' snapped her mother.

Judd's motivation to slap Solange was climbing. 'Tell us about the conversation you had with him.'

'What conversation? This is a *pub*. He wanted a drink. I gave him a *drink*.'

Judd wasn't about to let up. 'Did you ever serve him before yesterday?'

The resultant shrug sent Judd straight to push-mode. It wouldn't please Sarge but would give her some job satisfaction. She checked her phone. 'It's getting on for eleven o'clock. We'll see you at headquarters, Harborne, in twenty-five minutes. Get your mother to drive you.'

Maternal concern suddenly kicked in. 'Hang *on*! She's not going anywhere!'

'In which case, she had better start talking. Tell us what we want to know.'

The mother glared at Judd. Aware that the bar had quietened, its clientele hanging on the exchange, she looked at Watts, lowered her voice and pointed. 'Go through that door and round to the other end of the bar. It's quieter. She'll come through.' And to her daughter, 'You heard me! Get yourself round there.'

Watts and Judd were seated at a table when Solange reappeared. She dropped heavily on to a chair, pulling her sleeves over her hands, gaze fixed on a nearby window, her face a careful blank. Watts had his notebook out, pen poised.

'Tell us about Jack Beresford.'

She shrugged. 'What's to tell? He's dead old, is all I know.'

He studied the closed face. 'We can't find him. Wherever he is, he has no coat.' He watched the words sink in, saw the facial expression waver, went with something he guessed would really hit the spot. 'He doesn't know what's happened to his dog.' For the first time, she looked directly at him.

'What're you on about?'

'It was found inside Jack's place. Somebody fed it drugs.'

'What?' Her face flushed. 'You're saying somebody's *killed* it?'

The black-fringed eyes filled. She pulled at her long sleeves, blotting sudden tears, her face losing its faux self-assurance, plus several years, leaving Watts questioning whether she was old enough to serve in a pub. They waited it out. After a minute or so, Watts asked, 'Do you want your mother here?'

She raised her sleeve to her nose, sniffed. 'Get *real*.'

Reaching for a paper napkin from a small basket on a nearby table, Watts handed it to her. 'Come on, Solange.'

She dabbed at her eyes. 'It's bad about the little dog – he was cute – but I don't know anything about what's happened to Jack. I can't tell you what I don't know, can I?'

'Did Jack ever talk to you?'

'A bit. Half the time, I didn't listen.'

'In the half you were listening, what did he say?'

'I don't know!' More tears slid. 'He used to go on about some war when he worked as a policeman or something. Other times, he went on about the people living here. He was into being green, saving the planet, stuff like that. He said that if we did, it would be thanks to ordinary people, not the rich tossers who live here.'

'He actually said those words?'

She shrugged. 'More or less.'

'Sounds like he didn't have much time for some of the residents here.'

Solange was on her feet. 'He was right. They're a bunch of twats.'

They watched her stomp her way to the bar, go behind it and disappear.

Judd stood. 'I'll get her back, Sarge. I'm sure she knows more than she's saying.'

'Or she might not. I'm betting she's under sixteen and I could do without time-wasting complications, like her mother getting involved. I need to talk to the officers out searching for Jack. After that, I'll be talking to the local GP.'

'What about the woman who cleans this place? Shall I talk to her?'

'It doesn't look to me like she's here. Go to the church and have a chat with the vicar. He should be a mine of local information.'

Their departure from the pub was closely tracked through the pub's rear fence where Solange was standing next to a man. 'What did they want to know?' he asked.

'They were on about that old guy who's gone missing.'

'What did you say to them?'

'Nothing!' Not looking at him, she chewed at one of her fingernails. 'They'll be back. I'll have to talk to them—'

He grabbed her neck, causing her head to make sudden, sharp contact with a nearby wall, his face touching hers.

'You say *nothing* about me, got it?'

She pulled away from him. 'You *bastard*, Ryan. If my dad ever finds out what you've done, he'll see that you get *prison*.'

'Who's going to tell him? *You?* I don't think so.'

She heard him laugh, one of the first things about him that she had liked. Pulling at her jersey to cover her neck, she veered away and disappeared into the pub.

SIX

Same day. 12.15 p.m.

After a brief, dispiriting phone conversation with officers searching for Jack Beresford along the Rednal Road, then dropping off Judd near the church, Watts drove a short distance and parked close to Newton's health centre. With no immediate action possible where Jack was concerned, he was now responding to the possibility that somewhere, somehow there was a connection between Jack's death and that of Marion Cane. Even if there wasn't, Heritage was still expecting him to continue inquiries about her. He jabbed his phone, waited for the number to ring out.

'This is Detective Chief Inspector Watts. I want to speak to Mr Jessop, the solicitor.'

He listened as the cool female voice informed him that the solicitor was unavailable. 'Can I take a message?'

'Tell him I want to discuss Marion Cane's estate with him.' Adding his number, he ended the call, got out of his vehicle and headed for the health centre.

Inside, he was surprised to find so many people in the waiting area, mostly sixty-five-plus, all well dressed, some young mothers with buggies, a few others with toddlers. Kids' names drifted over to him. Zaza, Caspar, Skyla, others he couldn't get a handle on. He approached the reception desk and the woman there, her head lowered.

'I'm here to see Doctor Devereaux.'

She looked up at him. 'Do you have an appointment?'

'No.'

'If you want to register with us, I'm afraid—'

'Ring Doctor Devereaux and tell him that Detective Chief Inspector Watts, headquarters, Birmingham, wants to talk to him.'

She reached for her phone, spoke into it, keeping her voice low. When the call ended, she looked up. 'Take a seat, please. Doctor Devereaux will be out shortly.'

Watts left the desk to scrutinize nameplates on several closed doors. Locating the name 'Devereaux', he moved closer to it, smiled down at a square-faced infant waiting with its mother. It looked up at him, its lower lip starting to tremble. Devereaux's door suddenly opened and a woman emerged, followed by a man of forty-something. As the woman walked away, he beckoned to Watts.

'Come on in, Detective Chief Inspector!'

Feeling eyes on his back, Watts followed Devereaux into the room and took the chair he was indicating.

'How can I help?'

'I want some information on Marion Cane.'

The GP regarded him. 'You're aware that Ms Cane is deceased?'

'Yes. What can you tell me about her?'

'Not very much, I'm afraid. She had lived here for about eighteen months or so when she died of natural causes approximately six months ago. She wasn't a regular attender at the practice. If you want more, I'll need to look at her notes.' Seeing

Watts unzip his jacket, he turned to the desktop computer, tapped it, pointed at the screen. 'Here they are. Very limited, as I said. Is there anything in particular you'd like to know?'

'Did she have any specific health worries?'

'Ms Cane was a retired, professional woman. She consulted me twice, both within six months of her death.'

'Let's go with those.'

Devereaux's eyes fixed on the screen. 'She came in the first time complaining of feeling a little odd.' He nodded. 'I remember now. She struggled when I asked her for specifics but then referred to feeling confused, a little anxious, somewhat "absent" at times. I did the usual checks – blood pressure, balance and so forth – and found nothing untoward. I suggested that she try to reduce her anxiety and gave her some printed, self-help advice. Her next visit was – let's see . . . almost four weeks later. She didn't refer to those earlier symptoms but described some very brief episodes of dizziness and' – Devereaux pointed again – 'some memory difficulties . . .' He looked at Watts. 'My opinion was that she was still experiencing a degree of anxiety, for which I prescribed a low-dose fluoxetine. I didn't see her again. I suspected that stress was at the bottom of her reported symptoms, possibly related to the drastic change to her life due to ceasing to work and moving here.'

'Did she actually say that?'

'No, but she described her work in high-powered financial environments in the States and London. In general practice, one hears many accounts of experiential stress, most of which can be attributed to significant life changes. Her experience of living here in the Heights after what she had been doing for so many years would have been a significant culture shock, plus a marked reduction in the pace of her life.'

'The bit about reduced pace sounds like a good thing to me.'

Devereaux sent him a patronizing glance. 'No, no. Contrary to popular opinion, not all stress is *bad*, DCI Watts. It can give shape to a life, break up the day into tasks to be done and so forth. It can prevent the individual from becoming caught up in his or her thoughts, which I suspected was likely, given Marion's move to our peaceful area. I said this to her because during her second visit here she asked me if she might be losing her faculties. I reassured her on that and again conducted basic checks.

Her blood pressure was a little elevated on that occasion. I suggested the introduction of some specific routines into her daily life which might help dispel her anxieties. Following that second consultation, I requested our practice nurse check her blood pressure over the following two months.'

'And?'

Devereaux's eyes returned to the screen. 'Let's have a look, shall we? Yes, the practice nurse checked Marion's blood pressure on two separate occasions. It remained somewhat elevated. According to an entry by the nurse, Marion indicated that she was not taking the medication I had prescribed. I later learned that she had never collected the prescription from our pharmacy here. The nurse gave her dietary advice and that second visit was her last to the practice.'

'So, what happened? What did you do?'

Devereaux frowned, glanced at him. 'What do you mean, what did I do?'

'You didn't follow up on her not taking the medication?'

Devereaux sent him a smile that got nowhere near his eyes. 'DCI Watts, you'll have seen the number of patients waiting for consultation. We serve more than the immediate area of Newton Heights. As doctors, we do not monitor all of our patients' choices. Our job is to *advise, prescribe* and then leave it to individual patient choice what they do thereafter.'

'You don't think a bit of encouragement or persuasion might help?'

'As I just explained to you, it is not part of our role to directly persuade patients, even when what has been suggested is in their best interests. It's a case of *liberum arbitrium*, DCI Watts.' He inclined his head to him. 'Freedom of choice.'

'I'll be requesting a copy of all of her medical records at some stage.'

'I've examined them fully. There's nothing in them that would interest the police.'

'That's a judgement I'll be making, Doctor Devereaux.'

Five minutes later, Watts was outside, wondering if there was a Latin phrase for superior gits who get on people's nerves.

SEVEN

Feeling chilled, Judd walked under a wood-tiled archway and followed the rough gravel pathway into the churchyard. Avoiding small puddles, she continued along, sending glances to the gravestones on either side, mostly of different shapes and sizes, some fairly new looking in black, shiny stone. She slowed at one, the inscription on it sharp, easy to read. Her gaze moved to those on her left, many leaning at angles, grey and pitted, their inscriptions impossible to decipher. Continuing on, she followed the curve of the path, getting a glimpse of a low tiled roof beyond a fence off to her right, startled by sudden, high-pitched squeals, followed by the sound of a bell being rung. A primary school? Did Newton Heights have enough kids to warrant one? She recalled the pricey modern buggies she had seen, thinking that the well-off can have any number of children. Particularly if they don't have to look after them all day. Closing down the line of thinking, rounding another curve in the path, she got her first glimpse of grey stone walls and part of a square tower some way ahead.

Her footsteps muffled by a thick layer of dead leaves, she reached the church's two impressive wooden doors, one fitted with a sturdy, black metal ring. Unsure what else to do, she lifted it, cold and heavy, tugged at it, tried to turn it. She pulled, then pushed at the door. It remained closed against her. Frustrated, she glanced around, seeing that the path she had followed here diverted to the right of the church. The children's voices she had heard earlier were now gone. All was quiet. In her own garden, there was never this quality of silence. It felt thick. Like a blanket. Following the path, the low branches of thick evergreens reaching towards her, she came to the rear of the church. She had no religious belief. Back when she was very small and frightened inside a home which should have cared for her, she had asked inside her head for someone to help. No one did. *Go, figure.*

Directly ahead she could see a door that looked to be slightly open. Somebody had to be here. She recalled a recent visit to a

church in one of Birmingham's inner areas which had been
burgled and her surprise at the impressive value of the items
stolen from it. Sarge had referred to it as 'church plate', much
of it, silver. She liked churches. What she didn't have was any
liking for religion.

Reaching the door, she tugged at it. It opened further. Stepping
quietly inside, she found herself in a large storeroom. It smelled
of dust. Boxes of varying sizes covered much of the floor space,
some overflowing with toys, others heaped with leather-bound
books. Off to one side, plastic clothes hangers on wooden pegs
each supported a white, lace-edged garment. Briefly wondering
if the vicar was responsible for laundering them, she grinned at
the picture forming inside her head. No. That would be Mrs Rev.
Directly ahead were two tall cupboards obstructing much of her
view of another door, which she guessed led into the church
proper. Moving quietly in its direction, stepping between various
items, she was stopped, mid-step, by low sounds coming towards
her. A voice. Two voices, One low-pitched, persuasive, the other
lighter, a woman's, ending in a rich, intimate laugh, followed by
a series of other, muted sounds. A flush crept slowly upwards
from Judd's neck. Hidden from view within this jumbled space
of toys and hymn books, something very personal, very intimate
was happening. Shocked, embarrassed, she turned away in the
direction she had come, her foot nudging a box of toys which
immediately set off soft animal sounds, a sheep, a dog, a—

Barely breathing, eyes wide, face radiating heat, she went
quickly to the door she had come in by. Reaching it, she stepped
quickly out, pushed the door closed and leaned against it, chest
pounding, her head in freefall. She knew without doubt what she
had just heard. Sex. Inside a church. Despite her own zero belief,
she found the realization shocking and disturbing. Opening the
door a few centimetres, she listened again. Nothing. She quickly
turned away, lost her balance and fell back against the door,
causing it to bang shut.

'Steady.' A breathless, fifty-something man was holding her
arm, looking down at her. 'Are you all right? I do apologize for
almost knocking you down. It was entirely my fault. I was
completely focused on my timed power walk.'

Judd stared up at his reddened face, at the fitness watch he
was displaying to her, at the long coat, scarf and old plimsolls.

She brought her breathing under control. '. . . I'm OK. I'm fine. Actually, I'm looking for Reverend Partington.'

'Now, *there's* a happy coincidence. You've found him! Although rather more dramatically than I would have wished. How can I help?'

'I'm Police Constable Chloe Judd—'

'Of *course*. I heard via local gossip that there was to be some very low-level exploration of Marion Cane's death, and now, of course, the disappearance of poor Mr Beresford.' He pointed to the door from which Judd had emerged. 'This is the quickest way to my house, but if you prefer to talk to me alone, we can do so inside the church.'

Judd stared at the door. Whoever was inside that room might still be there. Her police role suddenly reinstated itself.

'Did you come past the main entrance to the church a few minutes ago?'

'No.' He pointed. 'I've just come from my house, which is in that direction.' He looked back at her. 'You're looking rather pale. Having almost knocked you down, I feel responsible.'

Judd tried to protest, but he continued, 'It'll take us barely minutes to get to my house if we go through the church, and we can talk there.' He opened the door and waited for her to come inside. Feeling out of options, Judd did so, ears straining for sounds of sex, half listening to his loud voice.

'This room is such an awful muddle! I keep meaning to ask the Ladies-of-the-Rota to tidy it.' He laughed at what Judd guessed was a small joke as he led her across the now silent room and out into the main body of the church, Judd giving a backward glance, catching sight of several hefty cushions on the floor close to the door.

Coming into the church itself, she found it lit only by weak sun coming through stained glass. She breathed fully for the first time in what had felt like several minutes, the vicar busily pointing out to her the sheen on dark wood, the glow of brass, the blue-brown floor tiles.

'It's lovely,' she whispered, still too distracted to take in the detail he was describing.

'It is, isn't it? Although I'll admit that the furnishings at my house are more comfortable for sitting.' He smiled down at her. 'And my wife makes *really* good coffee.'

They exited the church by the main door, which he secured, then walked a short distance along a tree-lined path to a large modern house. Opening the front door, he called out, 'Anna, it's *me*. We have a young visitor!'

A woman who looked some years younger than the vicar hurried into the hall, her face flushed. 'Would you believe, it's taken me an *hour* to get rid of your rota ladies. *Really*, Leonard, you should deal with— Oh, hello?'

'This is Police Constable Chloe Judd, Anna.' Partington smiled at Judd. 'Excuse me. I need to change.'

Half an hour later, Judd's mouth was full of cake, Mrs Partington offering coffee. 'Is that too strong for you?'

Judd swallowed. 'No, it's just as I like it. Thank you.'

It suddenly occurred to Judd that, away from the bish-bash and competitive humour of police headquarters, a bit of old-fashioned atmosphere was no bad thing. She retuned to Partington, who had reappeared and was now wearing a soft-looking yellow sweater and sheepskin slippers.

'Yes, Marion Cane was part of our volunteer group, our rota of helpers. She brought flowers from her garden in the summer and holly with glorious red berries in winter. I was pleasantly surprised by her willingness.'

'Why surprised?'

'If you had met Marion, you would have been surprised,' said his wife.

Partington took a coffee refill from her. 'My wife is referring to Marion's professional background. She'd had a rather exciting career prior to settling here. I did ask myself if she might be able to find a niche for herself within the church, and she did try, but unfortunately it wasn't to her liking.'

'Was she religious?'

'I wouldn't say so, no. She seemed to me to be a very private person and she certainly didn't fit the usual expectations of church helper.' He looked across at his wife. 'What do you say, Anna?'

His wife smiled at Judd. 'She certainly didn't. Frankly, I was amazed when she first indicated an interest in joining.' She stood. 'If you'll both excuse me, I have a lot to do, so I'll leave you to talk.'

She left the room, closing the door. Judd looked down at her notes, then up at the vicar. 'What impression did you gain of Marion Cane as a person?'

He considered the question. 'I would say reliable – trustworthy, of course.' He paused. 'Possibly somewhat lonely.'

'Did she actually tell you that?'

'No.' He sent Judd a glance. 'Given your official interest in her, I don't believe I'm violating a confidence when I tell you that one of the few times Marion asked to speak to me, which would have been several months before she died, she told me that her mood was extremely low.'

'Oh? Did she say why?'

'No, although I did wonder if she was missing her previous work life. That kind of high-powered environment would surely leave a huge gap when the work itself finished?' He smiled. 'Not that I have any direct experience, of course. At the time she spoke to me, my impression was that she hadn't discussed how she was feeling with her sister.' He sighed. 'But why would one automatically assume that a sibling should be regarded as appropriate or suitable for such personal unburdening?'

A question was knocking at the inside of Judd's head. 'As far as you were aware, did she have anyone in her life? I mean, someone she was in a relationship with?'

'I can't answer that, but I did wonder if the low mood she had indicated might be related to her living alone.'

'Did she talk to you about it?'

'No, and I didn't encourage her to do so.'

Having picked up a slight hesitation within his words, Judd asked, 'Any reason why not?'

'The impression I had of Marion was that she was – how shall I put it? – vulnerable.'

'Vulnerable, how?'

'My goodness, this is difficult – vulnerable to any show of interest in her that she might have misinterpreted.'

Judd quickly wrote, smiling to herself. It seemed that, despite his age and pleasant fussiness, he had picked up a possible sexual vibe from Cane and had avoided placing himself in what he considered might be an awkward situation. She looked up at him. 'Are you able to say anything about Ms Cane's mental health?'

'Her mental health? I'm not too sure how to answer that.'

'Did she ever mention to you that she felt anxious or worried?'

Judd waited, conscious of the loud tick of the grandfather clock still audible from the hall. Partington had the look of someone intent on choosing his words. His wife had come back into the room and was sitting quietly on the sofa. 'This is only my impression,' he said, 'but she did appear to be somewhat ambivalent about living alone in her house.'

'She actually told you that?'

His wife looked across at him. 'Leonard, this is a police matter. You have to share whatever you know with the officer.'

He looked at Judd. 'This is really difficult. I'm merely repeating what she said to me. It was around three months before her death. She came here and asked me if I could . . . it sounds as melodramatic now as it did then. She wanted me to perform an exorcism. At her house.'

Judd stared at him, her understanding of the word coming entirely from a film she had watched with one of her colleagues, Adrian Jones, aka 'Jonesy', as they shared a takeaway at her house some weeks ago, she outwardly mocking but secretly disturbed.

Partington was speaking again. 'We all have a spiritual side, of course, but I remain unconvinced of the notion that evil spirits can control people and places, and the bishop is aware of my stance. My view is that whatever ailed Marion at the time was possibly the province of psychiatry. She was upset at my refusal.'

'What did you do?'

'I gave her the contact details of our bishop and suggested she write to him to see if he could suggest someone.'

'Did she contact him?'

'The bishop said not, but she did talk to me on a couple of occasions when she was dusting and tidying inside the church. She became distressed both times. I got the impression that she thought the house was in some way bad for her, although she wouldn't or couldn't say how. Given what we now know, that she had heart disease, perhaps that worry I witnessed was too much for her in the end.'

'Was she particularly friendly with anyone in the church?'

'No one that I'm aware of.' He paused. 'How shall I phrase this? Marion was very accomplished in terms of her working life. A committed career woman in the financial industry who had risen high.' He smiled. 'When she arrived in Newton Heights,

I think she was viewed as a bit of an oddity and not without
envy, particularly by our female volunteers. They tend to be
somewhat older women who never had the kind of career oppor-
tunities Marion appeared to have had. I doubt they found much
in common with her, or she with them.'

'So, there was no one within the church she might have
confided in?'

'I can't think of anyone, no.'

'Are you in sole charge here?'

Partington smiled. 'This is a small community but I couldn't
do everything required without help. I have a deacon, Matthew
Redpath. He came here from Essex approximately five or six years
ago, having given up his accountancy job for theology training.'

'Where does Mr Redpath live?'

'Here in the Heights.' Seeing her surprise, he added, 'The
church is fortunate to be able to offer accommodation. If you
want to talk to him, he's a nice, helpful young man, although I
doubt he'll be able to tell you anything about Marion. Perhaps
if you wait to speak to him after the weekend?' He smiled.
'Weekends are our peak time.'

Judd smiled and nodded. 'I'll make it Monday. Do you have
any other helpers?'

Partington hesitated. 'Eric Brook has been with us as a theology
trainee for about eighteen months. He shares the house with
Matthew. His settling in has been a somewhat slow process. He
appears to enjoy very loud music. Gregorian chants,' he saw her
blank look, 'and something called "hot metal", which seems to
me to be a most unusual combination.'

EIGHT

12.55 p.m.

Watts was on his phone, Heritage's voice in his ear.
'How's the search for this elderly man progressing?'
'It's well under way, sir. I've got six local officers
who know the area and I've added eight of ours. They're searching

the open land around Beresford's house. If nothing's found, I'll extend their activity to nearby woods. I spoke with them fifteen minutes ago. Nothing to report so far.'

'This is extremely concerning, Bernard. Initially, my thinking was that Beresford might have become confused and simply wandered off, but what happened to his dog has put a different twist on the whole situation.'

'Sir,' responded Watts, recalling nothing in Beresford's demeanour which had indicated confusion, nor any tendency to wander.

'It's entirely possible that Beresford was feeling depressed and *he* gave the dog the sedative. I'm being realistic here. He's living alone. It's November. Dark mornings, dark evenings which begin in mid-afternoon, with nothing to look forward to until Christmas. Wherever he is, he needs to be found, and soon.'

Watts was still thinking of the bright-eyed Beresford he saw in the pub. 'He didn't look depressed to me, sir.'

Heritage sounded dubious. 'That kind of presentation of normality can precede suicide. If necessary, I'll send another six officers from here to add to the search. Keep me informed, please.'

'Sir. What about the Cane follow-up?'

'Keep on with it for the next couple of days. Report to me any progress, or lack of, and we'll discuss next steps if any are indicated.'

'Sir.'

Watts pocketed his phone, recalling Brophy's likely response to the situation they had here: a mix of high-octane stress, limited insight into investigative need, plus a chronic fear of media interest. Brophy had specialized in turning any event into a catastrophe.

'Give me Heritage any day,' he murmured, getting out of his vehicle into a cold Newton Heights and heading for a small row of shops close by. He went into the small café Judd had suggested and ordered coffee. She was already here, spoon poised above a cappuccino, a smiley face worked in chocolate on its foam, her notebook open. She looked up as he sat opposite.

'Get anything?'

He repeated what he had been told by the GP, about Cane complaining of dizziness and confusion, plus an indication of high blood pressure. Judd raised another foam-laden spoonful. 'That could go some way to confirming her death from natural causes.'

'Devereaux prescribed medication for her. He's from your "Come in, here's a prescription, now sod off" school of health-care. I'm wondering why an intelligent, professional woman like Marion Cane, who was aware of having some health issues, didn't take what he prescribed.'

Judd shrugged. 'She was an independent woman. She probably didn't like being told what to do. From what I've heard so far, Sarge, she sounds like she was a bit isolated here.' She watched him add three spoons of sugar to his coffee, shook her head as he stirred. She glanced around, lowered her voice. 'I've got something I think you should know about. Listen to *this*. I went to the local church earlier. The main doors were locked, so I went round the back. There's a sort of storeroom which was open. *Guess* what I heard.'

'The organist playing "The Stripper".'

She frowned at him. 'Actually, you're not far off. There were two people in that room and they were *at* it.'

He stared at her. 'You're having me on.'

'I am *not*. I'm telling you, they were going at it, hot 'n' heavy, murmuring to each other, laughing. Talk about *embarrassed*. I couldn't wait to get out. That's when I literally bumped into the vicar. He took me to his house.'

'I arrested a vicar once. Seventy years old, mild as you like. He'd just killed his next-door neighbour with an axe.'

She gazed at him. 'You're not taking what I'm saying seriously.'

'Yes, I am.'

'This vicar is in his mid-fifties, no axe, and his wife gave me coffee and cake. They were both really nice – the vicar and his wife, I mean. She looks to be a few years younger than him.'

'Did you mention the sex episode to them?'

She glanced quickly around the café. 'Of course, I *didn't*,' she hissed. 'I asked them about Marion Cane. Apparently, she wasn't religious but she did help maintain the inside of the church. He described her as trustworthy and level-headed—'

'That doesn't fit with what her GP said. According to him she was having dizzy spells and feeling anxious.'

'There's more.' She read to him the other details she got from the vicar.

Watts looked unimpressed. 'Exorcism? Nobody believes that rubbish.' He thought about what they knew of Marion Cane. 'Wouldn't you have to be religious to want an exorcism?'

'Don't ask me. I haven't got a clue. Anyway, the vicar and his wife were really helpful. He's aware of this quasi-investigation we've got into Cane's death.'

'Oh, yeah?'

'From some bishop or other.'

'Sounds like we're getting interest from some high places. You do know what this business with Cane is about, Judd? It's about her realizing her professional glory days are behind her and she's feeling frustrated and useless and, in all likelihood, depressed.'

Judd drained her cup. 'I think she was lonely. The women who live here, including the older ones who look after the church, didn't take the trouble to welcome her.'

'Who said?'

Judd's notebook snapped shut. 'The vicar, more or less. I've just remembered. He's got, like, an assistant, a Matthew Redpath. I'll talk to him on Monday if he's available.'

Watts pushed his cup away, started to rise.

She looked up at him. 'Where are you going?'

'To have a chat with the officers I've got searching for Jack Beresford. I want you to phone the GP surgery – here's the number.'

She took it from him.

'Have a word with the practice nurse, Tracy Wilson. Get her take on Marion Cane.'

'I'm getting the feeling that whatever I say to you sinks without trace.'

'Heard every word, Judd.'

On her way to the surgery, Judd detoured to the address the vicar had provided. Getting out of the car, she picked up loud music. Heavy metal. This was it, all right. The houses on either side were detached, but she was willing to bet that this level of noise travelled. She headed for the one on the left, a car parked on its drive. She rang the bell and waited, ID at the ready. The door opened. Before she could speak, the man standing there glared at her, then at her ID.

'At last! I've made countless complaints to the neighbourhood association here and nothing's been done. Come in and hear for yourself what it's like, living next door to *that*!'

'Mr—?'

'Travis. Dan Travis.'

'Mr Travis, I'm not here about any noise nuisance.'

He stared at her.

'I'm part of the police investigation into the disappearance of an elderly resident named Jack Beresford—'

'Never heard of him.'

'I'd also appreciate a word with you about the house next door.'

'Sorry, come on in.'

She stepped inside and followed him into what looked like a dual-purpose sitting room/office, given the comfortable-looking sofas and high-spec computer equipment. She listened, barely picking up sounds from the next house.

Travis also listened. 'I think he's turned it down, but when I was zoned in on work earlier, it was really loud, throbbing away.'

'Do you know the people who live there?'

'Yes. Two youngish guys. They're part of the local church. Which is why I couldn't believe the music when it first started.'

'You've met them?'

'Just Matt. He's one of the few positives about this whole place as far as I'm concerned. Hang on.' He went to one of the computers, and Judd watched him save whatever he was working on. He looked up, grinned at her. 'Newton attracts two types of people: high-earning, mid-thirties professionals, and retirees. I don't fit in. I'm twenty-one. I write advertising copy and rent this place from my dad, rather than fork out for an office. What was I saying? Oh, yeah – I like a football kickabout at the weekend. So does Matt. We use the small playing field beyond the school.'

'You mentioned two guys living next door.'

Travis eye-rolled. 'The second one is a whole other story. Eric somebody. It's *his* music you just heard.'

'Do you know anything about him?'

He shrugged. 'Only what Matt's told me. Like I said, the house is a church set-up. Matt's been here a few years, the other one getting on for around two years. He comes and goes, looks like a hippie, all flowery shirts and these red jeans he wears.' He pointed in the direction of the house. 'The music is unusual at this time of day. He usually chooses night-time to play it, like some bloody vampire— Excuse me. I think Matt's had a word with him about it, and it has quietened down quite a bit. But it started up again around an hour ago, when I needed to concentrate, so it got right on my wick.' He raised his hand, listened. 'Nope. Totally quiet now.'

NINE

2.20 p.m.

Having noted down the details from Travis, Judd drove to the health centre. Going inside, she spoke to one of the receptionists behind the wide sweep of desk. 'I need to talk with Tracy Wilson, your practice nurse, please.'

The receptionist looked up at her. 'And you are?'

'Police Constable Chloe Judd.'

She took a few steps away as the woman reached for her phone and spoke quietly into it. 'She *says* she's a police officer . . . looks about sixteen . . . OK. I'll ask. Excuse me!' Judd returned to the desk. 'What's this about, exactly?'

'Marion Cane.'

The receptionist spoke into the phone again, looked up at Judd and pointed across the waiting area. 'Room number three.'

Judd headed for it. The door opened before she reached it and a cheerful-looking woman waved to her. 'Come on in, PC Judd! I'm Tracy Wilson. What can I do for you today?'

Inside the warm treatment room, Judd took the chair indicated. 'I have some questions about Marion Cane who died a few months ago.'

Wilson nodded. 'I remember Marion. Such a nice person, she was, to talk to.'

Judd's spirits rose. 'Did you see her often?'

'Only on the two occasions when she came in here to have her blood pressure checked.'

'Were you aware that Marion had concerns about her health?'

'Yes. I got an email from Doctor Devereaux indicating that she had consulted him, describing confusion and anxiety and subsequently some dizziness and memory problems, which is why he asked me to check her blood pressure. The first time I did it, it was within normal limits. The second time she came it was elevated, but when I told her, she didn't seem bothered about it. She said that she wasn't taking the medication Doctor Devereaux had prescribed for her.'

Again, Judd found herself wondering why an already anxious woman hadn't shown concern about a rise in her blood pressure. 'What did you make of that?'

Wilson shrugged. 'My job is to listen to what people say and advise them. I did suggest to Marion that she should seriously consider what the doctor had said, but I wasn't confident that she would.'

'Did you form a general impression of her from those two visits?'

Wilson hesitated. 'You mean, beyond her health concerns? The impression I got from talking to her was that she didn't like living here.'

'She actually said that?'

'More or less.'

'What did she say?'

'Hang on.' Wilson tapped computer keys and pointed at the screen. 'She said that once she was inside her house, the front door closed, she felt, "restless and worried". She turned to Judd. 'Marion was a single woman. From what she told me about her experience of working in New York and London, her life must have been really full-on back then.' She laughed. 'I don't mind admitting I was envious just listening to her, and all that time she was earning a crazy amount of money.' Wilson sent a glance to the closed door, lowering her voice. 'Have you seen the house where she lived?'

'Only from the outside. Very impressive.'

'I'll say! When she came here for her first blood test, she was wearing Nike gear, but the second time she came, she looked *the* business. Not glam, just quiet-posh, if you get what I'm saying. She had on a long black skirt, a silky cream shirt, boots. She looked a million dollars, but tasteful, you know?'

'Did she seem at all unhappy that day?'

'No. I wouldn't say unhappy. A bit distracted, possibly.' About to add something, she hesitated and closed her mouth.

Judd waited. 'We need whatever information you're able to give us, Ms Wilson.'

'It isn't information, not in the way you mean. Just an impression. To me, Marion seemed very . . . emotionally needy.'

'What made you think that?'

The nurse shrugged. 'Just the way she presented. She must have missed having colleagues; a lot of them were men. You know, a successful woman in a man's world.'

'You're saying that she needed male attention?'

Wilson was now looking uncomfortable. 'I wouldn't go that far. As I said, it was just an impression.'

Judd looked down at the notes she had made. 'Was Ms Cane on her way somewhere when you saw her that second time?'

'I don't know. She was always well dressed whenever I saw her around the Heights. Even her running clothes were pricey by my standards. The very last time I saw her was the week she died. I was on my way here and she was walking. She looked a bit pale, tired, you know, but she said she was planning to go into Birmingham to the theatre later to see a play.'

'Did she say anything else about that?'

'Only that she knew the place in America where it was set.'

'How did she seem to you on that occasion?'

'A bit tense, I thought. I mentioned it to Doctor Devereaux, and about her looking tired.'

'What did he say?'

Wilson's glance moved from Judd to the door and back. 'I wouldn't want him to hear this, but he just brushed it off.'

'Can you remember when you last saw her?'

'That was it, the time I just mentioned, which was on the Monday. I couldn't believe it when I heard she was found dead on the Friday.'

Judd's head was now in overdrive. 'The house she lived in is really big. We know she had a cleaner. Was there anyone else she employed?'

Wilson shook her head. 'Sorry, no idea. I know about the

cleaner because she works at the pub here and lives not far from me.'

'Did Marion entertain much, as far as you know?'

'I don't, but I doubt it. From the few comments she made here to me, she wasn't into that kind of thing. Too stressful, she said.' Wilson laughed. 'I tell you, if I had a house like that, I'd be dragging people in off the street just to look at it!' She sighed, shook her head. As Judd closed her notebook, Wilson pointed to it. 'I've just remembered. She had somebody do her garden for her.'

'Name?'

Wilson's face changed. 'Ryan Bartlett. He lives in Longbridge. Styles himself as a landscaper. I wouldn't have him near my property without my valuables being under lock and key. That's if I had any, but you get where I'm going.'

Judd left the health centre and in ten minutes she had reached the row of small, independent shops again, one of them an estate agent. She gazed through its window at photographs of properties for sale in the area with gobsmacking asking prices.

'Hey, Chlo!'

She turned to see Ade Jones coming towards her, in black baseball cap, black-and-white chequerboard strips on each side, black coveralls and boots. 'Hey, Jonesy. You're part of the search for Jack Beresford?'

'Yep. Finished ten minutes ago on account of the light starting to go. We'll be back early in the morning.' He glanced at the estate agent's window and grinned. 'Thinking of moving here?'

She eye-rolled. 'On my pay?'

They fell into step, neither of them breaking the silence between them. Before the last investigation that they had both worked on, she and Ade had been good mates. They still were, but it had got complicated. A man she really liked – a man Jonesy had detested – had turned out not to be the person— *Just leave it.* She and Ade still shared the occasional takeaway at her house, but there was now a subtle distance between them.

'I was looking for you,' he said. 'Sarge asked me to tell you to call it a day. He'll phone you later about tomorrow.'

'It's "Sir", now.'

'I know. Want a lift home?'

'Please.'

*   *   *

Thirty-five minutes later, he dropped Judd outside her house, with no pushing to come inside. She watched him drive away. Halfway along her path, she turned at quick footsteps approaching. It was her next-door neighbour moving at speed along his path. 'Hi, Dennis—'

'Hey, Chloe. Sorry, can't stop. A quick shower and out. It's quiz night!'

When she first moved here, Dennis was without work, always ready to chat, while she, under pressure from the case they were investigating, invariably gave him the brush-off. Now, he had a job and seemed to have his life back on track, which she was glad about. She smiled to herself. *It's lucky you've got Sassy for company.* 'Good quizzing, Dennis! Knock 'em dead.'

She opened her front door, stepped into her house, closed it, dropped her bag on the stairs and walked along the hall. The little cat came racing to her with its familiar *miaow*-and-bell-tinkle combo and proceeded to climb up her trouser leg. 'Ow-*ow*!' She laughed, hugged the little animal. She had worked out when the injections Sassy had been given as a tiny kitten would be fully effective and she could go outside. Today.

'Did you get brave and try the cat flap I left open?' She scrutinized the small face, the big yellow eyes staring at her. 'You *didn't*, did you? You gotta be more out there, kiddo.'

She put the little cat down and headed for the kitchen, more *miaow*-tinkle following. Inside the kitchen, she eyed the floor and the litter tray and crouched to stroke her. 'Sassy, you're such a goo-goo-girl!' she whispered.

Straightening, she sighed. 'Instead of talking to myself about investigative stuff, I now talk Idiot to my cat.' Selecting a tin of cat food from several in the cupboard, she fetched the plastic dish and fork. 'Looks like it's just you and me, Sass.'

An hour-plus later, plate on the floor bearing evidence of curry sauce and rice, Sassy next to her asleep on her back, soft tummy rising and falling, Judd emailed Watts brief notes on what she had learned that afternoon, then began a search.

The small screen filled with the names of plays set in New York – *42nd Street, Hamilton, Rent.* The list went on. She did the same for Birmingham. None of them seemed to fit Judd's expectation of what might have interested Marion Cane. She could hear Sarge's voice inside her head: *We go with the evidence and what it tells us. What we don't do is knit stuff together or make assumptions.*

She put the iPad on the floor and listened to rain beating her windows, eyes closing. Her phone buzzed. She started, fumbled for it. 'Yeah?'

'Cheer up,' said Watts.

'Those have to be two of the most annoying words in the English language,' she snapped.

'I know. I got your notes. Just wanted to let you know that I'm leaving for Newton Heights early in the morning to get the search for Jack Beresford moving up a notch as soon as there's daylight. I want you to call in at that estate agent. Make it early, so it's quiet. Request details of Marion Cane's house. According to her sister, the agents still have a load of details and photos. I want all of it.'

'Why, exactly, apart from being nosy?'

'I want to know who Marion Cane was. We start with where and how she lived.'

TEN

Saturday, 16 November. 8.15 a.m.

Judd parked close to The Running Man. As soon as she was out of her car, she sensed a change of atmosphere from the previous day. People – probably residents at this hour – were standing close to the row of shops, some deep in conversation, others pointing in the general direction of Jack Beresford's house. Something was *up*. She checked her phone. Nothing from Sarge. Deciding that the estate agent could wait, she got back inside her car, drove out of Newton Heights and turned left on to the Rednal Road. Reaching Beresford's house, seeing no parked vehicles, she continued on for several minutes, eventually slowing when she saw several up ahead, including Watts' BMW. She parked behind them and got out, picking up voices including some shouts. Following their direction, she walked the long path between two fields, black Nikes drifting over softness. Seeing Watts some way off, she hurried to him. 'Sarge! Sir!'

He turned, waited. 'Have you got the estate agent's stuff?'

'Not yet. As soon as I arrived, I could tell something was up, so I came straight here.'

'We've found Beresford.'

She followed him towards thick tree cover and through it to a dull, dank area smelling of dead vegetation. Beyond the police tape, several officers with reddened faces were pulling on ropes, a metal stretcher with broad straps coming slowly into view.

'Is he OK? What's happened?'

'There's a deep ravine just down there. It looks like he fell into it in the dark.'

They watched as officers, Jonesy among them, carried the stretcher towards the road, their feet sliding, and on to an ambulance that had just arrived. Surrendering the stretcher to the paramedics, it was driven away, lights flashing, its short, piercing *wiu-wiu-wiu* splitting the air, fading to nothing, leaving a heavy silence. 'He's alive?' asked Judd.

'Deeply unconscious. The lads got him out as soon as they could. That's all we know.'

She gave Watts a steady look. 'The words he said to you at the pub. You *must* be thinking there's something in what's happening here, and if you're not, then I—'

'We don't run—'

'Before we can walk. I *know,* but there has to be some connection to Marion Cane.' She turned away from him, then back again. 'And that unsigned note is telling me that Beresford isn't the only one who knows something.'

'Unless he wrote it.' He checked his watch. 'Get to the estate agent and collect all that stuff I want.' He rummaged through his pockets, brought out his notebook, flicked pages. 'I've arranged to see Craig Jessop, Cane's solicitor, to ask him what her estate is worth.'

'Have you heard from Will?'

'Not yet, but Heritage is adamant that he wants him on this investigation.'

Judd drove back to Newton Heights, parked directly in front of the estate agent's and went inside. A woman seated at a pale-grey desk was talking on her phone. Judd walked around, listening to the posh voice, giving property photographs peripheral glances, looking at the woman, absorbing the details: smooth blonde hair to her shoulders, a ring on her left hand big enough to double as a weapon, a cream knit dress and soft-looking brown boots. Judd pictured the likely childhood that had produced it. *Horse-riding, private schools, mummy and daddy* . . . Definitely a gymkhana type.

Switching her face to pleasant, she approached the desk and waited. So far, she hadn't merited a glance. The call wasn't about to end any time soon. Judd fixed her gaze on her. 'I need to speak to you now, please.'

The call continued without pause. 'Mm . . . I know. You're *so* right, Caro. They're absolutely ghastly types.' She sighed. 'Look, someone's just come in, so I'll call you back in a sec . . . Ciao.'

Call ended, she sent Judd's mud-covered Nikes a glance then looked up at her with cool grey-blue eyes. 'Yes?'

'I'm here to talk to the owner of the business.'

'He's not here.'

'When do you expect him?'

'Tomorrow. Possibly.'

Picking up the satisfaction underlying the two words, Judd said, 'I need information about a house here.'

The woman's eyes travelled over Judd a second time. 'If you tell me which property you're interested in—'

'The house that belonged to Marion Cane.'

Immaculate brows slowly rose. 'We are handling that property and we have all of the relevant information on it in readiness, but as of now probate has not been completed.' The facial expression morphed from pleased to haughty. 'In case you're *not* aware, the asking price is likely to be in the region of two mill—' She stopped as Judd's ID appeared. Haughty was replaced by something that looked like disbelief.

'This is police business,' said Judd. 'I want all of that information, including printed details, plus photographs of the property, both internal and external. I'll take it with me.'

'You can't view the inside,' she snapped. 'Ms Cane's family is very specific on that point. The house is as it was when she died, still furnished, so there's a security issue—'

'Not for us, there isn't, and, yes, we can. We're liaising fully with Mr and Mrs Franklin.'

Their eyes locked. Judd watched the woman stand, which brought her to around five feet ten, tracked her languid sashay to a nearby door. Within a couple of minutes, she was back, her hands around a box file. It arrived on the desk with a solid thump, French manicured hands proprietorial.

'Keys,' prompted Judd. She watched a repeat performance, this time with a flounce and toss of blonde hair, listened as drawers were pulled open, then banged shut. The woman reappeared, dropped the keys on to the box file.

'Thank you.'

Judd left the premises, arms around the file, the keys in her pocket, thinking that height gave gravitas. At five feet two she didn't have any. What she did have was attitude when she was being messed with. Back inside her car, she opened the file. Uppermost was a letter from Jessop, Marion Cane's solicitor, to the Franklins, confirming what they already knew: Marion Cane's house would be up for sale once probate was finalized. She turned a few pages, not seeing anything that looked remotely relevant to Cane's death, then on to a slick-looking presentation file of glossy photographs to entice potential buyers. The first was an exterior shot. Despite having already seen the house from the outside, Judd's eyes stretched. She gave a long, low whistle. Impressive as it had been at first sight, her initial glimpse hadn't done it full justice. The place was jaw-dropping. Her eyes slid over the photo, then on to numerous other exterior shots. Reaching the interior photographs, she absorbed its internal scale, the design, the detail. She looked out at dullness and mist. There was only one word for Marion Cane's home. Breath-taking.

She turned back to a photograph showing the rear elevation of the house, her brows creasing as her eyes moved slowly over it. Glass. Way too much glass for Judd's liking. She was back in a summer-hot classroom, the teacher's voice drifting to her on the warm air, a few half-remembered words. *This is one of Aesop's fables . . . about a fox wanting to eat some grapes high above him . . . He can't reach them . . . Walks away, telling himself the grapes are sour . . .*

Judd grinned, seeing herself in the fox, dissing Marion Cane's house because it was beyond anything she could ever have. Sour grapes.

She leapt at the sudden opening of her passenger door.

Watts leaned inside. 'Aye-up, Judd. Stop talking to yourself. That the stuff from the estate agent?'

'Yes,' she snapped, 'and I wish you wouldn't *do* that.'

'Never knew anybody like you for losing herself in detail. I'm not cramming myself in there to look at it. Bring it with you.'

'Any news on Jack?'

'No.'

She followed him to his vehicle. Once inside, she said, 'Remember we passed Marion's house the other day? You will *not* believe what you're about to see. Take a look.'

She passed the photographs to him, heard his low, 'Bloody *hell.*'

She then brought out another small album and looked inside at the interior photographs, the first of a sitting room with what looked to be a mile-high ceiling. 'Holy *moly!*' She breathed, held it up, pointing, 'See *this*? Inside, there's a sort of glass balcony where the bedrooms are, looking down on to the ground floor.'

Watts glanced at it. 'Looks like a hotel foyer to me.'

'Her furniture's to *die* for.' She thought of Marion Cane. Rich. Successful. Dead.

Watts passed the photographs back to her. 'I want to see it, first-hand. I'll go to the Franklins, first chance I get and request the keys—' He looked up at a faint jingling sound. 'Where'd you get them?'

'Same place as all this.'

He dug in his pocket for his phone. 'I'll let Mrs Franklin know we're going over there.'

'When?'

'Now.'

A few minutes later, Watts drove on to extensive brick paving and they gazed out at Marion Cane's last home. Even on a dull November day like this, it was every bit as impressive as its photographs. Ultra-modern, despite its various roof elevations and rose-coloured tiles. Judd's eyes settled on the extensive windows. Hungry fox aside, her view was still that they were great for looking out. Just as great for looking in. Watts was searching his pockets. 'Franklin gave me the security code . . . *Got* it.'

Pulling a scrap of paper from an inside pocket, he looked down at what he had written, silently repeating it. They got out and approached the house. Watts inserted the key and gave the heavy door a gentle push. It swung slowly, silently open. He stepped inside. About to follow him, Judd stopped, her chest tightening at a sudden, insistent *tk-tk-tk*. She waited as Watts crossed the wide hall to a keypad and entered the code. It stopped. Judd breathed.

She stepped inside. Watts raised his latex-gloved hands to her, then moved away from her to the stairs. Pulling two gloves from her jacket pocket and putting them on, she hesitated, suddenly reluctant, then went further inside the ground floor and opened a door on the left. It too swung smoothly open. It was one of the rooms she had already seen in a photograph, its sheer height demanding that she look up, *up*. She did, to a ceiling seemingly suspended miles above her, the balcony she had seen in photographs running high along one wall.

She looked away and down, getting another sudden wave of dizziness that had become all too familiar in the last couple of weeks, this time followed by a tightening inside her chest. She took a few deep breaths. The dizziness stopped. Her eyes moved slowly over enviable furniture and on to a massive white sofa. She went to it and sat. She and Sassy would be small and lost on it. Sassy's paws, her own denim jeans, on *white*? Any furniture of this size would never fit through her front door, or any other part of her house. Hearing soft sounds as Watts moved around upstairs, she crossed the room, taking in Marion Cane's other furnishings. Pausing at an attractive cupboard, its doors of tinted glass, she carefully opened it. Books. She reached up, removed one. Not just any books. This one was a classic. She opened it. A first edition. *The Fall of the House of Usher.* She knew it from secondary school, remembered the atmosphere of it, the solitariness, the isolation, the sense of being trapped . . . All of it too close to her own early life experience. During the first reading by her teacher, Judd had fainted. That teacher, a great encourager of Judd, had accepted her time-of-the-month explanation. In subsequent lessons, Judd had sat, outwardly attentive, thinking on hold.

Replacing the book and closing the cupboard doors, she moved across the great expanse of wood floor to a thick, colourful rug. What had it been like for Marion Cane living here alone? She looked again at the high ceiling, wondering if there was anywhere in this whole place that invited a person to just curl up and revel in its warmth as a home. Would the heating being on make it feel different? Welcoming? She pushed her hands inside her pockets, seeing Watts suddenly appear above her, moving along the balcony and disappearing through another door. She crossed the room to a low, solid-looking table, several magazines resting on it. She picked up one of them, glossy and heavy. It was full of pictures of women in outfits no ordinary people ever saw in real life. She put it down, looked at others, months old magazines, among them something smaller, slimmer. She slid it out. The door behind her drifted silently open.

'Talk about throwing money about!'

She started, squeezing her eyes closed. 'Do *not* sneak up on me like that!'

'I wasn't, and there's nobody here but us. What's got you so tense?' He came to her. 'Find something?'

She shook her head. 'I've only been in this room so far. It's weird, but I don't feel that comfortable opening drawers and going through Cane's belongings.'

'Part of the job description.'

'I know, but . . . this place isn't exactly a crime scene.'

'This is where she lived and where she died, which is why we're here. Anything got your interest?'

She waved the slim item. 'This theatre programme. I like the theatre, when I get the chance to go. This is for a show that ran for a month in Birmingham. I didn't see it, but look at the dates.'

He did. 'And?'

'It fits with what the practice nurse at the surgery told me, that just days before she died, Marion Cane went to the theatre.'

'That's high blood pressure for you. A few blokes I worked with over the years had it. Never a day's illness, then *zap*, out like lights in their forties.' He clicked his fingers. 'Just like that.'

She grinned up at him. 'You probably sneaked up on *them* as well.'

She turned programme pages, read aloud, '*Wait Until Dark.*' She got a quizzical glance. 'It's the name of the play.' She pointed to the synopsis. 'It says here that it's set in New York in a place called Greenwich Village. This has to be the play Marion Cane went to see. It looks to me like she was missing her old life. I'm paraphrasing the plot here: one of the main characters, the husband, comes home from a business trip, bringing a doll – I hate dolls, just saying. This particular doll is stuffed with drugs, right? He goes out and some guys who are after the doll get inside the house, but what they don't know is that his wife, who's blind by the way, is inside—'

'Got it. It's a comedy. According to what Franklin told us, Cane was glad to leave New York and London behind.'

Judd looked up at him. 'Do *you* think something bad happened to her here, Sarge, in this house?'

'My jury's still out.'

She put down the programme, her gaze drifting around the room. It settled on a place on a nearby wall. 'I thought nothing from when Marion Cane was alive had been removed?'

'It hasn't.'

She pointed. 'Something's gone from there, see?'

He came and stood next to her, followed her extended finger. Taking glasses from an inside pocket, he put them on. It was the faintest of marks. The merest shadow on smooth, pale paint. A rectangular outline. 'She probably had a picture there and she moved it. It's what happens. You buy a picture, put it up, then change your mind and move it elsewhere. It's about living with things. You'll get what I mean when you've been in your place a year or two.' He looked again, seeing something just above the rectangle, a tiny indentation, smoothed and painted over with some skill. He pointed to it. 'Yep. She had a picture hanging there.'

Judd followed him from the sitting room and into a spacious kitchen of pale-grey wood and dark-grey drawer pulls, all topped with dark-grey granite, plus splotches of red from a coffee machine, kettle, toaster. More floor-to-ceiling windows. She gazed out at the dead garden, then at her own reflection, blonde, small. Alone.

'Sarge?' She went quickly to the door and into the hallway. He was halfway up the stairs. 'Don't just *go* without saying anything!'

'What's up with you?'

'. . . I just need to know where you're going . . .'

He looked down at her. 'Judd, this is no *Psycho* house. It's modern, worth a fortune and way beyond our combined pay scales. Come *on*.'

She started up the stairs after him. He was right. Money had been lavished on this place. Yet there was something lacking. She cast about for a word, came up with 'soul'. Following his suede shoes, she reached the landing and continued on to what looked like the main bedroom. Going inside, she stood in its centre and slowly turned. *Sumptuous* was the word. No expense spared. Times when she had eaten too much chocolate drifted into her head. Yep. It summed up this whole place. Too much. Way. Too. Much. The super-king bed with its heavy woven bedcover in scarlets and pinks, the pale, transparent drapes secured above it, looping downwards either side, pale satin pillows, cream wood shutters at the windows, ensuite bathroom, walk-in wardrobe. She went inside, counted eight pairs of top-of-the-range trainers, four more designer pairs. Whatever her health status, Marion Cane looked to have been well into fitness. Coming back to the bedroom, she was stopped by a framed sketch hanging on the wall above the bed. She stared at the fine curving lines forming a delicate oval, the subtle shadings of flesh tints, deepening to rose— Judd felt a sudden rush of heat to her face. If this is what had hung on the sitting-room wall, no wonder Cane moved it up here. Watts went past her, his eyes on the sketch.

'A bit abstract for my liking.'

She wasn't about to tell him what she was seeing: something female. Private. She shook her head, walked to a bedside table, pulled out a drawer. Empty. Bowing her head, she looked again. Not quite.

'Sarge? I think there are meds in here.'

She reached inside and brought out a small box. He came, looked at it, lowered his head and reached inside, bringing out three more. 'Eye drops. Nothing I've read has indicated that Cane had an eye problem.' She looked at the boxes. 'Those are over-the-counter, not prescription.'

'For what?'

'They soothe your eyes if they feel tired. They also help if you want the whites looking clear.'

'Again, for what?'

'Like, a date or something.'

She looked up at him. 'At fifty-nine, Marion Cane wouldn't be having dates, would she?'

'No, she'd be too busy falling to bits or being brain-dead, like everybody else who's fifty-plus.'

'I *never* said that.'

He gazed at the four small boxes. 'This stuff mattered enough to her to buy in bulk.'

Judd gazed down at them. 'I think Marion Cane had a man in her life.'

'I hope she did. We need to find him. It could open up our inquiries.' Watts carefully placed all four boxes in an evidence bag, closed the drawer.

Judd was looking around the room. 'I'm confused. I don't know where I am with this, looking at the life of a woman whose death was certified as due to natural causes.'

'We're following what Heritage asked us to do.'

'Did you speak to Cane's solicitor?'

'Briefly. According to what I got from him, the probate value of this house alone is massive, plus she had a lot in investments, which she would have, given the kind of work she did. He's already requested updated information from those companies and from her bank about all of her financial arrangements.'

Judd was looking dissatisfied. 'Here's something Einstein never said: Money plus man equals motive.'

He grunted. 'That wouldn't be a sexist comment, by any chance?'

'No. Realistic.'

'Leaving that well alone, do you fancy an early lunch?'

ELEVEN

They were inside The Running Man, this time aware of local attention on them from some distance away. Watts was waiting for his call to be picked up. Ignoring the looks coming their way, Judd lowered her voice, 'I don't think this place was a good idea—'

'Mrs Franklin? DCI Watts. Did your sister have maintenance people or decorators she routinely used?' He nodded. 'Yeah, mmm' – he wrote down details – 'thanks for that. No. Just a general question.' He ended the call. 'If Marion Cane needed interior work doing, she used somebody local. Ryan Bartlett. I've got his contact number.'

'Tracy Wilson, Devereaux's practice nurse, mentioned him. She said he was the gardener.'

Solange arrived with a bad attitude and their sandwiches, which she dumped on the table. 'Your coffee and tea are coming,' she snapped.

Watts watched her go. 'What I really like about this whole place is the welcome it extends to outsiders.'

Judd bit into her prawn salad on rye, and eye-rolled as he lifted two thick slices of white bread, browned sausages and tomato sauce just visible.

He chewed, nodded, pointing at it. 'At least they put together a decent sandwich here. None of that *ciabatta* stuff that's every-where. I've just remembered where I've seen Bartlett's name. It was on a board outside a house near to the Franklins'.'

They continued eating, ignoring occasional glances from distant customers. After a few minutes, their drinks arrived. Watts gulped his. 'I want to see this Bartlett and hear what he's got to say about Marion—' His phone buzzed. He reached for it and listened. It didn't take long. 'Thanks for letting me know.' He ended the call, lowered his voice. 'That was Connie. The hospital just phoned. Jack Beresford died without regaining consciousness. I want to look at the place where he fell while there's still some decent light.'

Thirty minutes later, they pulled off the road, parked close to other official vehicles and followed the rough pathway on foot. 'What did Doctor Chong actually say?' asked Judd.

'A head injury he sustained is believed to be the cause of death.'

Jones was waiting for them. As they neared, he said, 'I'll take you down the gradual route to the bottom of the ravine, Sarge. It's an old disused railway line and it's a really steep approach otherwise.' He glanced at Judd, nodded. 'All right, Chlo?'

'Yep.'

They followed Jones past the place where the old man had been hoisted by stretcher, then along and down a relatively shallow incline to the bottom of the ravine, Judd's attention caught by a narrow gleam of metal. She pointed. 'What's that?'

Jones looked to where she was pointing. 'It's a short run of the old railway track. Most of it has disappeared. That square thing over there is an old coal store.'

He saw Judd's frown.

'Steam trains ran through here years ago.'

'What are we looking for?' she asked Watts.

He had been asking himself the same question. 'Anything that looks like it might be relevant.' He looked around. 'Why would a man in his nineties come to this place, without a coat and alone at night? The short answer is he wouldn't. Somebody either brought or forced him here. The same somebody who drugged his dog, got Jack out of his house, not bothering with his coat because he *knew* Jack wouldn't be needing it. Let's hope the hospital post-mortem gives us something.'

Jones pointed to the nearby bank rising steeply upwards. 'That's where we managed to get him out.' He paused. 'He reminded me of my great-grandad.'

'Did Beresford speak at all while you were here?'

'Not a word, Sarge.'

They came to the taped area where Jack Beresford had lain. Watts got down on one knee, his gaze moving slowly over the immediate area. Despite the relatively early hour, the light was going fast. He patted his pockets. 'Torch, Jones.'

He took it, playing the sharp beam over thick grass and dead leaves. Pulling on a glove, he reached down, gathered small items, then looked up to see Jones holding out an evidence bag. Watts dropped the few items into it and got to his feet. 'Have a look for anything I've missed, Jones.' He looked up at an area of darkening sky visible above the trees. 'Better make it quick.'

Back in his office, Watts placed a pristine sheet of thick white paper on the table, carefully shook the contents of the evidence bag on to it, then looked to Jones, who added a few more items. Judd looked down at them, chin on fist, face judgemental. 'Sweet wrappers, scrap of paper, gum wrappers, plastic bottle caps, ring pulls . . .'

'We've been told that local railway enthusiasts collect litter there,' said Jones. 'I checked. The last time they were there was eight days ago.'

Judd prodded the items with a pen, then looked up at Watts. 'Were you hoping for anything specific?'

'No, but it's all of interest because it was where Jack was lying.'

She prodded again. 'I think we can rule out his chewing gum, drinking Coke and smoking.' Seeing their eyes on her, she shrugged. 'One of the basic words applied to the content of any scene is "relevance". None of this looks relevant to Beresford. How sure are we that it *is* a "scene" in the criminal sense? Just like we don't know for sure that Marion Cane was victimized.' She sent Watts a disgruntled glance. 'I'm just saying that I don't see how these bits of litter help us.'

Watts carefully gathered them together and replaced them in the bag, thinking how in the past she would drive him nuts with her enthusiasm for everything. Times change. Enthusiasm now tempered by experience. 'I'll get Adam to give it all a once-over. You, OK?'

She frowned, avoiding his gaze. 'Yes, why?'

'You've been looking a bit under the weather these last few days.'

The door swung open and Heritage came inside, followed by Traynor. Heritage broke the sudden silence. 'Any progress?'

Watts said, 'The hospital has confirmed that Jack Beresford died without regaining consciousness, which is all we've got until they do the post-mortem. In relation to Marion Cane, we're continuing to pull together a picture of her life.'

Heritage nodded. 'Will's here to give you some help on both.'

They watched Heritage's progress to the door, saw it close on him, each of them searching for something to say to Traynor. He looked thinner in the face than when they last saw him just days before. He spoke, his voice subdued. 'The university has insisted I take the two weeks' compassionate leave I've been offered, which I didn't request and don't want.' He looked at Watts. 'I need something to do, Bernard.' He ran his hand over his hair, gazing downwards, rather than at them. 'I need to be part of something.'

'You are, Will. We're glad to have you here.'

Judd was curbing a sudden impulse to go to Will and give

him a hug. She watched him sit as Watts supplied a quick update on the deaths of Marion Cane and Jack Beresford. 'Cane's death is still natural causes, but Beresford's might be shaping up as something more sinister. What links them for me are the words Jack said to me, plus the anonymous note. It's possible he knew something about Marion Cane or her death. It was her death that took us to Newton Heights in the first place. Oh, and we've got another possible connection for what it's worth: Jack Beresford's sons, who took over his business, built Cane's house and one of them lived in it for a while. Judd will bring you up to speed on where we're at while I get some coffee going.'

As Watts left the table, Judd looked at him. 'Are you OK, Will?'

'Yes, Chloe,' he said quietly. 'Shall we make a start?'

Judd began laying out all they knew so far about Marion Cane's life and what appeared to be the facts of her death, adding what else they knew of Jack Beresford in life and death. Jones added details of the search for Beresford, his eventual location at the ravine and the confirmation of his death. Traynor listened without making notes. As Watts returned with coffee, he asked, 'What's the initial view of each of these deaths? How about you, Chloe?'

She hesitated. 'I've been more involved with Cane. There were some physical health concerns – dizziness, anxiety, that kind of thing – possibly relating to her mental health, neither of which seemed to cause her GP any real concerns, but she died very suddenly at fifty-nine, and to me, well, it doesn't feel right. I know we don't investigate deaths on the basis of feelings, but it was Jack Beresford's comment to Sarge in relation to Cane, to "keep asking your questions", plus the anonymous note, which led to us becoming involved at all. Trouble is, there's no way of knowing what Jack was thinking when he said what he did.'

Traynor turned to Jones. 'Do you have any thoughts, Adrian?'

'Only that, until we know otherwise, Jack's head injury could be entirely due to his fall into the ravine.' He paused. 'The big question for all of us who were involved in the search for him is what the hell was he doing there?'

'Are there any theories on either of the deaths?'

Jones shrugged. 'I don't know much about Marion Cane and I flip-flop between Beresford's death being accidental or something criminal. That about sums up where I'm at.'

Judd nodded at Traynor. 'It's a similar story for me with Cane. Her death certificate says heart disease, but there are aspects of her life that I can't get my head around. As for Beresford, his being out there on his own, with no coat, makes absolutely no sense, so it has to be suspicious.'

Watts came to the table. 'We need to know more about Cane, but right now our primary focus is Jack Beresford.'

Jones looked to Traynor. 'We've started making some low-level inquiries about him with the locals. None of them are rushing forward to talk to us, with the possible exception of the vicar. He's been helpful, given his knowledge of Newton Heights. Our real difficulty is that it's essentially a bedroom community. A big proportion of the residents drive or take the train to work and return late. It's been difficult to find anybody who knows anything about Beresford. I'm anticipating a similar response, once we start asking about Cane.'

Traynor looked at each of them. 'Beyond what you've already said, is there any information so far that has claimed your interest?'

Avoiding Watts' gaze, Judd said, 'Yes. I went to the church a day or so ago. There's a room at the back. I went inside and there were two people there—'

'You don't *know* that for certain,' said Watts. 'You never saw anybody.'

'No, but I heard enough to know it was two people in some kind of sexual situation. Will has just asked for anything that got our interest. *That* got mine.' She looked around the table. 'How many times have either of you been in a church and actually heard sex going on?'

Jones grinned at her. 'Never, but it would get my interest.'

Traynor quickly wrote. 'You're not able to guess the identity of whoever it was?'

'No, I just wanted to get out of there.'

Traynor looked at each of them. 'What do you know about Marion Cane and her life so far?'

They gave him all of it, including the nature of the work she had had in the past, details of her health and information about the high value and contents of the house where she lived and where she died.

Watts waited for him to finish writing. 'How do you feel about talking to one or two people, Will? There's a young chap who is part of the church, and there's also Cane's cleaner. Neither has been spoken to yet.'

Traynor reached out for information lying on the table, a slight tremor evident in his hand. 'Before I get directly involved, I need to absorb everything you've told me about these two people who have died. I'll also want to talk to forensics officers who have attended the scene where Beresford died.'

Hearing his words, Watts got his first surge of optimism. Given Traynor's criminological skills, whatever case there was here, he had confidence that Traynor would find it. 'It's your call, Will. We've got trace evidence from the spot where Beresford was recovered—'

'It's literally rubbish,' said Judd.

'I'd like to see it.'

Watts reached for the phone. 'Adam's team has it. I'll let him know you're working with us.' After speaking a few words into the phone, he replaced it. 'Adam says to go straight up.' He and Traynor walked to the door together. Watts held out his hand. 'We're glad to have you with us again, Will.'

'Thank you, Bernard,' he said quietly. 'You're a good friend.'

They watched him leave, Judd biting her lip.

'How's he doing, Sarge?' asked Jones.

'As OK as anybody can be, given the news he's just had, but he's tough. Over the last few years, he's had to be. What're your plans for Monday, Judd?'

'I'll go and see Matthew Redpath, the church deacon. The vicar described him as helpful, which probably means pleasant but no help at all. At least he'll know a lot of the people who live in that place by name.'

'When you do see him, keep your opinion of "that place", plus churches in general, to yourself. On Monday, I'm going back to the pub to see what's-her-name . . .' He turned notebook pages. 'Theresa Yates, the cleaner there, who also cleaned for Marion Cane. At some stage, I also want to talk to this Ryan Bartlett, her gardener-handyman.' He checked the time on his phone. 'Are you on duty tomorrow, Jonesy?'

'No, sir. Back Monday.'

He looked from Jones to Judd. 'It's been a long week. Go on, you two. Enjoy what's left of your weekend.' As Judd got ready to leave, he lowered his voice. 'Make sure you get some quality downtime. You look all in.'

'I already told you, I'm OK.'

One floor up, Traynor took the plastic bag from headquarters' head of forensics. 'Thanks, Adam.' He gently shook the bag and separated the items with his pen, frowning at them, understanding Chloe Judd's description of it as 'rubbish', seeing little investigative relevance in any of it.

TWELVE

Monday, 18 November. 9.40 a.m.

Watts came into the lounge of The Running Man, picking up subtle smells of polish, not-so-subtle bleach, and a loud, continuous whir. Stools were up on tables, legs in the air, chairs moved to one side of the big room. A woman was dragging a vacuum cleaner, her arm moving energetically forward and back over the bright, patterned carpet. He called to her, 'Morning!' Getting no response, he followed the flex to the wall and flicked the switch.

The woman stopped, glared at the vacuum cleaner and delivered it a swift kick. 'Sodding, *useless* thing—'

'Theresa Yates?'

She whirled. 'Who are *you*? The pub's not open yet.'

'DCI Bernard Watts.' He held up ID. 'I'd like to talk to you.'

She stared up at him, letting the business end of the vacuum cleaner drop to the floor. 'What about?'

Sidestepping the question, he reached for two stools and carried them to the bar. 'Half an hour of your time should do it.'

With little show of enthusiasm, she followed him, flicked a duster at one of the stools and sat, her eyes fixed on him. Watts did some evaluation of his own: forty-plus, on the heavy side, wearing a tabard overall. He wondered what she had made of Marion Cane's house and, more to the point, its owner. Right now, she was looking apprehensive.

'Hurry up, then! I've got stuff to do and the landlord's wife is a bloody fault-finder.'

'Marion Cane.' He waited for a response. It took twelve seconds to arrive.

'What about her? She's dead.'

'Do you live around here?'

She gave him a sideways glance. 'Yeah, right. If I could afford it, do you think I'd be cleaning *here*?' With a heavy sigh, she swung to face him, plump knees showing below the tabard. 'I live in Dempsey, just this side of Longbridge. I do two mornings a week here, Mondays and Thursdays from eight to ten.' She half rose, peered across the bar to the door on the other side, head tilted in listening mode, then reached into her pocket and brought out a cigarette and a plastic lighter. Lighting the cigarette, blowing smoke to one side, she eyed him. 'I've seen police hanging around. Why do you want to talk to me?'

'Like I said, Marion Cane.'

'Why now? She's been dead months.'

'Tell me about her.'

A long drag on the cigarette and Yates blew more smoke over her shoulder. 'I loved my job at her place. She was a great person to work for, Marion. The best.'

'Go on.'

She shrugged. 'I cleaned for her for the best part of two years, usually on a Friday with an occasional day agreed between us. Not that you'd class it as cleaning.' Her eyes drifted over the saloon. 'Not like this dump. I loved going there.' She sighed, shook her head. 'What a life she'd had. She'd worked all over, you know. She had a really good head on her but she was nice with it. She'd make us tea or coffee and we'd chat.'

'What about?'

Another shrug. 'Sometimes about the jobs she'd had, the places she'd lived. She would ask me about my life. About Ralph and the kids. There was no side to her, if you know what I mean.'

'Was there ever anyone else there on the days you worked?'

Yates' eyes slid from his. 'Not that I recall.'

He made a mental note.

'It was you who found her dead.'

A long drag on the cigarette. She pinched it out, dropped it into the tabard pocket, waving away the smoke. 'That was a right bloody to-do, that was! I never had a key to the house, which I was glad about because I didn't want any messing with the house alarm. I always rang the bell and Marion would let me in. That morning, she didn't. I rang again. Same.'

'What time was this?'

'I'd say around half nine. I get the bus and it's often late. Have you seen her house?'

'You're outside, waiting to get in,' Watts prompted.

'The bloke who did her garden was already there, sitting in his van. He let me in.'

'He had a key?'

She gave Watts a look. 'He'd have needed one to do that, wouldn't he?'

'Got a name?'

'Ryan somebody.'

'Was it his usual day?'

'Couldn't tell you.'

'What sorts of jobs did he do at the house?'

Yates' eyes drifted away. 'Far as I could see, he pulled up an occasional weed and generally messed about, like there was a lot for him to do. I know that Marion did a bit of gardening when she felt up to it. That whole house and garden looked like they'd just been unwrapped and plunked down – know what I mean?'

Watts backtracked. 'You've said that this Ryan had a key and he let you into the house.'

'Yeah. He knew I worked for Marion and—'

'When he let you in, did he turn off the alarm?'

'Far as I recall, it wasn't on.'

Watts' interest in this woman was escalating and, so far, he was willing to accept what she was telling him. 'What did you do when you got inside? I want details.'

She leaned against the bar, arms folded, looking at him. 'It was just like any other morning, except that Marion wasn't about. I just got on with it. Went into the laundry, took washing out of the machine. Put it in the dryer. Came back to the kitchen, wiped some stuff off the floor tiles—'

'What stuff?'

She shrugged. 'Dunno. Just pink powdery bits, like Marion had stepped on something. She was very particular about that floor. I got a cloth, wiped it up, then washed the floor. By then it was getting on for quarter to eleven and still no sight nor sound of her.'

'Where was this Ryan?'

'Somewhere outside, as far as I know.'

'What did you do?'

'I was a bit hesitant. Marion had to be in because of the alarm being off, so I decided to check on her.' She looked away from him. 'She was in her bedroom, actually in bed, just . . . lying there. I didn't need to be told she was dead. I'd seen my two nans . . . but this was different.'

'How?'

'It was the way Marion looked. All neat, you know? Her hair just so. There were flowers in a vase on one side of the bed. I'd never seen flowers there before.' She looked up at Watts. 'This will sound barmy but, like I said, I'd seen my two nans, dead. I also saw them at the undertaker's place when they looked all right. That's how Marion looked. All neat and tidy, her face clean, except for what looked like a bit of lip gloss. I touched her arm.' She tapped the bar's surface. 'Colder than this, she was. It shook me up, I can tell you, although now I think about it, it was probably because she was so young. I'd never seen anybody that young who was dead.'

'Was she in poor health?'

She snorted. 'No! OK, she looked stressed at times, a bit tired, but physically she was in great shape, and I *mean* great shape, if you get what I'm saying.'

Watts said nothing.

'She walked loads and she did that Pilates stuff. She took classes.'

'Where?'

'Here, in Newton. She said her GP told her she needed to calm down a bit, not get so agitated.' The corners of Yates' mouth travelled downwards. 'Well, he would, wouldn't he?'

'Would he?'

'Course! He's a bit flash, that one. Into the money. His wife runs the Pilates classes. I bet they don't come cheap.'

'At the health centre?'

She looked scornful. 'She has her own studio where she teaches it. There's plenty around here with nothing to do and money to waste.'

'Tell me what you know about Marion Cane's life here.'

Yates hesitated. 'You're asking about her personal life?'

'I'm asking you to tell me anything you know.'

She lowered her voice, gave him a conspiratorial look. 'I can't give you chapter and verse, but I think she had somebody. A man.'

'A partner?'

'I wouldn't go that far, just somebody . . . occasional, you know.'

'Who?'

'How would I know! I was there two days a week, max.'

Watts was now slot-rattling between irritation and curiosity. Curiosity won. 'What led you to think she had a man?'

She gave him another look, this one triumphant. 'The wine glasses! The coffee cups! The little dish she used for nuts.'

'What about them?'

'They were in the dishwasher, waiting to be washed. Marion was a stickler with that machine. She rarely left stuff hanging around inside it. It was a Monday morning. This place wasn't opening that morning, a family funeral or something, and typical Marion, knowing I needed the money, she asked me if I wanted to do a couple of extra hours at her house.' She sighed. 'Whoever it was, he must have been there on the Sunday. *That's* the sort of man any woman would want: a drink, bit of a chat, then straight to it, no messing about with cooking—'

'When was this?'

'Now, you're asking. I'd say it was a few months prior to her dying.'

'Did she ever tell you that she was involved with somebody?'

'Course she didn't! We weren't on those kinds of terms, and Marion was a private person, but, trust me, there *was* somebody.'

Watts considered all she had said so far. She brushed ash from the tabard's upper chest area. 'Good luck to her, I say. She had a great figure and her *clothes* – they were something else. Why she wanted to live in this place never made sense to me. I know what would have suited her. One of them posh penthouse apartment places in the middle of Birmingham, the Jewellery Quarter. All the restaurants, bars and clubs close by, but no. She chooses Newton. To me, that's like being buried alive. I hope she did have somebody to liven things up.'

Watts asked, 'Got *any* idea who he might have been?'

'The bloke she'd got?' Yates shrugged. 'No, but I doubt he lived around here. If he did, it would have been all over the Heights, yet I never heard a whisper. Which I would have done, working in this place.'

'What do you know about her sister and brother-in-law?'

'Only that they live close by. I got the impression Marion didn't get on with her sister.'

'What about the brother-in-law?'

'I've hardly ever seen him. He came to Marion's place one Christmas to deliver something. I think his job takes him away a lot.' She grinned at Watts. 'I bet he's happy about that. That wife of his looks like a right misery. Nothing like Marion.'

'Any talk about them, as far as you know?'

'You mean, like gossip?' She shrugged. 'Far as I know, he wasn't around enough to be talked about and the same for her, really.'

He changed direction. 'Marion Cane was involved with the church here.'

Yates stared at him. 'She never mentioned that to me. She had no time for religion, far as I know.'

'She used to help with the upkeep of the church,' said Watts. 'You know, tidying, polishing, taking flowers there, arranging them.'

Yates sniffed. 'I wouldn't know about that.' She watched him flip his notebook closed. 'There was something, although I don't want to make a thing of it. It was nothing, really.'

The notebook opened.

Yates looked at her watch, sent a brief look around the large room. 'One time I was at Marion's and she seemed . . . how shall I put it? Worried. Confused.' She shook her head. 'That's too much. More like she was mulling something over.'

'And?'

'We were having coffee together at the time, and she's looking out of the kitchen window and she says to me, "Terry, do men say horrible things just for fun?" Well, I was a bit shook by that. I asked her, "What kind of things?" But she wouldn't say. Then she says, "You know, I thought I wanted a man to lean on but I've changed my mind."' Yates shrugged. 'That's what told me she'd had a man and she'd got rid of him. I wanted to ask her questions because I liked Marion and she did seem troubled— *That's* the word for it. Troubled'. But she just finished her coffee and stood up, which I took to be the end of the conversation.' Somewhere beyond the bar, a door opened, then banged shut. Yates stood. 'If that's who I think it is, I'd better get a move on.' She went to the vacuum cleaner and switched it on.

Watts left the pub wondering if he had just been handed something useful.

THIRTEEN

10.38 a.m.

Judd's phone rang as she hurried along the path through the churchyard. She reached into her pocket for it. It was Watts.

'I've talked to the woman who cleaned for Marion Cane. It looks like Cane had a man in her life at some stage.'

'Who?'

'She doesn't know. I'm just giving you a heads-up. See you later.'

'But—'

He was gone. She checked the time and slowed down. What he had said had got her interest. It posed more questions which needed answers. She walked on, wondering if the man was local. Somebody who came to see her on the quiet. Probably married. Her eyes drifted over gravestones. Stopping at one, she read the inscription: *William Archibald Beaumont. Born 15 February 1895. Died 10 October 1917. Age 22.*

Judd frowned. So young to die. She read on. William had had a son, born barely a month before he himself died. A lump rose in her throat. He had left a loving wife as well as his son. She gave her head a brisk shake. During the last couple of weeks, her emotions had been all over the place. 'Get a *grip*.' Another glance at her phone told her it was almost eleven.

Leaving the gravestones and their stories, she sped along the path, over wet leaves, past the looming evergreens towards the church and its huge main doors. One of them opened in response to a firm push. She went inside, pulled it quietly closed after her, followed by a resounding echo. She walked the long main aisle, all sound from outside muffled, the light low. The tension in her shoulders and neck slowly faded. All around was silence – dark, gleaming wood, a faint smell, like lavender. She moved slowly along, absorbing the atmosphere, the peace, getting a sudden, unexpected insight into Marion Cane's involvement here—

Organ notes ripped through the silence, hitting stone and hurtling upwards to the cavernous roof space. She stopped, her heart hammering. On a deep breath, she continued along to a shallow flight of steps, the music now filling the whole place.

A man was seated at the organ, his arms stretched to its keys, hands and feet moving, his face upturned. After several seconds, he stopped, the music dying slowly to nothing. He turned, looked at her, surprised. 'Hello! I apologize if J.S. Bach startled you.'

'No, I'm fine. No worries.'

He stood and came towards her. She noted the dark trousers and shirt as he held out his hand. 'Police Constable Judd.'

'Mr Redpath.'

He smiled. 'Please, it's Matthew. Your hand feels cold. I've got a small office just off to the side over there and it's a good deal warmer for us to talk than it is out here – if you're OK with that?'

'That's fine.' She walked with him, relieved that he was not leading her anywhere near the room where she had heard what Sarge was now calling 'shenanigans'. He pushed open a heavy-looking door, stepped aside for her to enter what looked like a study, then went directly to a small electric fire, adding another bar to the one already glowing. He turned to her, indicating a nearby chair. 'I'm afraid I can only spare fifteen minutes, twenty at a push. Is that enough?'

Judd's brief glances had told her that he was probably a decade older than her. 'That should do it.'

'You want information about Marion Cane. Shall I just tell you all I know? There isn't that much, but I'll start with a bit of context. I came to Newton six or seven years ago as a trainee, initially just a couple of days a week, then moved here full-time to a house the church rents, which is really good for me. I don't have a lot of money and there's no way I could afford to live in this area. I assist the vicar here as deacon, a kind of church jack-of-all-trades position. My father is a vicar and my plan is to dedicate my life to God and eventually have my own ministry.'

Judd felt a quick surge of embarrassment at the simple, unexpected sincerity of his words. Seemingly unaware of their impact, he smiled at her. 'I am getting to Marion. Leonard gave me some specific responsibilities here. One of them was to manage the church's rota of helpers.' He grinned. 'Initially, it was more a case of them managing me, until I became more confident. You wouldn't believe that a set-up like that has all the makings of high drama, would you? I suspect Leonard wanted to see how I handled it. He must have been satisfied because I'm still doing it. Marion Cane was part of that rota. Well, sort of.'

'How did that work out for her?'

He hesitated. 'I'm guessing that you know something of Marion and her life, so you'll understand when I say that she was as different from the other helpers as it is possible to be.'

'Are you saying she didn't fit in?'

'She really tried. It was more a case of the other rota members taking a certain stance towards her. That's not intended as a criticism of them. Marion was so different from any of them that they found it very difficult to understand and relate to her.' He paused. 'If it doesn't sound too fanciful, I'd say they found her a bit exotic.'

'Did it cause any specific problems?'

'Nothing beyond a few feathers being ruffled.' He grinned again. 'Particularly those of the longest-serving rota members.' He became serious. 'I liked Marion. I did what I could to make things easier for her by organizing the rota so that she was with the more amenable members.' He looked directly at Judd. 'It was my impression that Marion was seeking something from our small church community. I assumed it was peace of mind, although she never said so to me.'

'Did she find it?'

He shook his head. 'I suspected quite early on that her involvement with the church wasn't going to give her whatever she wanted. Unfortunately, that proved to be the case. She mostly discontinued her involvement with the rota but she still came here to dust and polish the interior of the church. I think it gave her a sense of calm.'

'Did she tell you that?'

'Not directly, but I would occasionally find her here, arranging flowers she had brought from her garden. She looked really happy on those occasions. It was good to see another person experiencing the profound peace of our church and God's presence.'

Judd made quick notes. He was probably around the same age as some of her force colleagues, yet worlds apart in the simple, sincere way he spoke about the church and his work.

'Could you give me an idea of Marion Cane as a person?'

He gave it some thought. 'I didn't know her that well, but I would describe her as very intelligent, very worldly in the sense that she was well travelled.'

'What was your response when you learned that she had died?'

'I was surprised. Shocked, I suppose.'

'Were you aware that she had some health concerns?'

'Leonard mentioned to me that she was experiencing anxiety, but nothing more than that. Anxiety is a common feature of our lives these days, isn't it?'

She nodded, thinking he had a point. 'Reverend Partington has said that he suspected Marion was lonely.'

'Really? He never mentioned that to me. Actually, it doesn't fit my own experience of her. She seemed to me to be a generally happy, enthusiastic sort of person, despite whatever worries she might have had.'

'Did you see her at her home?'

'Once.'

'Why was that?'

There was a brief pause.

'We have a church trainee here. Apparently, he arrived at Marion's house, wanting to talk to her. Leonard rang and asked me to go there and sort it out.'

Judd waited for more. When it didn't come, she looked up.

'Sort out what? Why?' She waited again as Redpath chose his words.

'Eric Brook. He's about thirty, thirty-one. A graduate from theology college. As an individual, I would describe him as not very worldly. He had seen Marion at church and I think she impressed him as someone he could talk to. Our job is to respond to parishioners' requests for help and support, not ask for it. Anyway, I went over to her house, found Eric there, had a quiet word with him and we both left. I think his suddenly arriving like that had startled Marion, but she was very understanding about it. I also talked to Eric and he understood that it wasn't acceptable to turn up at someone's home without invitation. It never happened again.'

'Was there any suggestion that Eric might have been attracted to Ms Cane?'

'I'm not aware of that. I think he was feeling very lonely and considered her to be a kind person he could talk to.'

Judd moved to what she considered a key issue. 'I've seen photographs of Marion Cane. They show her to be a physically attractive woman. I've heard her described as physically fit. I'm trying to understand what might have caused such a successful, confident woman to suffer anxiety issues. Her life here, compared to her experience of working in New York and London, would have been comparatively calm and peaceful. It might also have given her more time to think, to feel lonely and want some companionship. What do you think?'

He nodded. 'I know what you mean. Unfortunately, I can't offer any insights. In my experience, Marion was always pleasant but very reluctant to talk about herself and her life. I accepted that. Talking about one's problems doesn't appeal to everyone. I have wondered if I should have been more proactive, tried to encourage her to talk, but that isn't how we work here. And, anyway, I doubt she would have considered me as someone who could advise her.'

'But it occurred to you at the time that she had problems?'

'I wouldn't put it in those terms. I think I assumed that she missed the social aspects of her work, having colleagues, whereas here she wasn't working. That would have been a significant lifestyle change for anyone, possibly one she was struggling to adjust to.' He fell silent, then, 'My direct experience of Marion, such as it was, is that she was a cheerful, very competent woman, although I didn't get to know her well. You might do better to ask people of similar age to her.'

'Anyone particular in mind?'

'Unfortunately, no.'

Judd searched for an angle. Something that might touch on his personal perceptions of Marion Cane. 'Did her age surprise you?'

'No. Leonard had already given me some biographical facts to assist me to relate to her.' He glanced at his watch. 'Sorry, but are there many more questions?'

'Just a couple. Do you spend all of your time here in Newton?'

'Yes, except for when I stay over at my girlfriend's place in Birmingham.'

Surprised, she looked up at him. The possibility that he might be in a relationship hadn't occurred to her. The question was out before she had time to think. 'How does the church regard that situation?'

It was his turn to look surprised. 'Ours is a modern church,' he said quietly.

Annoyed with herself and her general ignorance about churches and religion in general, she asked, 'Does your girlfriend ever stay here?'

'Occasionally, if it fits her schedule. She works in Birmingham as an art restorer at the museum and art gallery there.'

Judd smiled to herself. He looked and sounded proud of his girlfriend. 'What's her full name?' She looked up at him. 'In case we need to speak to her in future.'

'Milly Adams.'

'What can you tell me about Jack Beresford?'

'Who?'

'He's an elderly man who lived along the Rednal Road. He died recently.'

'Of *course*. He was missing, wasn't he? I doubt he was a member of our church. Leonard never mentioned him.'

Judd went with her final question, one to which she thought she probably already had an answer. 'Did you ever hear or see anything which suggested to you that Marion Cane might have a male friend?'

He shook his head. 'Sorry, I can't answer that. My contact with her, such as it was, was limited to seeing her within the church.'

She closed her notebook. 'Thank you for your time, Mr Redpath. I hope I haven't delayed you.'

They both stood and he walked with her and along the aisle to the main doors of the church, where he turned to her, extending his hand. 'If you need to talk to me again, you know where to find me.'

She walked away, envying his quiet, understated confidence.

FOURTEEN

12.30 p.m.

Watts was waiting as Judd hurried to where he was parked and climbed inside. 'You're looking a bit pale still.'

'Stop with the fussing. I'm fine.'

'That's not what I'm seeing.'

'I'm *cold*. How convinced are you that Marion Cane had a man in her life?'

'From what Yates the cleaner said, it looks like she didn't lack . . . companionship.'

She sent him a look. 'If that's you being "subtle", I wish you wouldn't.'

He switched on the ignition. 'And good afternoon to *you*, Snippy. In anticipation of you going on about successful single women like Cane and their hard-fought independence, and whatever else, I'm talking human nature. There are indications that Marion Cane needed a man, so it should be no surprise that she had one.' He quickly reversed, swung the vehicle into a sharp turn, leaving Judd suddenly light-headed.

She swallowed. 'What indications?'

'A couple of used coffee cups and wine glasses in the dishwasher on a Monday morning, according to Yates. She found Marion Cane dead in bed, by the way.'

Judd's brows shot up. 'Nobody's mentioned a man before.'

'There's more. Yates worked for her for quite a while. According to her, Cane said a couple of things that got her interest and have now got mine.' He repeated the question Marion Cane had asked Yates, about men saying unpleasant things, and that she had decided she did not need a man. 'It's the best we've had so far. It tells us that, one, she had a man and, two, he was giving her problems. There's something else. When Yates arrived at the house on the day she found Cane dead, she couldn't get in because she didn't have a key. Cane would always let her in.' He looked across at Judd and waited.

'I give in. How did she get into the house that day?'

'Ryan Bartlett the gardener let her in. With a key.'

Judd rubbed her hands together. '*Yes*. I want to be there when you talk to him.'

'How did it go with the vicar's mate?'

'Matthew Redpath was very pleasant and open, but he didn't provide any gold dust if that's what you're hoping.' She pulled out her notebook. 'He knew Marion Cane because of her volunteering at the church. The vicar had suggested he try to give her some subtle support. From what he said, he didn't get very far, and I don't think he felt he was the best person for the job.' Seeing Watts waiting, she added, 'I get where he's coming from. He was probably in his early thirties when she came to live here. His view of Cane is that she was missing her previous work life but she looked happy enough when he saw her at the church. He also told me that the other women volunteers weren't very accepting of her—'

She rode out another small wave of dizziness as Watts navigated a tight left turn.

'Hardly surprising,' he said.

'But he didn't confirm the vicar's view that she was lonely. He described her as a mostly happy, enthusiastic person, possibly overthinking minor problems associated with changes to her life since she came to live in Newton Heights. By the way, he lives here in the village.'

He glanced at her. 'I thought religious types were all as skint as church mice.'

'The house he's living in is rented by the church. There's a trainee there called Eric Brook. *He's* got my interest. He went to Cane's house, wanting to talk to her.'

'So, what?'

'Not something he was supposed to do, apparently. Sounds

like he had seen Cane around the place and thought she was an understanding type of person. It looks like he's had some problems since he arrived in Newton.'

Watts sniffed. 'I thought church types gave support, not asked for it. We'll check him out. Anything else?'

'I mentioned Jack Beresford's name but Redpath didn't initially recognize it. Jack wasn't exactly a resident and he was no churchgoer.'

'Not a wasted morning for either of us. Yates has confirmed that Cane enrolled for Pilates classes run by Devereaux's wife, that she did a few sessions but they gradually fizzled out. Her view of the GP is that he's one for the money. Mrs Devereaux is away for a few days, but when she's back, I'll want to talk to her. Ask her about her contact with Cane, how well she knew her, what she knows about her life and general health.'

'Did the cleaner say anything about Marion Cane's involvement with the church?'

'No, but the impression I got from Yates is that Cane had no time for religion.'

Judd dropped her notes into her bag and stared out of the window. As they approached headquarters, they saw a small knot of people standing around the entrance. Watts drove swiftly past. They got out to raised voices.

'Detective Chief Inspector Watts! Are you able to confirm that West Midlands Police is about to start a full-on investigation of—?'

'DCI Watts! Got anything to say about a connection between the deaths of Marion Cane and an elderly resident—?'

'Have you called in Doctor Traynor, the criminologist, to assist—?'

Passing Traynor's Aston Martin, they went inside the building and on to Reception. Heritage was waiting for them. He walked with them away from Reception, keeping his voice low. 'Following my decision to raise your inquiries relating to Beresford and Cane to full investigative status, and against my advice, the chief constable decided to release a press statement this morning. Keep me informed of progress on both matters. In the meantime, *nobody* talks to the press.'

'Sir.'

Minutes later, inside his office, Watts was drinking strong tea and watching Traynor read through the information they had relating to both Marion Cane and Jack Beresford. Seeing him reach the last page, Watts asked, 'Any thoughts?'

Traynor took a few seconds to answer. 'Detail breathes life into any investigation.' He looked up at them. 'There's a lot here that's going to assist us to develop a picture of the lives and the deaths of Marion Cane and Jack Beresford.' He added, 'Good work, Chloe.'

Watts glanced at her, saw she was looking pleased. His own professional relationship with her didn't allow for much in the way of congratulatory stuff. He knew she needed it. He also knew that if she got it, she tended to become over-confident and likely to go off-piste, which had landed her in trouble in the past. Having been part of his investigative team for almost three years, there was a lot to recommend promotion for her. If it could be obtained on merit, she would have it by now, helped by a supportive pitch from him. In reality, there was a process to be gone through. Judd's problem was that she didn't want to declare her interest, go through the stages and risk failure. She was doing a good job, but in terms of promotion, she was going nowhere. He re-tuned to Traynor's voice.

'Full investigate status means you're now free to follow that detail wherever you wish, Bernard.'

'What's your current thinking on Beresford's and Marion Cane's deaths, Will?'

'Given Jack's wartime experience of police work, I think it's likely he sent the anonymous note relating to Cane's death. If I'm right, that act in itself suggests that he had sufficient confidence in his view to send it here, rather than to a small local police station. His subsequent death and the manner of it could well indicate that Jack himself was considered a real and significant threat by someone.'

Judd was looking animated. 'Put like that, this whole investigation is on the move, Sarge. We need a base in Newton. A place we can use to get every resident in to talk to us.'

Watts shook his head. 'I've seen the responses from home visits: a heavy investigative load that has got us precisely nothing.'

Traynor nodded. 'I've spoken briefly to officers doing those visits to what is essentially an influx of relative newcomers with little commitment to the area. In some ways, it's similar to the situation when I lived in Oxford and—' He looked away. 'Jack Beresford chose to approach you directly, Bernard. That suggests to me not only that he sent the anonymous communication but that he lacked faith in help coming easily from residents of that area.'

Watts studied the criminologist. 'Will, did you suggest to Heritage that he raise this to a full investigation in order to give it more traction?'

'I don't have that level of influence, and John certainly doesn't need that kind of guidance from me.'

'I need to ask you something else, Will. Are you up to being a hands-on part of this investigation?'

Judd's tension spiked. She had already seen a remoteness, a carefulness in the criminologist's face, the way he moved. As if he was worried that any sudden, unexpected action might break him. She had learned what had happened to his family soon after she started work at headquarters, had seen some of the effects of his post-traumatic stress. Those had lessened over time, to the point where she had more or less forgotten about it. She had also learned from her investigative work with Traynor that he knew his job. She sent him a quick look. He had to be around forty. She glanced at Sarge. She couldn't imagine the personal relationship between him and Connie Chong but had no such difficulty where Traynor and his partner were concerned. A chance sighting of Jess when she came to headquarters to pick him up had confirmed her view that the criminologist and his tall, well-proportioned partner were hot together. Jonesy had expressed a similar, more direct view—

'Earth to Judd!' She looked up at Watts. 'Are you listening?'

'You just said that we go with Cane's death being a possible homicide, while we wait for results of the post-mortems on Jack and his dog.'

Traynor smiled at Watts, his brows rising. 'What do you see as your main investigative problem, Bernard?'

'Marion Cane herself. A high-flyer in the US and London who has a personality change and becomes more or less a recluse in the Heights.'

'A dramatic change of location and lifestyle can cause adjustment difficulties, confusion, discomfort,' said Traynor.

Judd nodded. 'The church deacon I talked to said something similar.'

'I get that,' said Watts. 'There's still a lack of consistency in what we've been told about her. By now I should know who Cane was or what she was about. I don't. She was happy, then she wasn't. She was confused, anxious and lonely, then she's got a man. And running through all of that, I'm sensing something way off about her.'

Traynor sat forward. 'Her identity was firmly linked to achievement. Her decision to retire may have been the wrong one for her, compounded by her choice of a new home in a semi-rural part of the country. Looked at from that perspective, it isn't surprising that she would feel a disconnect, possibly some self-doubt.' He paused. 'But what is unusual is the relative speed and seriousness of her decline. I might find that less surprising if there was evidence of significant mental health difficulties in her past, but there are none as far as we're aware.'

'According to her GP, he's not aware of any big problems in her medical history, but now we've got investigative status, I'll make an urgent application for her medical records as soon as we're done here.'

'How about contacting as many of her past work colleagues as possible, particularly those in London, who are more recent than those she had in the US?' suggested Traynor.

'I'll start tracing them.'

'Come and see her house, Will,' urged Judd.

'I want to see it and to meet her sister and brother-in-law.'

'How about tomorrow morning?' suggested Watts. 'Give the Franklins a ring, Judd. Tell them ten thirty a.m. at the Cane house. I want them both there, if he's not flying off somewhere.'

She pulled a face. 'What are you hoping to get from them? We know what she's like – all talk without actually saying much – and he's Monosyllabic Man.'

'Make the call!' He was on his feet. 'We'll see you at Cane's house tomorrow, nine thirty, Will.'

'Where are you going?' asked Judd.

'To see Ryan Bartlett. On my own.'

FIFTEEN

Watts was on the move, reflecting on Traynor's knack of seeing the gist of an investigation. It was something Watts himself did as SIO, but for this investigation he had found it a slow process to reach that stage. He had heard nothing from Adam about the items found close to where Jack Beresford was discovered and the way Traynor had looked as they left headquarters was worrying. Tired, which was understandable, but the kind of tired verging on emotional exhaustion that he had seen in the past, when he was unwell. He needed Traynor on board. If, over the next few weeks, he was unable to continue with this investigation, he would be a massive loss. In which case, Watts had to get his own thinking straight, starting with likely motives in the event that Cane hadn't died from heart disease. Why would somebody want to kill this woman? Marion Cane had had money. A lot of money. And a will. And a sister and brother-in-law who didn't seem to have much time for her. As a motive, it was a possibility. He slowed, made a turn in response to sat-nav instructions. There was a second possibility. Ryan Bartlett's connection to Marion Cane through the work he did on her property. He was there on the morning she was found dead. He had a key to the house. This could be a case of where there's a woman with money, you'll find a man hanging around. A not too bright one in Bartlett's case. According to her cleaner, she had a man in her life, so far not corroborated. Whatever the reality, Bartlett had a possible motive plus opportunity to inveigle his way into Cane's life and relieve her of at least some of her money. Things might be starting to look up. He came to a stop, his eyes moving over nearby houses, settling on a semi-detached to his left. Whatever home maintenance and horticultural skills Bartlett might possess, he wasn't applying them here.

He got out of his vehicle and walked over uneven slabs to the front door. Banging on it with the side of his fist, he turned to look again at the houses on the other side of the road, all glossy paintwork, small trees in tubs. He was willing to bet that Bartlett wasn't top of anybody's good-neighbour list here. Behind him, the door creaked open. 'Whatever you're offering, we don't want it.'

Watts turned to the thin blonde woman framed in the doorway, one leg corralling a toddler intent on escape. 'Mrs Bartlett?'

'Yeah?'

He took out ID, held it up. Her face showed no surprise. 'Is Ryan at home?'

'He's at work.'

'Expecting him soon?'

Seeing her eyes widen, picking up the sound of a vehicle pulling up close by, Watts looked round at the van, then back. Without a word, she scooped up the toddler and walked away, leaving the front door open. In situations like this, Watts regarded an open door as an invitation to enter. He took the measure of the man who had just arrived and was now walking towards him, his facial expression a mix of uncertainty and truculence. Truculence was winning.

'Who the hell are you!'

Watts showed ID, his eyes fixed on Bartlett's face. One of the things he had learned from his early years on the force: you could pick up a lot from an individual's first sighting of police ID. Right now, he was seeing angry defensiveness.

'Whatever you're here for, you've got it wrong.' Bartlett jerked his thumb in the direction of Watts' vehicle. 'You've got nothing on me, so sling your hook.'

'Theft of building supplies, fly-tipping, more theft—'

'That's history!'

Watts' eyes moved to the house next door, one of its curtains falling quickly into place. 'In your position, I'd want to take this conversation inside.'

Raising his middle finger to his unseen neighbour, Bartlett went past Watts and inside his house, Watts quickly following him. In contrast with the outside, it looked well maintained, a sixty-five-inch plasma television dominating the small lounge, pricey sound system equipment next to it. Nowhere near as tall as Watts, Bartlett's shoulders and tattooed arms showed that he worked out. Sleeveless arms in November. A trend. A badge of something Watts didn't get. Bartlett was now facing him, arms folded, legs braced. 'What's this about? Make it quick.'

'Marion Cane.'

Watts saw his expression waver. 'What about her?'

'She died.'

'I know. So?'

'You did work at her house.'

'Yeah, I did. So what?'

'What do you know about her death?'

'Nothing, except she had a bloody heart attack.'

'Where were you the day she died?'

'That was months ago—'

'My information says you were at Marion Cane's house.'

Bartlett's eyes narrowed. 'That fat scrubber who cleaned there, right?' He pulled out his phone, his eyes fixed on Watts. 'That you, Chris? I've got plod here saying things I don't like the sound of . . . Yeah . . . yeah, OK.' He cut the call, pointed to the front door. 'On your way, *pal*. You want to talk to me, it'll be with my solicitor, Chris Young. *Got* it?'

Watts moved in his own time to the door. He had got it. Bartlett's legal representation was known throughout the city and its criminal fraternity for its zeal in defending the indefensible. He turned back to Bartlett. 'I'll be seeing you again. I hope you've got *that*.'

Traynor came on to his drive, stopped the car and waited for his heart rate to settle. It continued to surge, sending perspiration on to his forehead. He stared at the warm light radiating from downstairs windows. As their relationship had developed, Jess had created a haven here out of a mere house where he had previously been existing. That, plus some short-lived therapy and a lot of determination, had helped him take control of his PTSD. For the last three years, he had chosen to believe he was free of it, yet he knew that it was always there, ready and waiting to sabotage him. The recent news from Oxford about what had happened to Claire had unleashed a tsunami of grief, anger and anxiety as powerful, as awful, as anything he had ever experienced since Claire went. He brushed the perspiration away. Jess had suggested he take time off from his lecturing. He had refused. The university had now taken that choice away from him, at least for the next two weeks. He felt utterly lost.

His actions methodical, he got out of the car, fetched his backpack from the boot, activated the car's alarm. Letting himself into the house, he let the backpack slide to the floor, a tightness in his throat adding to the pain in his chest.

'Will?'

He looked up at Jess, his head starting to pulse. She held out her hand to him. He took it. 'Come into the kitchen with me,' she said softly. He walked with her, sat down at the island. 'Bernard phoned earlier. He's concerned for you, Will. I said you'd ring him back sometime.'

He didn't respond.

'Are you hungry? I'll fix us something and then you can rest—' She watched his head lower, his hands going to his face, shocked by the sudden wracking sobs filling the room. She had seen him upset, but never like this. She went quickly to him, wrapped her arms around him, held him. He clung to her, buried his face against her neck, then her chest, his shoulders heaving. They remained there for several minutes, Jess stroking his hair.

'It's OK, Will. I'm here. I love you.'

During the three years they had been together, she had told him often that she loved him. He had never reciprocated. He let his arms drop, still not looking at her.

'I know. Without you, I couldn't have— I wanted to tell you how I feel about you, Jess. I knew that Claire was never coming home, but it felt . . . disloyal to say it. I'm sorry. I should have done.' He reached for her, held her, his mouth against her neck. 'I love you, Jess. You know I do.'

She held him, knowing better than anyone the devastating impact his wife's abduction and almost certain murder had had on him, his young daughter, his life. 'You need to give yourself time to adjust to what's happened. Are you going to pull out of Bernard's case?'

He shook his head.

'It's a homicide case. People died. I know how it feels to be left without an answer.'

By nine p.m. they were in bed, Traynor craving her, needing her warmth, Jess holding him, all else slipping away from them.

SIXTEEN

Tuesday, 19 November. 8.15 a.m.

They took seats facing Ryan Bartlett and the austere-looking, pinstriped lawyer next to him. Bartlett smirked at Judd, getting a dead-eye response. Watts was silently reprising his years of professional experience of Christopher Young and the many cases that had brought them together. Young, the 'Get 'em off, no matter what' lawyer. Watts wasn't about to let that process start here.

'Thanks for coming in for this voluntary interview, Mr Bartlett.' Bartlett opened his mouth, then quickly closed it as his solicitor spoke, his tone world-weary.

'DCI Watts, you and I are both extremely busy. I'm here to ensure that you're not intending to spring any unpleasant surprises on my client.'

'What might they be?' Getting no response, Watts continued. 'Like I said, voluntary, but if your client prefers to make it formal, just say.'

Bartlett's face changed. His head spun to Young, who glanced at his watch.

'Let's proceed as things are. If at any time I believe my client's rights are being infringed, I shall, of course, end the interview.'

Watts watched the lawyer take a gold Mont Blanc pen from an inside pocket.

'PC Judd will be doing our note-taking. This interview is the result of information gathered by me.' He glanced at Bartlett. 'It specifically relates to the day Marion Cane was found dead at her home.'

Bartlett's legs started to jiggle. Young sent him a look. The jiggling stopped.

'Let us hear what you think you have, DCI Watts. My client and I could be out of here very soon.'

Watts focused on Bartlett. 'Where were you on the morning Marion Cane was found dead?' he asked, supplying the date.

Bartlett shrugged, the jiggle starting up again. 'That's months back. Not something I'd put in my diary if I had one.'

'We know you were at Marion Cane's house.'

Bartlett's eyes narrowed.

'No comment!' Young quickly intervened. 'Before we get ahead of ourselves, DCI Watts, if you can be more specific regarding your interest in my client on that particular morning, it might assist his memory of events.'

Again, Watts' eyes locked on Bartlett. 'You were at Marion Cane's house that morning in your capacity as her gardener-handyman. To be precise, you were outside it in your van.' He searched Bartlett's face for signs of dawning comprehension, not seeing any.

'What if I was? So, what? I *worked* for the woman.'

'What was Ms Cane like as an employer?'

Bartlett smirked. 'All right. Fussy type. Always wanting stuff just so. She paid well.'

'What time did you arrive?'

Bartlett glanced at his solicitor, then back. 'Not sure.'

'Seven o'clock? Seven thirty? Eight?'

'Dunno. Eight thirty, nine o'clock.'

'Had Ms Cane left you any instructions?'

'No. I just cracked on.'

'Tell us what you did that morning.'

Bartlett had lost much of his earlier defensiveness, his demeanour cocky now. 'Mm . . . let's have a think . . . That day, at a guess, I'd say I was doing the lawns, weeding, stuff like that.'

Watts studied him. 'What time did you leave?'

'Not sure. That scrubber of a cleaner was still there. Ask her.'

'When you arrived at the house each morning, how did you get in to start your work?' He watched Bartlett grow still.

'Marion would let me in.'

'Really? How about if she was in the shower? Or not fully dressed.'

Bartlett's colour rose. He looked at his solicitor. 'I don't like this, Chris! I don't like the way he's hinting at something—'

'You're looking a bit hot under the collar, Ryan. Why's that?'

'I don't like being accused. You've got *nothing* on me. Tell him, Chris!'

'Marion Cane's *house key* in your possession says that we

have.' Watts' attention moved briefly to Young, who had lost some of his poker face, then back to Bartlett. 'Tell us about the key, Ryan.'

'I *never* had one. You've got this from that cleaner. She's a *liar.*'

'So, what happened on the day we're talking about? Your last day of employment there, as it happens? How did you get into the house?'

'She let me in.'

'Who let you in?'

'Marion did.' His eyes shifted from side to side. 'I remember now. She comes down, opens the door for me.' Watts listened to more creative ad-libbing. 'Yeah, I remember now. She didn't look too good. I asked her if she was all right.'

'What did she say, Ryan?'

He shrugged. 'Something about being sick, like she had the flu . . . I offered to make her a drink.' Heedless of his lawyer's frown, Bartlett was now well into his stride. 'She said, "No, thanks, I'll be all right." I said, "No worries, I'll crack on then," and I left her and went into the garden.'

'How did you hear that Marion Cane had died?'

'I drove over to Newton, to the house, a couple of days later and saw the cleaner on her way to her job at the pub. She waves at me, so I stop, and she tells me that Marion's died. I was a bit shook up, I can tell you. Last time I saw her, she was . . . Well, she wasn't too good but . . .'

'The key, Ryan. Where is it?'

Bartlett reddened. 'What bloody key? I've told you I never had no key!'

'I'll ask you again. How did you get into Marion Cane's house that last morning?'

His lawyer intervened. 'I'd like a word with my client—'

'I don't need no *word*. I've told him exactly what happened!' He rounded on Watts. 'Like I said, she let me in. She wasn't well. I asked her if she was all right, then got on with what she paid me to do!'

'Was the gardening all that you did for her, Ryan?'

'DCI Watts' – the lawyer was shaking his head – 'if you have a legitimate question, rather than what sounds like unpleasant innuendo, please get to it.'

Bartlett's eyes flicked from Watts to his lawyer and back. 'Yeah! Like he just said . . . *exactly*!'

Watts eyed him for several seconds, taking his time.

Bartlett pointed his finger, giving his lawyer a furious look. '*See* that? He's trying to get to me! That's *harassment*, that is! *Tell* him, Chris!'

'If I accept what you're telling me, that Marion Cane let you into her house on the morning of the day she died, it would have been a miracle.'

'What's he on about, Chris?'

'In fact, if Marion had walked downstairs to let you into her house and tell you she was unwell, not only was it a miracle but she herself was late to the party. She'd been dead hours before you arrived.' He held out his hand. 'The *key*.'

Eventually, after a hasty conflab between Bartlett and Young, it arrived on the table. Watts looked at it, then up at Bartlett and charged him with obstruction. He followed them out of the room, the lawyer's face set. 'By the way, just so you know. The locks on Marion Cane's house are in the process of being changed.'

SEVENTEEN

9.00 a.m.

They watched out of the window, Young delivering what looked like some serious words to Bartlett, after which he turned, headed for his Range Rover and drove away, leaving his client staring after him.

'At a guess,' said Watts, 'Bartlett has just been told the legal definition of "person of interest".'

'You had him right there. Why didn't you move on to Cane's murder and his likely involvement?'

'He's streetwise with low self-control and an IQ slightly north of a bag of spanners. None of which fits with what happened to Marion Cane.'

They watched Bartlett get into his van and drive off.

Watts shrugged into his jacket. 'I'm meeting Will at Cane's

house. I haven't finished with Bartlett, so I want you here, squeezing all you can from the notes you took during his interview. Every nuance. Every inconsistency.'

'No worries. Whatever's there, I'll find it.'

Arriving at Newton Heights, Watts went into the pub to talk to the publican's wife, who grudgingly released Theresa Yates from her shift. Watt walked her to the BMW and drove her to Marion Cane's house. The Aston Martin was parked nearby, Traynor getting out of it.

At the front door, Yates waited for Watts to unlock it, looked at her watch. 'This'd better not take long! I've had to change my day to come in and clean up after some party or other, so there's a lot to do.'

Watts had the front door open. Despite what he'd said to Bartlett, the locks hadn't yet been changed. Stepping into the hall to the familiar *tk-tk-tk*, he entered the code and took a quick look around. It all appeared and felt the same as it had on his previous visit. Returning to the front door, he raised his hand to Traynor, who was approaching the house. 'Wait there, please, Mrs Yates.'

'Hang on! How long's this going to take? If I don't get finished before the pub opens, the gaffer's wife will expect me to stay, and I've got to get back to the school to pick up our Preston—'

'We won't keep you any longer than necessary.'

Traynor came inside, and Watts quietly gave him the gist of his interview of Ryan Bartlett. 'He never had the alarm code but he had a key to this house at the time Marion Cane died.'

They headed upstairs. All doors on the first floor were closed, as Watts had left them after his previous visit. They went inside Cane's bedroom, her bathroom, then on to the other rooms.

'Far as I can see, everything is exactly as it was when I was last here.'

They returned to the ground floor.

'I phoned Janine Franklin late yesterday to remind her about today and ask her about Ryan Bartlett. She told me that immediately following her sister's death, she informed Ryan Bartlett that he was surplus to requirements. She also told him she had installed cameras here, linked to her house. She's just confirmed that she never actually did it, but he didn't know that. It seems unlikely that he's been in here. If he had been, half of Cane's stuff would have been in his van and gone.' He went to the front door. 'Come in, Mrs Yates. Sorry to keep you. This is Doctor Traynor. He's a criminologist assisting with our investigation.'

Traynor held out his hand to her. 'Mrs Yates, our apologies for delaying your work this morning.'

She took his hand, gazed up at him. 'That's OK. Don't worry about it. I'll soon catch up if I get a move on.' Hearing the change of attitude, Watts' face set, recalling a couple of female officers describing a similar situation at headquarters: 'The Traynor Effect', according to them.

He turned to her. 'Mrs Yates, you've confirmed to us that Ryan Bartlett had a key to this house and that he used it to unlock the front door and let you in on the day you found Marion Cane deceased.'

Yates nodded. 'That's right. Marion gave him a key in case she wasn't ready when he arrived so he could get on with his work.'

'Bartlett was happy working here?'

Yates' eyes slid away. 'Suppose so.'

'What was Marion Cane's attitude to the work he did for her?'

She shrugged. 'She never said.'

'What was your opinion of Bartlett?'

She gave Watts a steady look. 'I don't want any of what I say getting back to him.'

'It won't.'

'He's a pig and an idle sod. Full of himself. God's gift, you know.' Her face flushed. 'A few months back, I was taking our Preston to the clinic in Longbridge. Bartlett was passing in his van. He stopped, offered me a lift. I said yes, only because our Preston struggles a bit with walking. Know what Bartlett said when we got in? He looked right at me and said, "I didn't know your lad was a cripple." Right in *front* of the lad! I was that upset. I told my husband when I got home. He found out where Bartlett lived and went round there. Told him to button it. After that, Bartlett barely spoke to me.'

Watts changed tack. 'Did Marion Cane have many visitors?'

'How would I know? I was here five hours a week. I don't have a clue what went on here when I wasn't.'

'No one dropped in when you were here?'

'Only once. Her brother-in-law came, but I told you about that. Anyway, Marion wouldn't have encouraged people coming on my cleaning day, would she? And she wasn't the kind who liked people just turning up.'

Watts was thinking of the photographs he had seen of Cane, the impression he had formed of her as an outgoing individual. 'Did she ever refer to having visitors to the house?'

She frowned. 'Like who?'

Seeing Watts' patience was now on the thin side, Traynor said, 'Mrs Yates, it could be of significant help to us if you can tell us about any conversations you recall having with Marion, during which she mentioned anyone visiting this house.'

Yates considered this. 'Put like that . . . one time, she mentioned that her sister and brother-in-law were coming that evening for a bite of something.'

'When was this?' asked Watts.

'I'd say a few months before she died. It was just chat between me and her. Hang on. It was about the time of our Preston's birthday in early January, which is hard luck on him because who's got the money—?' Seeing Watts' face, she added, 'It would have been around the first week of January.'

'Did she say she was expecting anybody else that evening, or any other evening for that matter?'

Yates' eyes followed Traynor as he paced. 'She never said anything like that to me.'

He stopped, turned. 'Did Marion ever mention anyone else coming to this house on any occasion – perhaps women involved in helping maintain the inside of the church?'

She grinned up at Traynor. 'You've not met any of them, have you? One or two were around Marion's age, but that's where any similarity stopped dead. She had *style*, Marion, *flair* – know what I mean? You should call into the church sometime, have a look at them. You'll see what I mean.'

'Did Marion ever mention any other members of the church?' asked Watts.

This got him a frown.

'I'm thinking of the vicar, or somebody like that.'

'Not that I recall. She said once that the vicar's wife had dropped by and encouraged her to bake cakes for some church shindig, but that was about it.'

'Did she?'

'Did she what?'

'Bake cakes.'

Yates looked scornful. 'You *are* joking. That wasn't Marion's thing.'

Traynor looked at her. 'What was her "thing", Mrs Yates?'

She shrugged. 'I didn't know Marion that well, but I can tell you that she was a really nice woman. Generous and kind. Which she rarely got back, by the way.'

Traynor and Watts exchanged a glance. 'How's that?' asked Watts.

'I don't want my name mentioned, but . . . that sister of hers . . . I don't know the woman, but according to what Marion told me, she seldom visited, although she doesn't live far away. Never remembered her birthday, which I thought was really bad. Marion was very generous to them with tickets for shows, nice presents at Christmas and the like. I think there was a lot of green-eye there, if you get what I'm saying.' She looked at them. '*Jealousy.* From what I've heard, they get the lot now – house, contents, you name it.'

'We appreciate your insights, Mrs Yates,' said Traynor. He came closer. 'We know a little about Marion's life here and also about her past life and career. What we're trying to do is get a sense of Marion as the person she was, living here, how she felt about this home, this area and her life, given the highly successful career she had had previously.'

She stared at him, saying nothing.

He continued, 'It would have been a massive change for her, living here, after those high-powered jobs she had in New York and London.'

'I get where you're going, but she never talked about it to me.'

Traynor persevered. 'There appears to have been two very different sides to Marion's life, one the outgoing, confident career woman working in what is probably still very much a man's world and the other, the woman who lived here. In this house. A woman who had few if any friends and who, we're told, was experiencing significant anxiety.' She watched Traynor slowly raise both his hands, hold them apart then bring them slowly together. 'I can't do it, Mrs Yates. I can't make those two people fit together without the help of someone like you who knew her.'

She gazed up at him, her neck turning pink. 'Well . . . there was some talk.'

'What about?'

'You hear things when you work in a pub. I never talked about Marion to anybody, ever. She was good to us when our Preston needed surgery on his knees. Nobody round here knows, but she found a surgeon for him.' There was a pause. 'She paid for it.' Her mouth quivered. She pressed her fingers against it. 'I don't want anybody knowing about that because *she* didn't want it known. Like I said, there was talk. About her having a man in her life.' She looked at Watts. 'Remember what I told you about the glasses and cups in the dishwasher? It was around that time that I picked up on something else. Just a snippet of talk.'

'We need your help, Mrs Yates. You need to tell us all you know,' said Traynor quietly. She looked at him, then at Watts. 'I don't want my name mentioned, right? I heard that Marion had a bit of a thing going with her brother-in-law a couple of years back. Not that I was convinced, mind you. He's hardly ever here, and when he is, he looks a right miserable sod.' She shrugged. 'That's it.'

Traynor broke the silence. 'Thank you for all you've said, Mrs Yates. We appreciate it.'

She gave him a quick nod, watched as he moved a short distance away then looked back to her. 'Do you recall seeing a computer, iPad, or similar device in this house when you worked here?'

'No. Marion said she'd had enough of all that caper.'

'What about a mobile phone?'

'She had one of those. It got broke. She told me she was carrying laundry into the kitchen and it slipped from her hand and smashed on the floor. I saw the pieces in the kitchen bin.'

'When was this?' asked Watts.

'I'd say a couple of months before she died.'

'Did she get another phone?'

'I expect so, although I don't remember seeing one.'

He looked at his watch. 'OK, Mrs Yates. Thanks for your time. We'll give you a lift back to the pub. If you think of anything else, I'd appreciate a call.'

'You're all right, I'd rather walk.' She took the small card from him, put it in her coat pocket. They walked along the hall to the front door. 'It feels strange being back here. It makes me sad, thinking about Marion. Even now, it's hard to believe she's not here anymore.' She glanced inside the sitting room and pointed. 'Where's Marion's mirror gone?'

EIGHTEEN

10.50 a.m.

Watts paced, then turned to Traynor. 'The Franklins live less than ten minutes away but it looks like they're not coming, so we'll go to them.'

Securing the house, they headed in the direction of the Franklins' place, Traynor asking, 'Any thoughts on what we got from Mrs Yates?'

'She's got an eye for you. If you're asking in relation to the case, she's solved one mystery for us. When I was here with Judd a while back, she noticed something was missing from the sitting-room wall. Eyes like lasers, that one. We didn't know what had hung there or what had happened to it. There's something else. What Yates just told us about Cane's phone getting broken . . . she used the word "smashed". That's got me wondering at the possibility of some sort of altercation occurring in that house, for which I've got two possible scenarios, one involving Bartlett and now another possibility. John Franklin.'

'Phones get broken by accident.'

'Ha! Tell me about it! I've had a few in my time. Ran over one of 'em. Another one ended up on the wrong side of a wall at Dudley Zoo – no, don't ask. Most people replace them immediately. It sounds to me like Cane didn't. Who lives without a phone? Judd would be off her head inside ten minutes.' They continued on towards the Franklins' house, Watts glancing at Traynor, thinking how much better he looked than on the previous day. 'I need to know what you're thinking, Will.'

'Marion Cane is emerging as a very complex, possibly secretive person.'

Watts nodded. 'If what Yates told us about Marion and John Franklin is reliable, that something was going on between them, it could explain the distance between Marion and her sister.'

'What's the husband like as an individual?'

'Ask me another. When Judd and I talked to them, he made a clam look mouthy. Apparently he travels a lot for his work. I was thinking that maybe he didn't know Marion Cane well, yet what Yates said is suggesting a very different scenario. The other thing I remember from when Judd and I saw them is that Janine Franklin showed zero emotion about her sister's death.' He pointed to the extensive low-level property coming into view. 'That's their place. I don't like bungalows.'

'For security reasons.'

'No. Five minutes after moving into one, I'd feel two decades older. Although, if what Yates said is reliable, it doesn't seem to have slowed John Franklin down.'

They walked the long drive to the front door, becoming increasingly aware of raised voices as they neared it, each moving to a higher register, the male voice drowning out the other. Exchanging glances with Traynor, Watts banged his first against the door. Sudden silence from inside was followed by what sounded like a door closing with some force.

'That sounds serious,' murmured Traynor.

Watts pressed the doorbell repeatedly. Muffled footsteps approached the door. It swung open. Janine Franklin was standing there, her face pale, a vivid red welt on its left side. Watts motioned her to step outside. She shook her head. 'He's gone.'

'Who's gone?'

'John, my husband.'

'We need to come inside, Mrs Franklin.'

They entered the silent bungalow. She watched as Watts came in and pushed two nearby doors wide, peering into each room. 'He's not here and the problem has been sorted.' She began to cry.

Traynor looked at her, his voice low.

'Mrs Franklin, my name is William Traynor. I think it's possible that you need some medical attention—'

'No!' She turned away from him.

Watts asked, 'Where's he gone, Mrs Franklin?'

'I don't *know*. He just left in the direction of the back garden, but I'm not taking this any further, so just . . . *go*.'

Watts headed further inside the property, reached the kitchen.

It was empty, an exterior door wide open. He went quickly through it and out into the garden, scanning the many trees and bushes around the perimeter fence. He returned to the house and secured the door. With a staying motion to Traynor, he went into the conservatory where Janine Franklin was now sitting. 'Is your husband anywhere inside this property?'

'I've *told* you. He's *gone!*'

She bowed her head and sobbed. He looked back to Traynor, saw the criminologist point to himself then in Franklin's direction, brows raised. Getting a nod, he entered the conservatory. Watts returned to the hallway, listening for sounds within the house, Traynor's voice now coming to him, calm and controlled.

'Mrs Franklin, if you need some help, we're here to give it, but first, can you tell us where your husband might have gone?'

She said nothing, just sobbed.

Watts came back, looked at Traynor, then out of the window. He tensed. John Franklin was standing in the middle of the garden, his arms at his sides, his face empty of expression and colour. With a further staying motion to Traynor, he returned to the kitchen, unlocked the door and stepped out, keeping distance between himself and Franklin.

'Easy, now, Mr Franklin. Let's keep things nice and relaxed.'

Getting no response, he moved slowly towards him, reached out and took Franklin's arm. The last thing he wanted was Franklin rushing the house. 'I want you to stand over here with me for a while.'

A good foot shorter than Watts, Franklin looked up at him, then away. 'It was all a misunderstanding.'

Seeing him start to sway, Watts steered him towards a garden chair. 'Sit down. It's best you don't go inside right now.'

Franklin sat, then slumped, his head down. Watts stood next to him, his hand resting lightly on Franklin's shoulder, sending Traynor a nod through the window.

'Your wife's a bit upset, Mr Franklin. What happened?'

'Nothing,' he whispered.

'Your wife has been injured. How did that happen?'

'Things got a little . . . heated—'

'Because of the *money*!' Janine Franklin was at the kitchen door, her eyes fixed on her husband, her facial expression one of fury.

Watts went slowly to her, keeping his own face relaxed. 'Easy now, Mrs Franklin.'

'*Marion's* money! Jessop, her solicitor, phoned early this morning to tell me he needed to discuss some "difficulties" relating to her will.' Her voice morphed into a high-pitched wail. '"Difficulties" doesn't *begin* to cover it! He says he can't locate any of it. It's *gone!*' She made a quick movement towards her husband, stopped by Traynor suddenly appearing in front of her.

'What have I said to you!' shouted her husband. 'Marion had well over a million pounds in investments. It can't have vanished! It has to be some—'

'It's nothing to do with *you!*' she screamed. '*You* had my *sister*, you bastard! *That* money is *mine!*' She bowed her head, wracked by sobs. 'I had . . . plans.'

Watts led her, unresisting, back to the conservatory. Traynor steered her husband inside and along the hall. Watts came into the hall where Franklin was now sitting. 'You need to tell us all of it, John.'

Franklin rested his head against the wall, eyes closed. 'There's nothing to tell,' he said, his voice weary. 'Just a small domestic incident.'

'I want to know about the money.'

Franklin shook his head, his face etched with exhaustion. 'According to Jessop, Marion had a lot of savings and invest-ments. It seems that, over the past twelve months, it was Marion herself who closed all the accounts. I don't know what she did with it.' His face creased in a parody of a smile. Watts studied him. He couldn't recall much of John Franklin's face from their previous meeting, given that he had been all but invisible, but he doubted it was anything like what he was seeing now. He took a few steps away, closed the door so that Franklin's wife wasn't able to hear, and came back to him, keeping his voice low.

'We heard what your wife said, about you and her sister. What did she mean, exactly?' Franklin opened his eyes. He looked drained. 'What do *you* think?' He struggled to his feet. 'But it doesn't matter anymore. None of it matters. I have to get out of this place. I'm suffocating . . . can't breathe.'

He was now at the front door, pulling it open. Watts decided to let him go. Allow some distance between him and his wife and the situation he and Traynor had just walked into. He watched

Franklin reach the Mercedes, open the driver's door and get inside. Before Watts could intervene, Franklin got out of the vehicle, leaving the driver's door open, and walked slowly away from the house.

Janine Franklin looked up as Watts reappeared. 'He's left, hasn't he? It's what he does whenever there are problems. He's been seriously depressed since my sister's death, but I was holding things together. It was the solicitor's phone call that caused all of this.'

'Is John on medication for depression?'

She looked scornful. 'He's incapable of making those kinds of decisions or doing anything to help himself.'

Watts gestured to Traynor. They went into the kitchen.

'Would you stay here with her, see if you can get anything else out of her? Now we know he's got mental health problems, I'll go and find him.'

As Watts left, Traynor returned to where Janine Franklin was sitting. 'Can I get you anything, Mrs Franklin?'

She shook her head. 'I'm my sister's sole beneficiary. When I heard that the money was gone' – she gulped air, a hand at her chest – 'I couldn't believe . . . Still can't. I was hysterical. That's when he hit me.' She looked up at Traynor. 'I don't want him in any trouble because of what's happened. There's been a lot of tension between us since Marion came here to live.'

'Mrs Franklin, what your husband did to you earlier is an assault.'

'I won't make a complaint against him.'

'That's your choice. One of our priorities is to ensure that you're safe here.'

'I understand.' She glanced up at him. 'I found your colleague's manner extremely authoritarian.'

'Detective Chief Inspector Watts carries a lot of responsibility in the kind of situation we came into here. You are aware that West Midlands Police now has an official interest in your sister's death?'

'Yes. It's *ludicrous*. There was nothing mysterious about either my sister or her death.'

'It could help us if you talked about her, the person she was, from your experience.'

'Help you, how? With what? We were just sisters who had nothing in common. We didn't talk. We had nothing to say to each other. She probably talked more to her solicitor or whoever else was non-related, and don't ask me for names because, apart from Jessop, I don't know – except for that coarse-looking woman she had to clean her house. Right now, all I want is to be left *alone*.'

'It's best if I stay here.'

'If you must, but I don't want you asking me more questions.'

Watts moved along the road away from the Franklins' house, scanning the area for signs of John Franklin, trying to anticipate where he might have gone. He should have asked Janine Franklin if her husband had any specific contacts, possible friends living nearby, although, from what they knew about his work-related travels, it seemed unlikely. He walked on, his eyes scanning either side of him. He slowed. His breathing steadied. Newton-bloody-Heights. Not a soul in sight. Where were the owners of these big, pricey houses? Answer: somewhere else, earning more money to add to what they already had, those that weren't probably giving instructions to cleaners or au pairs. It suddenly came to him that he actively disliked the place. He was sick of what he saw as its introspective self-satisfaction; that if all was fine here, nothing else mattered. He gazed ahead. Marion Cane's house was just beyond the curve in the road. He followed it round, watched it come slowly into view through fine mist, standing alone, backed by woods, weak sun on its massive, blind windows. He headed towards it, seeing a car arrive and park outside, a small figure getting out of it.

'Aye-up, Judd,' he whispered on reaching her.

She sent him a look. 'I've been trying to ring *you*—' He put his index finger to his lips. 'What's going on? What's happened? I've been through every word that waste-of-DNA Bartlett said and I'm telling you that he's top of my list of sus—'

'Come over here and *zip* it!' he hissed. They were very close to the house now. 'Did you notice anybody walking around when you drove in here?'

'Like, who?'

'Stay there. *Don't* move.' He went to the front door, stopped, listened. Not a sound. There was nothing to confirm this was Franklin's destination. No reason that Watts could see that would have led him here. Aware of Judd moving closer, he made a staying motion. She stopped, whispered, 'What's *happened*?'

'You're sure you haven't seen a lone man on foot?'

'I just this second got here.'

'There's been trouble at the Franklins' place. On the face of it, literally, it's ABH.'

Her eyes were huge. 'Who—? Not "The Silent One". It had to be a sudden, violent response after years of browbeating – *not* that I'm condoning violence, just telling it like it sounds—'

'*Shut. Up.*'

She closed her mouth.

'You didn't see any sign at all of John Franklin as you drove into this place?'

'No.' She looked up at the house. 'You think he could be here?'

With another staying motion, feeling in his pockets for the key, he put his hand to the door. It yielded. He and Judd exchanged glances. With yet another staying motion, he turned back to the door and gave it a push.

'Hello? Mr Franklin?'

His words bounced off walls, spiralled, struck the distant ceiling and faded to a dying echo. 'Mr Franklin? This is DCI Watts . . . I'm alone, OK? I'm coming inside.' He stepped into the cavernous hallway, called Franklin's name again. It reverberated off walls and glass. Both Franklin's emotional state thirty minutes or so earlier and Watts' years of experience were telling him that this was the kind of situation that could easily place any officer in deep trouble. Aware that his nearest available backup was some distance away along the Rednal Road, he pulled out his phone, selected a number. A brief pause and he spoke, his voice low.

'I'm at Marion Cane's house in Newton Heights. Front door open on arrival. Soon as you can.'

Ending the call, ears straining for sound, he glanced at the stairs to one side. If Franklin was on the first floor it wouldn't be a good idea to suddenly appear up there. Better to stay on the ground floor for now. He moved silently towards the closed sitting-room door, listening for any indication of movement inside. All was quiet.

'Mr Franklin? John? We need to talk. You need some help.'

Still nothing. He reached for the handle, pushed it slowly downwards and released it. The door moved smoothly away from him. The room looked the same as it had when he was last here. Except for John Franklin resting against the cushions of the massive sofa. Watts went closer, looked down at him, at his bright red scarf, at the white sofa, wondering who had painted the vivid stripes exactly matching the colour of Franklin's—

He backed away, his heart pounding his chest, eyes fixed on John Franklin, a man of few words, who now had an extra 'mouth' cut into his own neck.

'Sarge?'

'Holy *sh*—!'

'Sarge! What's happened?'

He turned, blocking her line of sight with his bulk, but not before she had looked beyond him into the room.

NINETEEN

12.05 p.m.

White-suited figures swished back and forth, ghostlike, yet purposeful. Watts was standing close to an open window, deep-breathing as he watched the familiar routine. Photographs. A lot. Of the whole massive space. Walls. Floors. He avoided looking at the vivid, arterial sprays covering the sofa. A stretcher supporting an open body bag moved past him with a rhythmic squeak, one of its wheels wonky. He left the room and the house and went to Judd who was still half sitting in the open doorway of her car. He had seen her look better. She watched him approach.

'No need to say it,' she murmured. 'I should have stayed outside.'

'You all right?'

'Yeah . . .'

He turned from her. 'I'll be a few more minutes.'

'Stay away from the back of my car,' she whispered.

'What?'

'Most of my breakfast's there.'

He was halfway to the house when he heard a quick scamper punctuated by retching. The rest of Judd's breakfast had arrived. He continued on and inside the house, picking up the *whir-click* of cameras, flashes of light visible at the edges of the slightly open door. In the hall, Jones was coming down the stairs. 'I came as soon as I got your call, Sarge. I've checked upstairs. Superintendent Heritage is here. He wants a word.'

'Thanks. Give it fifteen minutes, then take Judd back to her house. Have Reynolds drive her car.'

'She won't stand for that—'

'She will.'

Smoothing his hair, a quick shoulder flex, and he walked inside the sitting room, now filled with purposeful activity. Heritage's attention was fixed on the sofa as John Franklin's body was carefully lifted from it, placed on the open body bag, zipped and wheeled from the room on another series of squeaks. He looked up. 'You found him, Bernard?'

'Sir.'

'Why were you here?'

Watts gave a quick overview of his and Traynor's visit to the Franklins' home, the indications of a domestic disturbance and John Franklin's abrupt departure. 'Traynor stayed with Mrs Franklin while I went to look for him. Both were in a highly stressed state when we arrived. From the verbal exchanges between them, it appears that there was a relationship between Mr Franklin and his sister-in-law, Marion Cane. That's all I can tell you right now, but Traynor might have more. He's still there.'

'I sent two officers to the house as soon as I had the basic picture.' His eyes moved over the bloodied sofa. 'Do we know what he used?'

Watts gestured to a SOCO who came to them, blood-smeared evidence bag in hand. 'He must have had it on him when he left the house – or got it from his car.'

Heritage peered through it at the knife and its carved handle. There was no doubting the capability of the blade inflicting the horrific injury on Franklin's neck. Getting a nod from Watts, the SOCO took it away. 'I'll go back and see Mrs Franklin. Try to establish if there's a knife like it missing from the house.'

'You'll officially inform her what's happened?'

'Yes. The house is close enough for her to be aware that something's going on here. I've alerted Traynor but asked him not to divulge anything to her. I'm hoping he's encouraged her to talk. There's probably a lot she can tell us.'

Heritage's eyes moved over the ruined sofa, then away. 'I take it Will is OK.'

'He is, sir. He's looking better than he did yesterday.'

'I want to know everything you learn from Mrs Franklin.'

Watts was pulling November damp deep into his chest, glad to be out of the Cane house, away from the sight and smell of death. The Franklins' house was gradually coming into view through the murk, its lights glowing. He was hoping that Traynor had calmed her down. It wouldn't last, given the news he was about to deliver. Reaching the front door, he nodded to the uniformed officer standing there, continued inside and on to the back of the house, another officer visible beyond the conservatory. Seeing Watts, Janine Franklin got to her feet, Traynor sending him an almost imperceptible head shake. Enough to tell Watts that she knew something was up but nothing specific. It was his job to deliver the specifics.

'Just tell me,' she said.

'You need to sit down, Mrs Franklin,' said Traynor.

After a brief hesitation, she did, her eyes fixed on Watts who sat opposite.

'There's no easy way to say it, Mrs Franklin. I'm sorry to have to tell you—'

'He's finally done it, hasn't he? Let me guess. He's thrown himself off somewhere or under something?'

He gave her minimal detail, pausing to give her time to absorb it. She didn't speak. 'Mrs Franklin, on behalf of West Midlands—'

'I've just realized where he did it.' She looked up at him. 'It was in her house, wasn't it?'

Watts felt his tension climb, waiting for the impact of what he had just told her to hit, guessing Traynor was thinking the same. They were on their feet as she moved to the door.

'I want a cup of tea.'

Watts encouraged her to sit. Traynor went to make the tea.

She gazed calmly out at the dull garden. Watts let the silence run on. Traynor appeared with tea.

She looked at them. 'Please, have some tea, both of you.'

Watts eyed her. He'd witnessed all kinds of reactions to sudden, life-changing events. Franklin's response was a first. She sounded as if she had invited them here for a social chat.

'Whatever John's done to himself, it was only a matter of time. There's something else. I don't want either of you to be under any misapprehension where Marion and I were concerned. I doubt I ever loved her, or she, me. The truth is I didn't like her. I'm sure that feeling was mutual.' She looked up at Traynor. 'What I've just said doesn't surprise or confuse you?'

'No.'

She gave a low laugh. 'A quiet man *and* an honest one. A very rare combination in my experience. Your colleague doesn't get it, does he?'

'DCI Watts hasn't heard what you said to me earlier.'

'You'll tell him?'

'Yes.'

'There's no need. I'll tell him myself.' She looked at Watts. 'When I married John, Marion was living in New York. She came back for our wedding. We had a party two days before. I saw them talking, laughing together. My sister was successful, well-off, attractive – all the things you already know about her. There was something else about Marion that *I* always knew. She needed sex, like you and I need tea in the early morning, a glass of something soothing in the evening. She was *hot*. Sexually hot. After the wedding, she returned to New York, and seven days after *that*, my "new" husband flew there on business. As soon as he came back, it was obvious to me that he had been with her. In the years before Marion tired of New York, his business trips became more frequent. He was spending as much time as he could in my sister's bed. After she returned to the UK to work in London, it was much more convenient for them. They continued to see each other regularly. His credit card statements, which he tried to keep from me, were an excellent indicator of what was happening. I have to say, they were discreet, but the fact is they had sex at every opportunity that presented itself. I don't think Marion cared if I knew, but John kept up the pretence.'

She took a deep breath.

'John was no Lothario, believe me. I could have told him that she would tire of him, eventually replace him. My sister was very self-focused. She needed men. She used them. That is, until she tired of them. When that finally happened with John, he was devastated. Not that he admitted it to me. He wasn't about to admit anything. Too afraid that he would be left with nothing. I think he actually believed that the relationship would start again, once she was living here.' She shook her head. 'It didn't. By the time she moved here, she would have replaced him, although don't ask me who with because I don't know. For Marion, having sex with my husband was of no consequence. I never dignified it by calling it an affair. He was a man and Marion needed *a* man. That's all there was to it.'

'Did she ever acknowledge the relationship to you?'

'She didn't need to. She knew that I knew, but it was never discussed between us.' She sipped tea, her face calm.

'You are saying that your sister replaced your husband with another man but you have no idea who that was.'

She didn't respond.

Watts sat forward. 'The identity of that individual could be very important, Mrs Franklin. Can you recall any fact, any suspicion as to who he might have been?'

She studied him. 'My guess is that it was someone local.'

Watts and Traynor exchanged looks. 'Local to?'

'*Here*. Newton Heights.'

'Can you suggest a name?'

She smiled. 'You still don't get it, do you? It comes down to *anyone* and *everyone*: Devereaux, the GP; Marion's creep of a solicitor, Jessop, who also owns the estate agents. Now, *that* would have been a good cover, wouldn't it? Who else? How about the common little man who did gardening and maintenance work at Marion's house? He's definitely a contender. He invariably removed his shirt at the first hint of warm weather and strode my sister's property like a *bantam*.'

She sent a quick glance in Traynor's direction. 'Marion was a pushover for a good male physique, but I wouldn't rule out any possibility because I knew my sister very well where sex was concerned. She joined Devereaux's wife's Pilates class. A very attractive woman, Vanessa Devereaux.'

Watts glanced at Traynor. 'Are you suggesting—'

'I'm not suggesting anything, merely going through all of the available options.'

Watts had already done some checking. 'Those were group Pilates classes that your sister joined.'

She raised her brows, gave him a look that suggested he was half-witted. 'Maybe she also had one-to-one sessions.'

Traynor broke the silence. 'Mrs Franklin, you appear to suspect any number of people, possibly of both genders, on the basis that your sister knew them.'

'Proximity and a pulse were sufficient for Marion. She was a powerful force when she wanted something. Or, someone.'

'So, how can you be sure that once she came to live here, the relationship with your husband did not continue?'

'Because of John's behaviour. His moods. He was devastated.' She gave Watts a direct look. 'Tell me what he did to himself.'

'Before we get into that, is there somebody living nearby we can call to come here—?'

'Do I *look* like I need anyone fussing around me? For goodness' sake, just tell me what he did.'

'He injured his throat using a knife.'

She slow-nodded. 'With a black handle carved with leaves.'

Watts' eyes were fixed on her. 'You're familiar with it?'

'Oh, yes. Very much so,' she said softly. 'They're maple leaves on the handle. Some years ago, John told me that a Canadian colleague took him hunting and he was impressed by a knife he had. During one of his rare loquacious moments, he described it to me. Told me how much he admired it. He didn't buy it, of course. *She* did. I'm guessing she ordered it online during the time she was living in London.'

Traynor's eyes were fixed on her. 'I have a question, Mrs Franklin.'

'I thought you might.'

'It might distress you.'

'I doubt it.'

'Do you have any idea why your husband would go to *that* house to do what he did?'

She closed her eyes, let her head drop back. 'It's so obvious it hardly needs saying. It's where Marion *is*.' She stared up at them. 'You just don't get it, do you? She's *still* there.'

*　　*　　*

They were outside the house, Traynor preoccupied, Watts deep-breathing. 'What she said about her sister. I don't trust any of it, but it's obvious she loathed her.'

Traynor did not respond immediately.

'Will?'

'Jealousy and rejection are corrosive and extremely damaging. I'm not convinced by all she's told us, but it's possible that the picture she's given us of her sister is her way of reconciling those negative feelings.' He looked at Watts. 'By portraying her sister as sexually powerful and indiscriminate, she's able to absolve John Franklin of much of the responsibility for what happened between him and her sister. It also meets her need to exonerate herself for what she sees as her failure to keep him.'

Watts absorbed Traynor's words. 'What she said about Cane's house and her "still being there". I don't want Judd hearing that. She's got imagination to spare and she's already nervy and off-colour, sticking with me like a shadow whenever we're inside it.'

They walked on, Traynor silent, his eyes fixed directly ahead. Watts' phone clamoured. It was Heritage.

'Sir.'

'I want to see you in my office at seven thirty tomorrow morning.'

Call ended, Watts turned to Traynor, seeing how tired he was looking. It took him back three or so years, to when he and Judd, a raw rookie, had gone to see him where he was living alone in deep countryside to ask for his professional help on a homicide. What they found was a man obsessively searching for his missing wife, restless, driven, post-traumatic stress tightening its grip. That situation had radically changed when he met Jess, his current partner, and moved house, his PTSD remaining mostly dormant. Until the recent news from Oxford.

'Will, you're looking done in—'

'Don't tell me I need to rest.'

'You *do*, mate. You need to give yourself some more time to deal with the news you've had or, chances are, you'll be no use to this investigation.' He got no response.

Watts reached for Traynor's arm. 'Go home, Will. Have a couple of days' break. Do what's right for yourself and for Jess.'

He watched Traynor walk away, querying for the first time if this kind of investigative work, which Traynor was so good at, was also damaging him.

He got into his vehicle, eyed himself in the mirror, seeing the exhaustion etched in his own face.

TWENTY

Wednesday, 20 November. 7.25 a.m.

Heritage was seated at his desk when Watts came into his office.

'Sit down, Bernard. I want to discuss Will with you. As you know, he and I go back a long way because of what happened to Claire. Having to tell him that her remains have been found was difficult, to say the least.'

'Sir.'

'You've worked with him on previous investigations and achieved very positive outcomes. He's expert at what he does. What I need to hear from you is whether you think he's up to handling the Newton Heights investigation.'

'If you're asking whether I think that right now he's able to fully commit to it, the truth is I don't know. This investigation is moving fast and yesterday's events were difficult for everybody. I did suggest he take a couple of days off, but I doubt he will. What I do know is that we need his expertise and he wants to give it.'

Heritage regarded him in silence for several seconds. 'This is a complex case you're leading. I want you overseeing Will's involvement. I need to know if it's not working out. I don't want to see him deteriorate in the way I've witnessed in the past. If you think my request is going to make things difficult between you, I need to know, now.'

Watts was fully aware of the pressure Heritage was under. He also knew that the role of overseer didn't sit right with him. 'Will's a colleague. A friend. There's nobody better at what he does. I like to be straight with whoever I work alongside. I'm not comfortable with the role you've outlined for me, and he'd sense in a nano-second what I was doing.'

Heritage's eyes were fixed on his. 'I appreciate your honesty. Anything else?'

'Yes. As and when I see him next, it will be business as usual on the case for both of us.'

Heritage nodded. 'I understand. Getting back to the investigation, you've selected your key officers?'

'Yes. I'm briefing them on all recent events in the next half an hour, but there's something I want you to consider.'

Heritage waited.

'Marion Cane's cause of death was identified at the time as due to natural causes. She's now emerging as a very complex woman whose life was very complicated. The more we learn about her, the more questions I have about her death. There's one way to get answers. An exhumation of her remains.'

There was a brief pause. 'I'll think about it. For now, we keep that to ourselves.'

They were on the second floor, inside what was now the incident room, Watts looking at his ten officers, his attention briefly settling on Judd, Jones, Reynolds and Kumar, whom he regarded as the nucleus of his team. He had already laid out to all of them that this was now a full investigation into the Beresford homicide.

'There's little in the way of leads for Beresford, so that's our priority. Due to a continuing lack of clarity around the cause of Marion Cane's death, we continue to explore that as well.'

'What about the Franklin suicide, Sarge?' This from young Reynolds, whose confidence, along with his physique, had noticeably developed in the last eighteen months.

Watts responded, 'Doctor Chong has confirmed it as a suicide. In terms of this investigation, Jack Beresford's death is the main investigative issue, but we remain open to *any* information relating to John Franklin and Marion Cane.' Watts studied them, the public face of his investigation. 'When you're in Newton Heights, I want you listening to all you're being told with those three names at the front of your heads.' He tapped the table. 'Beresford. Cane. Franklin.' Getting a chorus of 'Sarge', he reached for a sheet of A4, held it up.

'You've all seen this. The anonymous note that initially focused our attention on Newton Heights. You also know what Jack Beresford said to me: "Keep asking your questions". He *knew* why we were in Newton Heights that first day. He was telling me that Marion Cane's death was suspicious. It could have put him at risk.' He decided to say nothing about Traynor's involvement in the investigation. It was very likely that some of them had picked up concerns about his health. In his experience, every team was a gossip shop. He wasn't about to feed it.

'You've also got my identification of one person of interest. Ryan Bartlett. Handyman to Marion Cane. Make some subtle, local inquiries about him in Newton Heights and around the Longbridge area where he lives. Recent information indicates the possibility that there was sexual involvement between him and Cane. That needs subtle exploration. While you're doing that, you'll be looking for any connection between Bartlett and Beresford.' His eyes moved slowly over each of them. 'There's a lot to do. Best get started.'

Watts was back in his office, preoccupied with the investigation's first official briefing. He had kept mostly to the facts. The next half hour or so of informal talk among his officers would show them the complexities they were facing. Hearing the door open, he went to the worktable where Judd, Jones, Reynolds and Kumar were taking seats.

'I don't want to hear any gripes about the complications of this investigation. The whole time you're exploring Beresford's life, keep your thinking wide open to anything, *anything* relating to Cane and John Franklin. Whatever ideas you get, you run past me. And while you're doing all of that, you say zip to the media. By now, they'll be all over John Franklin's death and making what they see as connections. We give them nothing.'

He ran his hand through his hair, thinking that some acknowledgement of the investigative challenges might not come amiss. 'There is an issue with Marion Cane, but her official cause of death still applies. You ask general questions about her. The same for John Franklin, despite his death being a suicide.' He pushed copies of a list to the middle of the table, pointed at it.

'I want some people talked to. First, Devereaux, Cane's GP. He certified Marion Cane's death as being from heart disease, despite the physical symptoms she reported to him prior to it not pointing convincingly in that direction. He prescribed medication for her anxiety. According to her medical records, she never collected it, yet she was in possession of Valium, not commonly prescribed nowadays and there's no indication so far that Devereaux provided it. Where did she get it? Check known drug suppliers with even tenuous links to the Newton Heights area. Devereaux's wife teaches Pilates. Cane attended some of her classes. She's not been spoken to yet.' He paused, looked at each of them, wanting to gauge receptivity. So far, so good. 'The local vicar might be a source of information. There's also a deacon, Matthew Redpath, who's lived there for the past six or seven years, and Eric Brook, a trainee, who's been there a couple of years, plus some day visits to help him get to know the place. Available information suggests there might be a mental health issue where he's concerned, so he's got my interest. He needs talking to, but we'll discuss that before direct contact is made with him.' He looked around the table. 'Reynolds, your name might be in the frame for that. It needs a sympathetic approach.'

'Sir.'

Watts' attention moved to Judd. 'Bring us up to speed on what you got from Redpath.'

'I've met him once to establish what he knows about Marion Cane. According to him, she wasn't religious but she was involved in maintaining the church, which is how he got to know her. She wasn't particularly welcomed by established helpers. He seemed doubtful that the health problems Cane was said to be experiencing were serious, suggesting that she was simply dealing with a significant change to her lifestyle. I got nothing from him to suggest that Cane had confided in him about any other problems she might have had. I found him easy to talk to, so I'm wondering if she might have discussed them with him and he's being discreet. If he does know more, a bit of encouragement might help to get him talking.' She looked at each of her colleagues. 'We're all aware of historical difficulties in obtaining information from churches, but that situation has now moved on in terms of safeguarding and sharing information with statutory agencies. Both Redpath and Leonard Partington, the vicar, have been open to questions. My impression is that Partington gives quite a lot of responsibility to Matthew Redpath, which makes Redpath a reliable source of intel. All of the people mentioned as having been spoken to need a further visit to confirm the consistency of what they're telling us.'

Watts nodded. 'A heads-up in relation to Jessop who was Cane's solicitor. Janine Franklin is sole beneficiary of Cane's estate, but apparently there is some current difficulty in locating Cane's investments. From what we know so far, it appears that it was Cane herself who reinvested her money. She would have had the financial skills to do it. I'll be seeing Jessop, who strikes me as a busy, elusive type, so listen out for any comments about him. I want a couple of you talking to the people who run the local pub. In that line of work they're likely to hear talk, but not necessarily recognize or appreciate the significance of it. That's your job, to check it out.' He looked up. I want all local residents visited.' He heard groans. 'I know. Thankless task, involving some late visits to the male population of the Heights who leave it in droves in the morning in order to make a few quid – probably a *lot*. Kumar, I want you starting social media searches.'

'Sarge?' said Reynolds. 'I heard what you said about Marion Cane's money, but shouldn't Janine Franklin be regarded as a person of interest? She would have anticipated inheriting her sister's estate. She's only just found out that it might not happen.'

Watts nodded. 'Keep her on the back burner for now, given what's happened to her husband. When she is seen, it will be Judd who does it. Franklin's not an easy woman to talk to but she's given us information about her sister, Marion, which suggests she was—'

'A bit of a goer.'

Watts saw grins on most of the faces. 'Thanks for the interjection, Judd. I was about to say "sexually promiscuous", although Will Traynor is not fully convinced of it. Right! Get yourselves organized and over to Newton Heights.'

He watched them go, Judd following, her face closed. She had seemed on the ball just now, but there was definitely something going on with her other than the impact of Franklin topping himself. He had considered keeping her back to ask, but it wasn't the right time. He reached for the phone, tapped a number, waited.

'Hello, Jess. How's Will?' He nodded. 'I know. A difficult time for him. How are you?' Another nod. 'I've got some news for him. I've asked John Heritage to apply for exhumation of Marion Cane's remains, although that's under wraps for now.'

He nodded. 'Yeah, if you'd tell him. Thanks, Jess.' He put down the phone, his hand and his eyes staying on it. Traynor was taking a day to rest. Better that than getting exhausted and dropping out of the investigation.

Outside Watts' office, Jones was talking to Judd. 'Come on, Chlo. You've been moody for days. What's up?'

'Right now, I'm trying to get past you and to the loo!'

'Moody's the wrong word. More like worried.'

'Just— Leave it, Ade.'

She walked away, not wanting to talk to him or anybody else. Less than a minute inside the deserted ladies' loos and she was out again, her thinking in freefall.

8.35 a.m.

Jones was in Newton Heights, eyeing the Range Rover Evoque sitting on the drive next to a BMW 4-series convertible with cream upholstery. He adjusted his face as the front door was yanked open, a tall, well-built male in a formal suit giving him an irritable look, a female voice coming from somewhere inside the big house.

'I've *got* the kids' lunchboxes!' He eye-rolled, and said to Jones, 'I'm gone in five minutes. Make it quick.'

Jones held up ID. 'Sir, we're in the neighbourhood making inquiries—'

'If it's about some old man who's gone missing, I'll save you the trouble. I never knew him. We don't know anybody here.'

Seeing the door starting to close, Jones raised his hand to it. 'Like I said, sir, we're making inquiries. In the last few days, do you or any other adult living here recall seeing anybody walking along the Rednal Road? It runs past the turn-in to Newton—'

'She wouldn't have noticed anything and neither have I. We never take that road. Our route is always in the direction of the city.' He lifted his hand, displaying his left wrist.

Jones' eyes settled on a large watch with multiple dials.

'Have you got the slightest clue how much you're costing me, hanging about here?'

Jones smiled, lightly tapping the rolled-up list against his own forehead in quasi-salute. 'Thank you, sir. I appreciate your time.'

Walking away from the house, muttering, 'Wanker', he spotted

Toby Reynolds some way ahead and picked up speed. 'Got anything, Tobes?'

Reynolds waited for him, keeping his voice low. 'Zero. What is it with this lot? They live here but that's about it. Their heads, eyes, interest, *everything* is miles away. Not a single one so far has even asked me a question.'

Jones elaborately raised his arm and frowned at his Casio watch. 'You've just cost me . . . about fifty pence.'

Reynolds grinned at him. 'What're you on about?'

'It's what some big I-Am just said to me. How many more have we got?'

Reynolds consulted his list. 'Nineteen, no, twenty. I can't stand this whole place and everybody in it. Let's just crack on, get it done.'

5.10 p.m.

Watts was inside the post-mortem suite, watching the smooth, coordinated movements of Chong and Igor at the steel examination table, cleaning up after a road traffic fatality. A strong jet of clean water pushed some that was not so clean along narrow gullies towards the drain. Pulling off gloves, dropping them into a bin, Chong looked across at him. 'I thought you wanted Heritage to agree to an exhumation?'

'I did. I do.'

'Your face is saying otherwise.'

His phone rang. It was Traynor. 'Will, how are—'

'Theresa Yates, the woman who cleaned for Cane. Confirm to me exactly what she said about Marion Cane's appearance when she found her dead.'

'Hang on . . .' He thumbed through pages of notes. 'She said she looked neat and tidy, better than she expected—'

'She referred to there being flowers in the room?'

'Yes. On the bedside table. She noticed them because she'd never seen flowers there before.' He waited out the pause. 'Will?'

'Somebody wanted to memorialize Marion Cane in death.'

'Meaning?'

Traynor was gone.

*   *   *

Watts came into his office to find Judd sitting in a pool of light, smooth blonde hair curving around her face. She looked up. 'I thought you'd left.'

'I've just had a call from Will.'

'How is he?'

'Not sure.'

'He needs to take a couple of days off.'

'Try telling him.' He sat heavily. 'The first day of official investigation and I'm already knackered.' He looked across the table at her. Nineteen when she first arrived at headquarters about four years ago. He still didn't know a lot about her, yet what he did know was more than most here. She had had a foster mother who died and left her money she had used to buy a small house in a reasonable suburb of the city. She also had a couple of brothers she didn't like and hadn't seen in a long time. These brothers were on Watts' mind. If one or other of them had made contact with her, it might explain her edginess. This was no idle speculation on his part. He needed her on this investigation. Fully on it.

'Judd, as your senior officer, I have a responsibility to you' – he paused as she stood and reached for her phone, not looking at him – 'and I've noticed you're looking a bit distracted. I'm wondering if there's something on your mind—'

'No.'

She shrugged her way into her jacket. He watched her to the door and out.

TWENTY-ONE

Thursday, 21 November. 6.50 a.m.

Inside his office, Watts was on Google, querying the word Traynor had used about the flowers left beside Marion Cane in death. He thought he knew the meaning but wanted confirmation that he was on the right lines. It arrived onscreen: *Memorialize: To create something that signifies remembering or honouring a loved one or event—*

'Morning, Sarge!' Kumar and Reynolds came in and sat opposite him, Kumar sending meaningful glances to Reynolds.

'How did the house-to-house go yesterday?' asked Watts. 'Anything of interest?'

Reynolds shook his head. 'Nada, Sarge. Not a single resident of that place gave us anything. They're either inside their posh houses or they're somewhere else, with zero interest in what happens in Newton.' He got another glance from Kumar. 'Have you thought any more about putting Cane's sister on the persons-of-interest list, sir? She stands to gain a fortune from her sister's death.'

'You've talked to her?'

'No, but according to Chlo, all Franklin talked about was how much her sister was worth and the people she intended to sue if she doesn't inherit the lot.'

'Which she might not,' said Watts. 'You'd think if she went to the trouble of killing her own sister, she would have checked out how she stood in terms of her sister's estate. Which reminds me. I need to get hold of Jessop, Cane's solicitor.' He stared straight ahead for several seconds, shook his head.

'Sarge?'

'Suspicions of Janine Franklin don't make much sense. If they did, it would mean that Cane's and Jack Beresford's deaths aren't connected. Franklin's a very unhappy, jealous woman, but I don't see her killing Jack's dog, getting *him* to that ravine and pushing him into it.' Another headshake. 'I think Marion Cane herself suspected that she was in danger.'

'She might have done, if her sister was at the bottom of it.'

Getting a sudden tightening inside his head, Watts asked, 'Anything from the searches I requested?'

'No, Sarge,' said Kumar. 'All the usual social media searches in respect of Cane yielded zip. Whatever she might have been into, she didn't share or access it online. Are we planning to do the same for other residents?'

'Possibly, in time.' Watts' eyes moved to Reynolds. 'Any results for Rednal Road CCTV in relation to Beresford?'

'No, Sarge. It's been out of action since' – he looked at the printed details he was holding – 'the start of this year.' Seeing Watts' face change, he added, 'They said it's low priority, given the relatively low volume of vehicle and pedestrian traffic on that road.'

'Tell that to somebody walking along it in the bloody dark!' Watts was on his feet as Judd arrived. 'With me, Judd.' And to Reynolds and Kumar, 'I'll give you two a lift back to the Heights.'

After dropping off the two officers, they drove to the Cane house, left the BMW's warmth and walked in fine rain to the front door, an officer standing to one side of it.

'Anything?'

'Nothing, Sarge. Quiet as the— Very quiet.'

'Your replacements should be here in ten minutes.' Watts' phone beeped. Pulling it from his pocket, he spoke into it, holding out the keys and alarm code to Judd who looked down at them as if they were potentially venomous, possibly explosive, and didn't take them. 'Where are you, Jones?'

'I've just come from seeing the vicar, Sarge. He didn't have a lot to say about Marion Cane. I was planning to do a few more calls to householders, but it looks like a lot have already left for work—'

'We're at the Cane house. Come over.' He pocketed the phone, eyes fixed on Judd. 'Is this sudden aversion to keys something I should know about?'

She gazed up at him, mute.

'In your own time. I like standing about in the rain.'

'I was about to say that I think you should lead.'

'That'll be a first.'

She tracked his broad shoulders as he opened the door, went inside and deactivated the alarm, then followed him into the big, silent house.

He turned to her. 'We're here to search this place, room by room. I want all of Cane's personal stuff, her letters, notes, cards – in short, any and *all* communications that we can find.'

'Most people communicate using technology.'

'That's one of our problems. Her phone was smashed, then chucked away. Got the bags I gave you?'

She held up the stout roll. He took it from her, tore off several.

'The dining room is yours. I'll search the sitting room.'

She made no move.

'Judd!'

'I *heard* you.'

He watched her go, then headed for the sitting room. He hadn't wanted her in here. The signs of John Franklin's self-destruction and its impact on the huge sofa were now concealed under pale-grey sheeting, courtesy of SOCOs. He approached shelving at the far end of the room, eyes drifting over book spines. Slipping on gloves, he reached for one, drew it out, opened it at random and began reading, brows together, the corners of his mouth moving downwards. They had been told Marion Cane liked sex. Her choice of reading said that she had a liking for romance. He fanned pages, looked at the space the book had left. He agreed with Traynor's observation of Cane as secretive. It was one of the reasons they were here. He pulled out more books, held up each one, fanned pages, watched them drift, then placed each one on the floor. Reaching into the shelf space, he felt around, locating nothing that might help fill in the blanks of this wealthy, successful, anxious, confused woman who had wanted then apparently feared this house. Judd's mention of technology highlighted its absence in Cane's life. There was no indication that she had replaced the smashed phone and no iPad or similar device had been found here. It made no sense. He headed to the hall.

'Judd?'

'Yes?'

He went into the dining room where she was kneeling at low shelving. 'My impression of Cane is that she was a technically savvy type, so how likely is it that she had just that one phone and nothing else?'

She looked up at him. 'Depends if it was an iPhone.'

He waited for more.

'The iPhone has been around for years but, back in the day, when that bloke invented it, he told everybody it was the only device they needed. Since then, they've improved out of sight, so yes, it makes sense to me that she had nothing else.'

'So how come she never replaced it?'

'Dunno. Too busy? Too distracted? Or maybe she found she preferred to be without it.'

He returned to the sitting room, went to a small table close to the bookshelves and pulled open its single drawer with one latex-covered finger and looked down at one entirely low-tech item.

'Sarge— Sir?' Judd was standing at the door. 'There's nothing in the dining room— She leapt as the doorbell sounded.

'That'll be Jonesy,' said Watts. 'He's come to give us a hand.'

He watched as she went to the door, having noted how pale she was looking. Something was clearly up. He wouldn't ask. Likely, a female issue. He might get Connie on to it.

Jones came into the sitting room, his hair damp, eyes drawn to the sheet-covered sofa, then to Watts. 'Where do I start, sir?'

'We're looking for items of communication – notes, letters, cards, anything sent to Marion Cane. I've searched in here, Judd's done the dining room. Both of you go upstairs and do an in-depth search of each bedroom, including every single item inside her wardrobes: footwear, bags, pockets of her clothes – you both know the drill. You're looking for whatever might tell us something about Marion Cane that we don't already know. I'd be glad of something as basic as a bus ticket that shows she led a normal life here.'

'I doubt buses were her style,' Judd murmured.

'Get going. Oh, and search the kitchen, including any cookbooks.'

As they disappeared, he lifted the small item from the drawer, crossed the room to the floor-to-ceiling sitting-room window, pulled a chair closer and opened it at the letter 'A'.

Twenty minutes later, the sound of the doorbell brought him to his feet. He left the sitting room for the hall and opened the door. A man wearing a three-piece suit and an apprehensive look on his face stared up at him. 'I want to see the officer in charge.'

'You're seeing him. Who are you?'

'Craig Jessop. Marion Cane's solicitor.'

Watts stepped back, opening the door wider. 'I've been trying to contact you, Mr Jessop.'

'I heard. That's why I'm here.' He looked around the hall. 'Is there somewhere we can talk? It won't take long.'

'Here is fine.'

'I've come to assist the investigation into Marion's death.' He pulled some papers from an inside pocket. 'You're aware there's been some delay in obtaining probate for Marion's estate. There's nothing irregular in that—'

'Glad to hear it.'

'But I just wanted to explain the situation. Here.'

Watts took the three A4s from him, glanced at each of them.

'They're copies. You'll see from them that they confirm that it was Marion herself who made changes to her investments, as she was absolutely entitled to do, of course, although she didn't inform me.'

Watts looked down at figures with a lot of zeros. 'What's your point, Mr Jessop?'

'My point is that movement of funds was nothing to do with me. I also have this.' He produced a folded sheet from another inside pocket. 'It's a copy of a document I got her to sign after she informed me of her decision. It states that she alone initiated the changes without prior consultation with me and without my advice—'

'That was forward thinking, Mr Jessop. Expecting something to happen to her, were you?'

'What?' Jessop's face heated. '*No*, of course not. It was to protect *me*, in case her decisions resulted in financial losses. I didn't want to be held in any way responsible. Which I wasn't.'

Watts folded the papers, guiding Jessop to the front door. 'I'll hang on to these, Mr Jessop—'

'But—'

'Until we have Ms Cane's signatures examined and verified, after which I'll be in touch.'

He closed the door on Jessop, looked at each of the sheets again. Help offered to the police was sometimes self-serving. Another thought quickly followed. If Jessop was on the level, where was Cane's money now?

2.35 p.m.

Watts was frowning at a single medium-sized evidence bag sitting on the big worktable in his office, its contents visible through clear plastic, all of it collected by Judd, Jones and himself from their search of the Cane house: postcards, presumably from her New York days: the Flatiron Building, Trump Tower, the Empire State Building. Not one of them written on. Memorabilia. *Memorializing.* One or two other items depicted office buildings in London. He recognized The Shard, not because of its shape but because of the money he'd paid to go up it with Connie. Once up there, all he got was vertigo and a misty view, but Connie had enjoyed it. A postcard of the Royal Albert Hall. A single photograph showing a woman recognizable as Marion Cane at what appeared to be an animal sanctuary, small cages behind her, in her arms a small, amiable-looking animal with massive ears, and Marion smiling widely at her photographer. He took it out, studied Cane in life. Casually dressed. Blonde hair loose to her shoulders, youthful, happy. He turned it over. Nothing on the reverse. Turned it back again, staring down at the smiling face, his thoughts drifting to a bureau at his own house, crammed with stuff relevant to both Connie and himself. Cards. Letters from her mother in Hong Kong. Their bank statements. A couple of letters from his daughter containing news and photos of her life in Brussels with her husband. Documents relating to the house he and Connie shared, birth certificates, passports which ought to be locked away. His eyes stayed on the relatively few items they had found at Cane's house.

'Will the real Marion Cane step forward.'

Judd glanced at him. 'If you're into some kind of weird séance-y thing, I'm not in the mood.'

'Tell me what you think you know about Cane.'

She considered this. 'Rich. Independent. Good looking for her age. A bit on the moody side. We've been through all—'

'Now tell me what you don't know.'

Her brows slid together. 'That's impossible . . . OK, OK, let me think.' She did. About the death of her foster mother. Always there when needed. Loving, no matter what. She wished she was still here. At fifty-seven, her foster mother was terminally ill, then gone. She swallowed, shrugged. 'We're not satisfied that she died from heart disease. So, we're knocking ourselves out looking for an alternative reason. But people in their fifties *do* die. They're fine, and then they get ill. Marion Cane had high blood pressure and some heart disease, though her GP wasn't particularly arsed about it.'

'Anything else you don't know?'

Judd was silent then, 'Yes. Her. I don't get *her*. I've seen films set in the kind of financial set-ups she worked in. They look well crazy, all go-go-go, but we're told she loved it.' She looked up at him. 'Yet the next thing we know, she arrives in the Heights, buys a massive house, has it kitted out like it's part of a telly programme, and what does she do next? She lives in it like some . . . hermit.' She breathed. 'It feels like whatever I learn about her, the less I know *her*. The word "secretive" has been used about her. How about she was involved in some kind of risky goings-on when she lived in America? Getting it on with men, making enemies, causing jealousy where she worked?'

Watts looked dubious. 'If it's something that far in her past, why did nothing happen to her while she was in the US? My impression is that she was a hard worker who fitted right into that type of setting: women in spike heels, smooth-looking blokes wearing Rolexes, walking about and yacking—'

'I can't believe you're still catching up on *Suits*.' She sighed. 'Look, it's no good asking me about her or her life. I don't know anything about finance. Until eighteen months ago, all I had was a Post Office savings account, showing fifty quid max at the end of a good month.' She frowned straight ahead, pushing back her hair. It swung smoothly back into place. 'To me, the key to her death, to understanding *her*, is *men*. Marion Cane liked them a lot and they liked her right back.' She looked at him. 'How about, when she worked for these high-flying finance companies, she had a sideline?'

'As in?'

She leaned forward, voice lowering. 'How about something very private, involving "dating"?'

He stared at her.

She gave him an impatient look. 'You *know*. A kind of club where people with money and professional reputations to protect . . . *mingle*. She knew a lot of people and maybe she made introductions in a way which felt safe: what happens in the club stays in the—'

She watched his face change and nodded.

'*Now* you're getting it. If that's what she was into, it could fit with her being a goer *and* getting murdered. She knew names. *Big* names.'

Watts shook his head. 'Again, why wait till she's living in Newton-Bloody-Heights to kill her? And, by the way, Will's expressed doubts about what Franklin said about Marion being promiscuous.'

He stretched his arms, laced his fingers behind his head. 'It's got to be simpler than that. At least, I bloody hope it is.' He looked at her. 'Where do you keep your documents, Judd? Your passport, bills of sale for your car, stuff like that?'

'I'll tell you on the understanding I might have to waste you. I had a little safe installed at the bottom of a cupboard in my bedroom. I get what you're saying. You're thinking Marion had a hiding place. What if Jessop, her solicitor, knew where it was, got his hands on details of where her money was?'

He let his arms drop, told her about Jessop's sudden appearance with an explanation for what had happened to Cane's investments. 'I don't like the bloke, but I'm inclined to believe him.' He looked at her. 'Ryan Bartlett is still top of my list.'

'Her bit of rough? He doesn't seem to me to have enough savvy to get his hands on her money—'

They looked up as the door swung open. Watts was on his feet. '*Will.*' He went to him, hand outstretched. Traynor gave a brief smile which didn't quite reach his eyes. 'I wasn't expecting you, mate.'

'I need to be here, Bernard.'

They sat, Watts quickly bringing him up to date on the investigation. 'It's not good. Progress is at a standstill for Beresford, despite the lads talking to over fifty households so far, and not much better for Cane.' He pointed to the floor. 'If things don't change and soon, I can see both joining the cases already down there, in "Still Active". We both know what that means. A cursory glance through the files every few weeks or so and that's it.' He looked at Traynor. 'If you've got any ideas on how to progress this investigation, I want to hear them.'

Traynor stared down at the table. 'My advice is to focus on Marion Cane herself. She's the key. She's also an enigma. Successful. Wealthy. Socially confident. Anxious. Friendless. We need to understand that inconsistency, that change, the reason for the slow, steady dismantling of her contacts. Her life.'

Judd looked from him to Watts, then back. 'How about her experience of life in Newton caused her to rethink the choice she made to live there? She's got a shedload of money, she liked men, or so we're told, and now she's feeling trapped, *Or* she had a bad experience – say, in London, maybe the Heights – and now she's on her guard, she's reducing her social contacts, *but* she still wants a man.'

'I can put a name to one likely "bad experience",' said Watts. 'Ryan Bartlett.'

Traynor's attention was fixed on the table, his arms folded. 'One would anticipate her taking considerable care with her choice of partner, considering only those men she viewed as of equal financial weight and professional success to herself.' He looked at Watts. 'But we can't assume she never made an exception.'

'Exactly.' Judd looked at each of them. 'Bartlett is in her garden, shirt off, and she's, like, wanting to keep her hand in—' She glared at Watts, who was trying to breathe between coughs, one hand raised, his voice hoarse.

'Coffee . . . down the wrong way.'

Undeterred, she continued. 'What about Janine Franklin herself? She's jealous of her sister's success, her money, while she's mouldering away in Newton Heights with her beige husband who's dared to go over to the other side.'

'The what?'

'He was "in bed with the enemy". Janine Franklin had a lot of scores to settle and she could have settled all of them by killing her own sister.'

'*Evidence*,' snapped Watts. 'Ryan Bartlett is already a person of interest and I've got a couple of officers following him wherever he goes.'

Judd frowned. 'I'm beginning to see where this investigation is heading. There'll be loads of judgements made about Marion Cane and the choices she made as a woman.'

'Nobody here is—'

'I don't mean *us*. I'm talking about the media when they really get hold of this investigation.'

A silence built in the room. Judd looked at Traynor, his eyes fixed in what Sarge called his 'see everything' stare. She reddened as the blue eyes settled on her. 'I'm saying that she'll be rubbished for liking sex and men. If it turns out that she was in a relationship that went wrong, the attitude will be judgemental, not sympathetic.'

Watts thought about it. 'If she had started a relationship, it could explain the changes in her. She's unsure, suspicious, needy even. He's pushing. He wants to move into her place. She resists the idea and then *he* finds out she's been busy rearranging her finances. *He* gets the hump about it and things turn bad between them.' He shook his head. 'If he's not from the Heights, he could be anywhere, which means we're back at square one with no idea who we're looking for and no forensic evidence.'

'Cane was no fool,' said Judd, 'but if she was lonely, it's easy to imagine her being vulnerable to some smooth-talking type.'

'I doubt that,' said Traynor. 'Yes, her life appears to have deteriorated during the time she lived in Newton Heights, but I'm not convinced by the picture of her as careless in her sexual choices, and I'm very reluctant to accept what her sister says about her without verification. All we know for sure is that she was an independent, successful woman who had a relationship with her sister's husband. She had already had years of independent living. There needs to be a focus on what was happening in her life in Newton Heights to cause such a radical change in her behaviour.'

'I've changed my opinion of her as a goer,' said Judd. 'I'm with Will on this. I think something happened between the time she moved to the Heights and when she died. She changed from a really sociable person to a shadow of what she was.'

She sighed, gazed at the floor, then reached down. 'Hang on.' She straightened, holding up a small rectangle of paper. 'This looks like it's part of the stuff we found in her house.'

Watts took it then passed it to Traynor, who studied both sides. '"*You are confined by the walls you build. Trust me to free you.*"'

Judd frowned at it. 'I've got no time for that stuff – that "kitten on a rope" rubbish: "*Hang on in there*". We have to sort our own problems out.'

'It looks like Cane was a fan—'

The phone rang. Watts reached for it. It was Heritage.

'I've arranged the exhumation and confirmed it to Mrs Franklin as Marion Cane's next of kin.'

'How did she take it?'

'Not thrilled. Families rarely are, but she says she wants to know what happened to her sister.'

'Thank you, sir.'

He put down the phone. 'We've got ourselves an exhumation.'

TWENTY-TWO

Saturday, 23 November. 3.05 a.m.

Judd and Watts left the warmth of the BMW and walked across the churchyard in their heavy coats, leaves scattering around their feet, chill damp against their faces. Watts gazed up at a fuzzy segment of moon, the square church tower outlined against cloud, then down to the long, black vehicle up ahead, windows impenetrable as it reversed slowly into position. He and Judd watched as Igor, Chong's pathology assistant, got out and headed towards the large white tent now standing on land to the rear of the church, Connie's small, unmistakeable outline lit from within it.

'Sarge?'

'Yes, Judd?'

'What's happening?'

'Can you hear sounds of digging?'

'Yes.'

'That's what's happening.'

'What happens when it finishes?'

'I go and talk to the environmental health officer.' He looked down at her. 'He's the bloke you didn't like the look of when we arrived. When he's finished his paperwork, he and I will check the details and we'll both sign it. You'll stay here.'

'OK.'

After a further twenty minutes of watching, of listening to sounds of digging, a quietness settled on the scene, hooded SOCOs now moving purposefully inside the tent. A figure in head-to-foot white emerged, one hand raised in Watts' direction: the EHO.

Watts went to the tent, added his name to a list and followed him inside. The air was clammy with condensation, the odour of damp and rot strong now. Marion Cane's coffin had been raised and was resting on planks. Watts and the EHO approached it, checked printed burial details with those on the brass plate on its lid. Watts' eyes moved slowly over it. It looked to be in good condition following its six months' burial. He watched Chong conferring with two SOCOs. Turning, she nodded to Igor who left the tent, then returned, pulling a sturdy wheeled platform. A further quick examination of brass fittings by the morose-looking EHO and the coffin was lifted on to the platform and wheeled slowly, carefully out of the tent, six officers following it to the black vehicle where they lifted it inside. A brief pause as Igor unfolded a black velvet cloth and placed it over the coffin: a nicety observed by somebody who never knew Marion Cane. Igor secured the tailgate and drove the vehicle slowly from the churchyard and away.

Watts emerged from the tent, drawing more damp air into his chest. In his twenty-five-plus years of service, he had attended three exhumations prior to this one. He looked across at Judd standing alone. This was her first. She looked cold. No colour in her face. His gaze drifted further, looking for Traynor, not finding him. It had crossed Watts' mind earlier that his attending the exhumation wasn't the best idea. He walked to Judd. Her eyes were still fixed on the direction in which the pathology vehicle had faded a couple of minutes before.

'Come on. I've got a flask of tea with added benefit.'

She followed him to the BMW. They got inside. He fetched a small thermos from beneath his seat, opened it, half-filled a plastic cup and offered it to her.

She didn't take it. 'What's in it?'

'Tea and a drop of single malt.'

'I don't drink that stuff.'

'A night like this, make an exception. You look like you could use it.'

She took it from him.

He produced a second cup which he half-filled and drank, staring at nothing, picking up a series of small coughs, followed by a quick intake of breath. 'All right?'

'Mm . . .' More silence. 'You don't drink much, do you, Sarge?'

'No. I spill most of it.' He glanced at her. 'That was a joke.'

'I got it.'

'Feeling better?'

She nodded. 'We've talked a lot about Marion Cane. About how successful she was before she came here, how she kind of faded away, and now . . . she's inside that box we just saw.'

Watts started the engine. 'Finish your tea and I'll drive you home.'

TWENTY-THREE

6.30 a.m.

Traynor was inside his university office, looking down at the tremor in both his hands. He gripped them together. He was here to work. To block all thoughts of Claire by substituting another dead woman in her place. Marion Cane. The realization threw his heart against his chest. The previous evening, he had regained his focus, had reread all of the available information on her. Dissatisfied with the 'natural causes' explanation of her death, aware of the need for more exploration, he had decided on a methodology that might help him reconstruct events surrounding her death, including her behaviour and responses leading up to it. A psychological autopsy. He had conducted these in the past, in situations where the investigation of a death continued to raise questions. Those individuals who had had direct involvement in Marion Cane's life in the lead-up to her death had been questioned by Bernard and his officers. None of the information obtained had provided Traynor with a clear understanding of her or her state of mind prior to it. He needed to revisit those individuals, ask questions about her final weeks and months which are psychological rather than evidential.

Reaching for his iPad, he began constructing a list of those he considered persons of interest: Guy Devereaux. Vanessa Devereaux. Craig Jessop. Ryan Bartlett. Janine Franklin. Reverend Leonard Partington. Anna Partington. He paused, added Matthew Redpath, solely on the basis of his brief contact with Cane. On that same basis, Eric Brook's name also needed to be included, despite the trainee's reported psychological difficulties and his currently unknown whereabouts. Obtaining information from him might be both time-consuming for the investigation and distressing for Brook himself. Traynor added a question mark to his name. In any event, neither the trainee nor Redpath the deacon fitted Traynor's expectation of Cane's killer.

Reaching for a copy of Marion Cane's death certificate, signed by Devereaux in his role as her GP, he read the printed words referencing heart disease. There was no comment on the degree of seriousness. None on the suddenness of her death. Experience told him that, even at this stage, there were still three possibilities which must be considered. Natural causes. Suicide. Homicide. The exhumation would hopefully provide an answer. Three years before, Traynor had been asked to evaluate a death where the possibility of suicide had been raised. He had met with all those who knew the deceased, either personally or professionally, gathered their responses to his questions and ultimately provided his opinion that an alternative explanation required exploration. Renewed police efforts had eventually identified subtle indicators of foul play which had led to the arrest and subsequent conviction of a family member who eventually admitted to murder. A psychological autopsy might lay to rest Traynor's own doubts around Marion Cane's death.

He looked at the few names Bernard had found in Cane's address book. He had to establish, where possible, if any of them had known Marion Cane during the time she lived in London and also following her relocation to Newton Heights. Settling on one name, he glanced at his watch. *7.10 a.m.* Not too early to ring someone living and working in London? He reached for his phone, listened to his call buzz several times. It was picked up.

'Have I reached Jenna Carrington?'

'That depends who's calling,' was the cool response.

Realizing the abruptness of his words, he said, 'I do apologize. My name is William Traynor. I'm a criminologist working with West Midlands Police.'

'I'm Jenna Carrington. What's this about?'

'A few years ago, I believe you were a work colleague of a woman named Marion Cane?'

'Yes, I was. We both worked for the same finance firm.'

'Ms Carrington, your contact details were in Ms Cane's address book. I need to ask – were you and she close friends?'

'I don't know about "close", but we got on really well during the time we worked together. After she left the firm, we rather lost touch.' She paused. 'How did you come by Marion's address book?'

'I'm sorry to have to tell you that Marion Cane died about six months ago.'

'*No.* I had no idea! Oh my— What happened? Was it an accident?'

'I'm part of the police investigation that is exploring her death. May I ask you a few questions about her?'

'Yes, of course.'

'Do you have any observations to make on her as a person, her personality?'

'I need to give it some thought . . . I'd describe her as a warm person, also very efficient. Conscientious. What stands out for me is her warmth. Yes. Warmth and kindness.'

'Can you recall anything specific about her behaviour during the time you knew her?'

'Apart from what I just said, I'd say that she was very friendly, very sociable. It was clear when you were with her that she really loved being with people, socializing with them, you know?'

Traynor absorbed this. 'Do you have any general comments to make about her as a colleague? Or a friend?'

'Yes. I'd say honest, straightforward. You knew where you were with Marion. As I said, she was open. Gregarious.'

'Do you recall ever experiencing any difficulty in understanding her, either what she said or how she interacted with you?'

'No, sorry. I don't recall anything like that. None of that sounds at all like Marion. Like I said, she was honest, warm. Very outgoing.'

'Do you recall the last time you spoke to or saw her in person?'

'Yes, very clearly. By then she had quit working and was living in the Midlands. We hadn't seen each other in quite a while, but she rang me to say she had bought a house and invited me to visit her for a weekend.'

'When was this, exactly?'

There was a short silence. 'Sorry, I need to think – I'd say it was around eighteen months ago, perhaps a little less. I stayed with her from the Friday afternoon to the Sunday afternoon. I'd have to check exact dates.'

'Can you tell me about those days you spent with Ms Cane?'

'Of course. It was lovely to see her again. I was pretty new to finance work back then and Marion was so kind to me, really helpful. She was a great person, very highly rated by the firm. I've just thought back to when I started working there. I didn't know anyone. Guess what Marion did. She organized a welcome party for me.' She fell silent. 'Are you saying that her death is a police matter? That makes no sense at all. I just can't believe she's dead. She had to be in her mid-fifties when I knew her – a really confident, vibrant person.'

'Are you able to say any more about the weekend you spent with her in the Midlands?'

'Yes. I thoroughly enjoyed it. She was living in this village, which to me seemed like heaven compared to London. And her house! It was *beautiful*. Not all of it was furnished but she'd got one of the guest rooms done and everything was so tasteful. Just typical of Marion. She was full of plans for it.'

'What kind of plans?'

'Oh, you know. The decoration she wanted, the furniture she was ordering, the way she wanted the garden.'

'Did she mention anything more specific?'

'No, but she was at the stage where she couldn't wait to spend money on it, make it her home for the foreseeable future . . . This is *so* sad.'

'Did she introduce you to any local residents?'

'One or two as we walked around the village. I don't recall any names, but we met the local vicar and his wife.' She laughed. 'Marion had a wicked sense of humour. Afterwards, she joked about them, about how unsuited they were together.'

'Do you remember any specific comments?'

'Not really. My impression was that she thought him fuddy-duddy and described his wife as "fit". Actually, I remember thinking that he was rather sweet— Oh, I've just remembered. We met the local doctor. He was very pleasant. Marion had nothing much to say about him. I don't think she had any contact with him professionally. Why would she? If you had seen Marion back then, you would get what I'm saying. We went on a proper country walk while I was there and she wore me out!'

'Did you keep in touch?'

'For a while, yes, mostly through texts and emails.'

'When was the last time you actually saw her?'

'That weekend. I got promoted soon after, which meant I was

working longer hours, but I emailed Marion about the promotion because she was a kind of mentor to me.'

'When was the last time you spoke directly with Ms Cane?'

'At a guess, around eight months ago or thereabouts, and . . .'

Traynor waited. 'Ms Carrington?'

'Actually, you've got me thinking. Around that time, the tone of her texts changed. Nothing obvious, but they were quite short with much less humour and energy in them than I remember. I phoned her one day to see how she was. She sounded distracted. It felt like she was having difficulty following what I was saying. I asked her if she was OK. She said she was fine but she sounded like, I don't know, a reduced version of herself. I did ask her directly if there was anything wrong. She said no, that she was a little worried about something but she thought it would all sort itself out.'

'Did she give any details about that?'

'No, and it was clear that she didn't want to talk about it. I called her a couple of times after that but didn't manage to speak with her. I also texted her but she didn't respond.'

'Was that surprising to you?' He waited as Carrington thought about it.

'I think by that stage I had re-evaluated our friendship and decided that it had run its course. I was working, she wasn't, she was living the best part of a hundred miles away – it's what happens to friendships over time, isn't it? Particularly work-based ones.'

Traynor carefully framed his next question. 'From your direct knowledge of Marion, did her tone during that final time you did talk with her convey anything to you?'

'As I've said, I thought she sounded worried, distracted. Look, as you're working with the police, I don't want to mislead you by overstating anything. All that I've described are just my impressions of that time.'

'If you had to choose another word to describe Marion during that call, what would it be?'

He waited out the pause.

'My first choice was going to be "disturbed" – that there was something upsetting her, but thinking back to my conversation with her, the word doesn't convey what I was hearing.'

Traynor said nothing, not wanting to impinge on this woman's thought processes. He heard her draw a shaky breath.

'I'm probably overthinking this now, because it sounds too dramatic, but the word in my mind is "frightened".'

Call ended, Traynor gazed from his eighth-floor inner-city window at the slow Sunday build-up of traffic far below, the single word reverberating inside his head. If Carrington's recall was accurate, what specific forces or events had produced the changes she had described in Marion Cane? Based on what he knew of Cane, undoubtedly an intelligent woman, why hadn't she sought help? If she was fearful, was it possible that the source of that fear was too important to her emotionally? Or physically too close?

He went back to his desk, gathered information together, placed it inside his backpack, reached for his jacket and left his office for the nearby lifts. He needed more information to test his thinking. The lift arrived. He stepped inside, saw his mirrored reflection, looked away.

7.20 a.m.

Watts was in his new ultra-modern kitchen, trying to recall from the array of glossy white cabinets the location of plastic lunch-boxes when Connie appeared in pink PJs, her pixie cut spiky. She came to him, laid her head against his upper arm.

'All right?' he asked. Not a real question. More a verbal base-touching.

She grinned up at him. 'I remember Chloe Judd being fazed by that when she first arrived at headquarters. I told her it was basic "Birmingham", intended to cover all situations and even-tualities, that it took me a while to get it.'

He looked down at the perfect oval face. 'When do you start work on Cane?'

'I've cleared my list for this morning so I'd better get moving.' She left the kitchen and he pulled at a random chrome handle. A deep drawer slid effortlessly towards him. Lunch boxes.

'*Bernard?* I just remembered. In case you're planning another visit to Marion Cane's house, the biohazard clean-up team are due there, so make it another day.'

TWENTY-FOUR

Carrington's words were inside Traynor's head as he drove. If Marion Cane was in fear, it was unlikely that it related to her past work history. 'If' and 'unlikely' resonated inside his head. He needed more. He needed something approaching certainty. He was on his way to Newton Heights to talk to people who knew her while she lived there. Fifteen minutes on, he parked and approached the low-rise property. He had phoned half an hour before. She had agreed to see him. Passing the two parked cars, he reached the front door, rang the bell and waited. It was opened by Franklin wearing a long dressing gown, her arms folded against the morning chill.

'I've changed my mind. I don't want to talk to you.'

'Mrs Franklin, don't you want justice for your sister?'

She glared at him. '*You* people. It's just another investigation to you. You have *no* idea what it's like to lose somebody!'

His head tightened. 'We need your help, Mrs Franklin.'

She held his gaze, then turned and walked away from him. He stepped inside. It felt cold. Unopened post littered the hall floor. He followed her to the kitchen where she was opening wall cupboards, one after another. Reaching inside one, she took out a bottle, set it down with a sharp click, followed by another search. Finding a glass, she poured brandy into it, looked up at him. 'Do *not* presume to judge me.'

'That's not what I do.'

'*Really?* It seems to me that that's exactly what you and that officer you work with do constantly. Make judgements. Ask questions. Make *more* judgements. If that's why you're here, you can leave right now.'

'I do have some questions.'

She pushed past him, glass in hand. 'Well, so do I, as it happens. I want to know what made the police decide to exhume my sister.'

He followed her. 'We need to know exactly why she died. I've come here because I need to understand your sister and her life.'

'Ha! Yet another man who's fascinated by my sister. Will it never end?' She was inside the conservatory now, its huge windows a vista of dullness and damp. She sat, took a mouthful of brandy. 'What is there to understand? Her death certificate said heart disease.' She looked up at him, glanced at her watch. 'You've got ten minutes.'

He took a seat some distance from her, his first question general. 'I'm interested in your perceptions of Marion—'

'Really? I've got *plenty* of those.' She swallowed more brandy, sat back, giving him an appraising look. 'You're thinking about the last time you were here and how I was. How I took the news that John was dead.'

'Mrs Franklin—'

A single tear suddenly appeared, tracked its way slowly down her cheek. 'You can have *no* idea what it's like to be with a person for years and suddenly they're gone. Yes, we had problems, and yes, John was away a lot, but he always came *back*. To *me*. The police sent a liaison officer here to see how I was, if I needed "support". She talked to me about the shock of sudden death—'

Traynor was watching her mouth move, knowing the words from his own experience, all of them melding into a litany of heartbreak, loss, flashbacks, detachment, pessimism, and, finally, his way of dealing with it, which was to block it all. Until he couldn't and he had needed psychiatric support. It had helped. Had carried on helping. Until the news just days ago that an Oxford field had given up his wife, and he knew he was falling again—'

'Doctor Traynor?'

He looked up. She was frowning at him. He pulled his thoughts together. 'Are you able to tell me about your sister's daily routines, her habits, any changes you might have noticed in the months leading up to her death?'

'I can't help you with that. I didn't see her regularly.'

'Did you ever observe changes to her physical presentation?'

'No.'

'Can you tell me something about your sister's personality?'

'Yes. Marion was selfish. Her needs came before everyone else's. End of story.'

'During the times you and she did have contact, did you notice anything specific about her behaviour in the months before she died?'

'I noticed she was a bit on edge— No, *don't* ask me *when*, I don't have the least idea.'

'Do you have any general comments to make about her?'

Her eyes drifted slowly over his face. 'My sister was very consistent in all she said and did. Pleased with herself. With her life. With what she had *achieved.*' She sipped more brandy.

Traynor knew that what he was about to say was risky, but it needed saying if he wanted to move this process forwards.

'Mrs Franklin, my impression is that you experienced your sister's work, her life, her presence here as a criticism of you and the life choices you had made.' He saw her mouth set, a slow flush washing over her neck.

'I don't recall asking for your opinion and I won't justify what you just said with a response.'

'Have you any observations to make of Marion as a sister?'

'Two-faced. Mean. How about treacherous, disloyal, deceitful, back-stabbing?' She took a breath. 'Does that tell you what you want to know?'

'Were you aware of Marion using medication or alcohol on a daily basis during the time she lived here?'

Franklin stared at him, raised her glass, pointing at him. 'Very good. You mean, like her sister. I *don't* drink, except in some special circumstances, such as my husband deciding to slice open his own throat.' Her gaze wavered. 'Marion didn't drink, except for an occasional wine. The only medication I knew of was something she told me that the GP here had prescribed, but she had no intention of taking it.'

'When did she tell you that?'

Franklin shrugged. 'Not sure. A few months before she died. She mentioned to me that she was having mood swings. Again, don't ask me for details. I don't have any. I wasn't interested.'

'During those last months, do you recall experiencing any difficulty in understanding Marion, in terms of what she said or in the way she interacted with you?'

She gazed at him. 'Haven't you got it yet? I *never* understood my sister, but I can tell you how she "interacted" with my husband.

As often as she could and in all of the ways it was possible to do so.'

'How did you come to that realization?'

'I observed *her* when John was around. *That* told me all I needed to know.'

'Do you recall the last occasion you and your sister spoke together?'

'Yes. She told me she intended to see Devereaux again. Get his opinion on something or other. I wasn't paying attention.'

'Did you directly observe any changes in your sister near to the time of her death?'

'Like what?'

'Was there anything in addition to the quick shifts of mood you mentioned?'

'Marion was moody when she didn't have a man, or at least the prospect of one.'

'How did that show itself?'

She rested back her head, gazing at him. 'One question begets another in your world, Doctor Traynor. All I noticed was that she stopped jogging during that last couple of months. On the odd occasions I did see her, she looked . . . restless.' She glanced at Traynor. 'But she was still very much herself. One morning I saw her standing outside her house with Bartlett, her gardener. Gardener, *ha*! That's a bloody *joke*. She was looking down at him as he got into his van, all eyes and teeth. I didn't need to be told what *that* meant.'

'When was this?'

She shrugged. 'If he was there, it was probably early springtime.'

'Can you be explicit about what you observed in your sister that day?'

She gazed at him and smiled. 'Come *on*, Doctor Traynor. I'm sure you're a very worldly man. You know about my sister and how she lived. Her *needs*.' She swallowed more brandy. 'If Marion had seen *you*, you would have been on the receiving end of that same treatment, believe me, and you wouldn't be asking me all of these bloody questions.'

'Is it possible that she was in some kind of difficulty and was asking Bartlett for help?'

She put down the empty glass, ran her finger around its rim, emphasizing each word. 'My sister had only one "difficulty" and she knew how to ask for help with *that*.'

'Do you think it's possible that that aspect of your sister's behaviour placed her at some personal risk?'

Franklin's head came up. She stared at him. 'Placed her . . . Ah, I see what you're getting at. You're referring to her money.' Her eyes swam. 'You *must* promise me that the police are going to investigate what's happened to it—'

'I wasn't referring specifically to money and, as a non-officer, I can't make that kind of commitment on their behalf. Is it possible that your sister placed herself at risk from men who might harm her?'

She closed her eyes, whispered, 'Is there no end to this? Marion *always* believed that she had the world by the tail. It was in every aspect of her behaviour, the way she spoke, the way she moved, her voice, her laugh. What I'm saying is that my sister probably went after any man she saw who fit a key requirement: the ability to get it *up*.' She laughed, leaned back, her eyes on his. 'You're sure you won't have a drink, Doctor Traynor? Just a *tiny* one?'

'Thank you, no.'

She got slowly to her feet. 'Then, *go*! Leave me alone! I've got . . . things to do.'

Inside his car, Traynor opened his window, pulling cold air into his chest, wanting to be rid of the resentment and jealousy he had just heard, thriving beyond death.

TWENTY-FIVE

10.05 a.m.

Watts reached for Marion Cane's address book, his eyes on Judd. 'All the names in this need to be checked against whatever papers and communications we took from her house. We need linkage. I'll settle for a name or a single reference to *anybody* who might have been in contact with Cane, say, in the last twelve months of her life.' He stood. 'I'm going up to forensics to see if they've got anything for us. I'll be a few minutes, in case Will arrives.'

'They'd have phoned if they had anything.'

He headed for the door. 'I'll still ask.'

She reached for the address book and a pen, pulled the plastic evidence bag of small items to her side of the table.

He was back in fifteen minutes. 'They're under pressure up there. I'll go again, later. How's it going?'

'None of what we got from the house includes sender's addresses or contact details.' She pointed. 'This note is from an Alicia Lessing, thanking Cane for an invite to her London place for dinner. Inside this Christmas card, somebody called Miriam has written, "Merry, merry! Let's meet up in the New Year!" Two birthday cards, both "With love", one from somebody named Christy, the other from . . . *Jocasta.*' She shook her head. 'It's a different world down there, Sarge. None of those names feature in her address book. And who writes letters and cards, anyway, when you can just zap an email or a text?'

He reached for the address book, flicked pages. 'There's a couple of numbers here without names.'

He rang one, then the other. After a couple of minutes, he put down the phone. 'One unobtainable. The other some old gasbag who kept insisting I'm a plumber and wanting to know when I was coming to fix her downpipe.' He sat back, rubbed his face. 'Jesus *wept.*'

Judd shoved back her chair. 'Almost every word you just said was sexist or ageist.'

'Probably. This *highly unusual* bad mood of yours is telling me that today is unlikely to get a lot better.'

'Sarky.'

The door swung open and Traynor came into the office.

Watts nodded. 'Morning, Will.'

Traynor's phone beeped. He took it out, looked down at its screen. 'Hi, Tom. Thanks a lot for getting back to me so soon.'

They listened to the questions he was asking his caller. Whoever it was, he knew a lot about the technology associated with financial trading. After a few more minutes, Traynor nodded into the phone. 'You too, Tom. Thanks a lot for your help.' He ended the call. 'Tom Holland, one-time criminology colleague of mine, now an intelligence analyst specializing in serious and organized crime, drug trafficking and financial crime relating to banking and other sectors.'

Watts and Judd exchanged glances.

'A couple of days ago, I gave him two names: John Franklin. Marion Cane. Neither has featured even peripherally in any investigative work in which Tom's department has been involved over almost two decades. I also included the firms each of them had worked for in London and, in Cane's case, New York. Neither ever registered a blip of interest for Tom or his intelligence colleagues. I talked to Marion Cane's sister earlier. She confirmed that Marion was prescribed medication but didn't take it. She didn't identify what it was. She also said that Marion intended to consult her GP again but was unaware of the reason.'

'That Devereaux is a git,' fumed Watts. 'Maybe he's not telling us all he knows.'

'Franklin also recalled once seeing her sister in conversation with Ryan Bartlett outside her house early this year. The impression she had of her sister's behaviour suggests that Cane was conveying sexually explicit signals to him.' He paused. 'But, as I've said, I question how balanced Janine Franklin's observations are likely to be, given her negative feelings towards her sister.'

Watts rubbed his hands together. 'I hear you, Traynor, but my take on Bartlett is that he's a git *and* a liar—' His phone rang. He spoke into it briefly, ended the call. 'The examination of Marion Cane's remains is starting in ten minutes.' He tracked the criminologist to the door. 'You're not staying, Will?'

'No.'

They watched him go through the door and out.

'What do you think, Sarge?'

'He's dealing with enough death right now.'

'He is all right, though?'

Watts rubbed his big hands over his face, let them drop. 'Do you remember when you first started work here and we both went to see him?'

Judd nodded.

'You asked me a similar question. I had no answer then and I haven't now, but we're lucky to have him on this or any other case because he gets results, no matter what he's got going on.' He was on his feet again. 'I'm going to the PM suite— *No*, Judd, not you.'

'But—'

'You've never attended an examination of exhumed remains, and I doubt this is a good time for your first. You look like you're coming down with something. Stay here.'

The door opened and one of the officers from Reception came in holding a large envelope. 'For you, Sarge.'

He took it, opened it, placed its contents next to Judd. 'Here's a job for you. Marion Cane's medical records.'

Watts walked into the post-mortem suite, not looking at what was lying on a nearby examination table. Chong was in full-body scrubs, plus face shield. She held one out to him. 'I've got three road traffic victims waiting, for which I have to fully change, so I need to move on Cane.' Reaching for a clipboard, she looked at Igor. 'Confirm the deceased's name and details, please.'

'Marion Cane. Fifty-nine years old at death. Resident of Newton Heights.' He added her date of birth and grave location details.

'Exactly what I have here. Always a good start.'

Watts looked down at the remains now separated from coffin and burial garments. So, this was Marion Cane, whose name was inside his head when he went to bed, and still there each morning. 'She looks . . . good, considering.'

'What you're seeing is the effects of embalming. Igor, read out the details from her death certificate, please.'

Her eyes moved slowly from the feet to Cane's head as he did so. Pulling down a ceiling-mounted light, she placed her gloved hands on either side of it and applied gentle, systematic pressure to the underlying skull. Over the next several minutes, she conducted a similar process on the rest of the remains, her words picked up by the tiny microphone suspended above the table. 'Confirmation of no gross evidence of damage to the skeletal structure.'

She took a magnifier from Igor. 'Beginning whole-body examination for minor indications of interference.' She moved the magnifier slowly over the remains. 'This is going to take a while. I need to . . . thoroughly examine the skin, including that behind the ears and between the toes for anything that might suggest marks left by needle jabs or similar.' The room was silent as she continued the methodical search. After several minutes she straightened, shook her head.

'No visible abrasions, no cuts and no puncture marks evidenced.'

Reaching for a scalpel, she applied it, starting in the central upper chest area. Major internal organs slowly appeared within the opened chest cavity. She glanced up at Watts. 'I'm about to collect samples for toxicological analysis. In case you're not aware, the embalming process can potentially affect any results I get from them, but I'll still follow my usual sampling routine on the off-chance that if there was anything awry about Marion Cane's death, I'll be able to identify it.'

Watts absorbed her words. 'Whose decision was it for Cane's remains to be embalmed?'

Chong leaned towards the printed information Igor was holding towards her. 'Her sister, Janine Franklin, arranged it.'

Watts' head shot up. 'Franklin couldn't *stand* her sister. Had no time for her when she was alive. Why would she go to the trouble and expense after she was dead?'

'I rang her when I first learned that embalming had occurred. She told me that Marion had always taken great pride in her appearance and she wanted to do that for her in death.'

He shook his head. 'No, no, no, that's total bull. There had to be some other reason.'

Chong glanced up at him. 'If I'm following your thinking, I have serious doubts that Janine Franklin would be fully aware of the toxicological impact of the embalming process on her sister's remains and samples taken from it. Unless she worked for an undertaker.'

'Or researched it online.'

'Point taken.'

As Watts left, Chong harvested samples, then stepped away from the table, pulling off gloves and dropping them into a nearby bin. 'I want you to close for me, Igor. After the three RTAs, you'll be free as a bird.'

He looked gratified. 'I need to be out of here by six. We're going to see *Dark Mirror*.'

'Sounds more attractive than that assault course race you both did last week. A horror film?'

'More psychological. Lisa Vidal is in it. Jed likes dark-haired women.'

'How's that work for Jed?' she asked absently.

'It's a Judy Garland thing.'

She straightened, glanced down at Cane. 'I'm always heartened when I see hair more or less intact.' She pointed. 'She had nice hair.' Her glance moved to the face, still identifiable as the woman she had been in life. 'A very attractive woman.'

'I'll be forty next birthday,' said Igor, sounding subdued. 'Fifty-nine is starting to sound a bit young to die.'

'I *definitely* get that.'

She took the several tissue samples she had gathered, now labelled, to the refrigerator, placed them inside and closed the door on them.

TWENTY-SIX

Early evening

Traynor came into a comparatively muted headquarters and went directly to the second floor. Opening the frosted glass door of the forensic department, he walked into the extensive, well-lit room and raised his hand to return a greeting from Adam Jenner, Head of Forensics. The atmosphere here bore some similarities to the labs and cognitive research suites of Traynor's postgraduate years. It felt something like home. 'Thanks for waiting, Adam. I've begun a psychological autopsy of Marion Cane's death. Any physical evidence you've found could be useful to that process.'

'No problem. You want to know about the items I had removed from Marion Cane's house? They're over here.'

Traynor followed him to a long table, where Adam pointed to the mirror in its ornate frame. 'I've been to the house and checked the dimensions of the outline on the wall in the sitting room, including the position of its main fixing. I'm confident that this mirror hung in that room at some stage, probably for a relatively significant period of time.'

'Which suggests it was probably there for most of the time Marion Cane lived in that house.' Traynor looked down at it, then up at Adam, brows raised.

'Feel free, Will. It's been fully processed.'

Traynor ran his hands lightly over the carved frame, then leaned forward to examine the glass itself, his eyes moving slowly over it. 'I don't see any damage—' He pointed. 'There's something . . . some marks, here and . . . here.' Taking a magnifier from Adam, he leaned closer to the glass, tracking the narrow marks on several areas. 'I'm seeing fibres. It looks like something was stuck to this mirror at some time and the fibres adhered.'

'Exactly,' said Adam, indicating a colourful item lying on a nearby table. 'What you're seeing is transference. Some of the fibres on that mirror came from that rug which was also in Marion Cane's sitting room.' He pointed at the mirror. 'The dimensions of these marks suggest they were made by something roughly seven centimetres in length with a narrow adhesive strip.' He looked at Traynor. 'Care to take a guess, Will?'

Traynor gave the marks another close look. 'Some kind of label?' He looked up. 'How about Post-it notes?'

'That's my thinking. I heard Bernard refer to Marion Cane suffering confusion prior to her death. Maybe she used this mirror as a repository for reminders to herself. I do something similar using a noticeboard in my kitchen.' He grinned at Traynor. 'I'm guessing you don't need one. One difference between us, Will, is that my mind's not a steel trap.' He reached for a folder, removed several high-definition photographs.

'We've analysed the fibres. Take a look.' He pointed. 'These here are wool. They match the colours of the rug. Others, like these, are man-made polyester.'

Traynor looked at each of them. 'How about these?' He pointed at another enlargement, colour claiming his attention.

'More natural fibres, all uniformly short, predominant colour dark red, suggesting a soft yet robust fabric. My money's on jeans.'

Traynor looked at him. 'You're certain of that?'

'Enough to take it to court if required. Want to see what else we have?' He reached for another folder, opened it.

Traynor looked down at a single trace item, a transparent sheet holding it in place.

'A single hair. Often, it's all we get. Unfortunately, this one has no intact root sheath to give us DNA.'

'I'm still impressed.'

'Trace evidence doesn't cut much ice with Bernard if it doesn't give him the identification he wants. I'm ready to write my report, once we've fully examined the rug. It might yield a hair complete with root sheath, but please don't tell him because he'll be up here, pushing.'

'Have you had an opportunity to look at the eyedrops recovered from Marion Cane's bedroom?'

Adam reached for a plastic box, opened it and brought out one of the four small white containers. 'We've done a basic examination, which hasn't revealed anything of interest. They're over-the-counter eyedrops, all four of them still sealed and not subjected to tampering of any kind. Speaking non-scientifically, they suggest to me that Cane was highly motivated to look her best at all times and anxious to ensure she had a reliable supply. I'm straying into your territory here, Will.'

'I agree with all you've said. If anxiety had a chemical component, you would have found it all over her house. What about prints on the containers?'

'Good question. None.'

Traynor looked up at him. 'Sorry?'

'The small boxes bore smudges conducive with say casual handling in a retail environment, but there are no forensic indications that Marion Cane or anyone else directly handled any of the actual containers. I was thinking of checking with Bernard if there was any indication that Cane had a foible around hygiene as a possible explanation for the absence.'

'Not that we're aware. What about Jack Beresford? Is there anything you're able to add about his death?'

'Sorry, Will. Nothing.'

9.45 p.m.

Traynor was at home inside his study, having read through the minimal information gathered by officers from residents of Newton Heights. Most had had little awareness of either Marion Cane or Jack Beresford prior to the recent police involvement in the area. It confirmed for Traynor his view of Newton Heights itself. Not a village. A gathering of financially well-off people with little personal investment in the area in which they lived, who had chosen it because of the access it gave them to Birmingham's vast motorway network. He was thinking about Cane, once a highly successful financial trader, and Beresford, a prosperous builder. Linked by a house built by one of Beresford's sons, which Cane eventually bought. A house she had reportedly loved. Until her perception of it changed radically over time.

Beresford had also involved himself early on in the investigation. Described as a reserve police officer during the Second World War, his words to Bernard indicated that he believed there was something about Marion Cane's death that required investigation. The anonymous note, a copy of which Traynor was looking at, reinforced what Beresford had said. Had he written it? Whatever the true nature of the links between them, they were both now united by an investigation into their deaths.

Keep asking your questions.

To Traynor, those few words were an encouragement, spoken by one 'officer' to another, for Watts to persist with his inquiries into Marion Cane's death. His eyes remained fixed on them. If not for the evidence that Jack had been murdered, Traynor might have doubted their relevance. There were no such doubts now. Someone had struck ninety-two-year-old Jack on his head, sending him plummeting into blackness. If Jack suspected there was something amiss about Marion Cane's death at the time it occurred, why hadn't he gone directly to the police? Bernard's recall of the scene in the pub strongly pointed to Beresford going out of his way to approach him. Had this elderly man seen or heard something that meant nothing to him at the time Cane died but which had acquired a significance over time?

He returned to what they had been told about Marion Cane in the months before her death, her restlessness, the anxiety, confusion, self-doubt. Yet days before her death, she had felt sufficiently well to go to the theatre. There was no CCTV evidence of her arrival there, no confirmation from busy theatre staff on duty that evening that anyone resembling Marion Cane had occupied the aisle seat which was purchased in cash a month earlier, as was the seat next to it. No member of staff recalled taking that payment, nor anyone sitting beside her during the evening's performance. Traynor knew the theatre, the gold-filigreed library close by, the thronged road running past, the soaring office blocks, the art gallery, municipal buildings. A busy, often hectic scene, particularly in the evening, Marion Cane's presence unnoticed, then gone.

He turned to Cane's medical notes. They contained no reference to Cane experiencing eye problems, but Chloe had highlighted Devereaux prescribing medication for anxiety. They still did not know how she obtained the Valium found in her tissue samples and those he had discovered beneath her mattress. Was her possession of them an indication that she was in contact with risky individuals? He selected a photograph on his phone, one taken by Chloe. It depicted his own arms supporting the heavy mattress in Cane's bedroom, Valium tablets clearly visible in a neat line on its base. He shook his head. It had made no sense when he first saw them. It still didn't. If Cane had accessed them illegally, this was in the privacy of her own home. Why did she feel the need to conceal them? Was it possible that she wished to avoid taking them, yet wanted them easily accessible at times of significant need?

Having read through the medical records and, like Chloe, finding little of interest in them, he stretched his arms to release tension, felt the dog twitch at his feet. He reached down, absently stroked the soft fur between its ears. He was convinced that Janine Franklin's emphatic view of her sister's sexual behaviour was a bid to excuse her husband's sexual infidelity with Cane, mitigation of his complicity. Chloe Judd might be right that judgement of female behaviour could be operating here. But if Marion Cane *was* sexually needy, might that, alongside her Valium use, have increased her vulnerability as a woman? The familiar dull ache deep inside his chest was back. He reached for his phone, tapped on a number. Watts' voice sounded half-asleep in his ear.

'Will? What's up? It's after midnight.'

Traynor closed his eyes. 'Bernard, I'm sorry. I didn't realize how late—'

'Something on your mind?'

'Yes. You need to rethink your investigative direction.'

'Hang on—'

'Search records for other deaths in Newton.'

'Will, listen to me. You need to slow down—'

'You heard what I just said. Follow it up!'

He bowed his head, aware of Jess's warm hands on his

shoulders, breathed in the scent of her. He spoke, his voice unsteady. 'Bernard, you need my help. You need to do as I suggest—'

Jess took the phone from him, spoke a few words into it and ended the call. 'You can't go on like this, Will. You need to give yourself time to process the news you've had.' She watched him stand, saw the tremor in his hands as he tried to bring a semblance of order to the information covering his desk. 'If you don't, you're going to be ill again.'

'What I *need* right now is justice for *somebody*.'

She reached for him, made him turn to face her. 'You think that by doing that for Bernard's case you can stop feeling guilty about what happened to Claire?' She felt him tense. 'It *wasn't* your fault, Will. You're such a clever man.' She whispered, 'Why would you even think that? You need *time*. Time to accept what happened to her—'

'*Never*. Whoever . . . hurt her . . . is out there somewhere, living his life!'

Seeing his upset, how close to the surface his emotions were, she knew she had to say it. 'Do you remember when we first met, Will? I do. This is exactly how you were dealing with Claire's disappearance, searching for her, wanting to find her, hoping she was still alive, wearing yourself to a shadow, despite all the indications inside your house that something terrible had happened to her. Yes, you *were*, Will.' She gazed at him. 'You were constantly searching for her and for the man who took her. You know it's true. John Heritage led that investigation. *He* knows it. It didn't work then. It won't work now. All it will do is leave you exhausted and *broken* and I can't stand by and watch that happen.'

He turned away from her. 'This isn't about Claire. It's about Marion Cane and I've got work to do—'

'This *is* about Claire! Driving yourself so hard on this case won't change what happened to her! She'll still be *gone*, Will!' Getting no response, she walked away from him. 'You know I love you but I can't do this anymore. Claire is gone and I'm *here*, yet I'm starting to feel . . . invisible. I'm going to bed.'

Traynor was lying on the sofa in his study, his mind closed against the scene with Jess and her distress. She was right about his inability to respond to her in the way she needed. He understood. His loss wasn't hers. He glanced at his phone: 4.36 a.m. Hearing a rhythmic thump, he reached out and stroked the dog. 'Shh, Boy.'

Throwing back the duvet, he went in boxers and T-shirt to his desk. He should ring his daughter. Check how she was after the news he had given her about her mother. His head felt like a water-filled balloon about to explode. In the last day or so, he had overheard a whisper at headquarters that Heritage was planning to put additional pressure on the investigation in a make-or-break bid to get a resolution in the Beresford case. Heritage himself was under pressure. If what Traynor had heard was reliable, Bernard's investigation was now in trouble. Traynor was convinced that Cane's death was also a homicide. Eric Brook pushed his way into Traynor's thoughts – young, disturbed and in Newton Heights at the time Beresford died. If Brook was psychotic, he would not have needed a motive for murder that made sense to anyone but himself. He needed locating. Bernard had not fully given up on Jessop as a potential suspect and was planning to involve officers from the fraud team to explore Cane's finances at the time she died. He also regarded Ryan Bartlett as a contender in her death.

Traynor's thoughts returned to Jack Beresford. A once-wealthy man, he had gifted his money to his family during his life and was content to live simply. He paced the room, picturing Jack's quiet life, walking his dog, visiting his local pub where he sat quietly by himself, an elderly man who did not encourage social contact, who lived out his days in chosen isolation.

Keep asking your questions.

Solitary and unobtrusive as he was, Jack believed those words had to be said and had chosen to say them to Bernard Watts, a serving police officer. Jack wasn't killed for what he had. He was destroyed because of something he either suspected or knew.

Traynor reached for the clothes he had brought down the previous night while Jess was sleeping, dressed and left the house.

TWENTY-SEVEN

Monday, 25 November. 7.15 a.m.

Judd peered through mist at *For Sale* signs outside a couple of
distant homes, her eyes moving over extensive gardens, double
garages, a couple of triples way over there, several high-end
vehicles on the move to Birmingham's city centre, London, or
who-knows-where.

*It's unreal, this place. Give me bog-standard suburbia with its
parking problems, my little terraced place and Sassy waiting for
me—* Another thought arrived, this one weighted with negative
vibes. *I wish I was there right now, checking every five minutes
that my whole life isn't about to implode.* She closed her eyes.
Just buy a damned test!

'Judd, if you're thinking this is how today's shaping up, me
talking and you standing about, looking gormless, *think* again.'

'Sorry, Sarge – Sir.'

'We're on borrowed time with this investigation.'

She stared up at him. 'Who said?'

'Heritage, who else? Get yourself in gear. I want another talk
with Janine Franklin, if she's up to it. See if she can identify
somebody, anybody we don't already know about who was a
friend of Cane's.'

'I don't think Cane "did" friends in the last six months she
lived here, but there is somebody who knew Cane when she first
came here, who talked to her. She might have something to tell
us.' She pointed to the small row of shops some distance away.
'Gymkhana, the estate agent.'

'We'll have a quick word, although my experience of estate
agents is that their primary interest is the selling, never the people
involved.'

She sped after him. 'Wait! It's too early.'

'I find "early" a good time to shake people up.'

They walked the short distance to the double-fronted premises,
Judd's attention on a window directly above it, a woman pulling

back curtains, a shadowy figure standing close behind her. 'Sarge. Did you see him?'

'I did.'

Reaching the door, Watts gave the glass several sharp taps. Judd's eyes were fixed on the dim interior. She had a score here that needed settling. A light went on and a woman appeared from the back of the premises pulling a pink bathrobe tight, her long blonde hair loose, face irritated. Gymkhana. Reaching, then bending to disengage bolts, she opened the door a fraction, ignoring Judd.

'We're not open yet! It's only—'

'You are, for us.'

Seeing Watts' ID, she opened the door wider. 'You could at least let me get dressed!'

The sound of something heavy making contact with the floor above took their eyes ceilingward. Watts got breezy. 'This'll take no time if we crack on.'

Judd watched a mix of disdain and arrogance arrive on Gymkhana's face, guessing that Sarge's lilting Birmingham accent had told her all she needed to know about him: not too bright and easy to get rid of. Judd smiled to herself. *Big mistake.*

Watts asked, 'What can you tell us about Marion Cane, her life here and her death, Ms Cargill?'

'Why on earth are you asking *me*? I know nothing about the woman.'

He took a few paces past her, gazing around the premises. 'You might want to reconsider that. When Marion Cane first arrived here, you sold her a very pricey house.' He turned to her. 'Your commission alone would have made it memorable.'

Now seated at her desk, Cargill tossed her head. 'Newton is *full* of expensive properties. I don't recall—'

Arriving at her desk, he placed his big hands on it and looked down at her. 'You met Marion Cane more than once to clinch that big a sale. You showed her around that house. You chatted to her. You would have wanted to know about her, what she hoped for or wanted, so that *you* could convince her that *that* house had her name on it.'

'That's my job and she didn't need any convincing—'

'Did your boss meet her?'

He watched her grow still. 'No, he didn't. He leaves everything to me—'

'Exactly my thinking of the set-up here. Now you can tell us everything about that first day you met Marion Cane.'

Judd had watched Cargill throughout this exchange and knew that she was seething. And defensive.

'There's nothing to tell! She came inside. Said she was interested in buying the house and that's exactly what she—'

'Was one of your "For Sale" boards outside it?'

'No.'

'So how did she know it was available?'

'I'm a property agent, not a mind-reader!'

Watts slow-nodded. 'What I want from you is a full account of how things went the first time Marion Cane arrived at these premises. You don't know her. She comes in, a total stranger by all accounts. She expresses an interest in buying a house worth a cool two million-plus, and *you* decide, there and then, that she's no time-waster. How did that happen?'

Cargill looked away from him. 'You're probably unaware of it, but there's a psychology to selling. It was the way she looked. Her presentation, her clothes, everything about her confirmed her as a potential purchaser.'

'When was your next contact with her?'

'The following day I showed her around the property.'

'Keen, was she?'

'Very. That house is totally vulgar, both inside and out, but she loved it.'

Watts waited, seeing hesitation, guessing at an internal struggle between remaining only minimally helpful and volunteering additional information. 'I'd seen her before. She was staying with some relative here. She wasn't the type one could easily ignore.'

'How's that?'

'The clothes, the hair. Everything about her! It all demanded that you look at her.' The corners of her mouth moved downwards. 'Frankly, given her age, I thought her tasteless and overdone.'

With a glance at Watts, Judd asked, 'What gave you that impression?'

Cargill didn't look at her. 'It wasn't an "impression". She had a certain style which was vastly overstated. Much like the house she was wanting to buy.'

'You showed it to her,' prompted Watts.

Cargill sighed, now exhibiting signs of boredom. 'It's what I *do*. After barely half an hour inside, she wanted it.'

'How did she come across as a person?'

She gave Watts a steady look. 'She was just another wealthy client. She would have paid anything to get that place.'

'Why was she so keen?'

Cargill shrugged. 'She said it was exactly what she was looking for, went on and on about people she knew in London she was going to invite there once she moved in.'

'Any names?'

She tossed pale blonde hair away from her face. 'I wasn't paying attention. All I heard was that she wanted to show it off. My job was to close the sale.'

'Did you get the impression she had a partner?'

'No.'

'Ever hear anything on those lines after she moved into the house?'

He watched a second internal struggle start up. 'Just some talk after she died about her and her brother-in-law.'

'You'll have heard what's happened to him.' Getting no response, he glanced at Judd. 'Nasty business that.'

'Very nasty, Sarge.'

Cargill remained mute, tracking Watts now on the move, tapping his pen against his notebook.

'Was anybody else after the house?'

'I don't recall. It was a hectic selling time. I can't remember every detail of every property I show—'

'My only interest is in *that* house. Any other potential buyers?'

Cargill gave him a bored glance. 'For the Beresford house, no.'

He did a slow turn, brows raised. 'How do you know it was the *Beresford* house?'

'It's what older residents here call it,' she snapped. 'Jack Beresford owned the land. One of his sons built the house.'

Watts came closer, his eyes fixed on hers. 'What do you know about Jack and his son?'

'His family are builders. He started the company years ago. End of story.'

'The customers you get in here—'

'Prospective *clients*.'

'Have any of them talked about what happened to Jack?'

'Why on *earth* would they? A lot of them are new to the area.'

'And the others? Those who aren't?'

She shrugged. 'There was some talk when he first disappeared about why, how a man of his age could go missing. He didn't even own a *car.*'

Hearing the disparagement, Judd's eyes fixed on her. If there was any chance of Sarge requesting this woman come to headquarters for interview, she wanted to be part of it, on her own turf, with Gymkhana well rattled.

'That family is well-off – I mean, totally loaded – yet he lived in some *ghastly* old shack on the road that runs past the Heights, which was ridiculous. Completely la-la, if you want my opinion.' She stood, went to the door, pulled it open. 'That's it. That's all I know.'

They left the premises, the door closing abruptly on them. They walked away from it, Judd's voice a low hiss. 'She's not going to help, unless we get her in for a talk at headquarters.'

'No grounds and no point, far as I can see. Her interest in people starts and ends with how much money they've got.'

'You saw who was hanging about upstairs?'

Watts was reflecting on what was probably the cosiest of bedfellows for an estate agent. A solicitor. 'Oh, yes.'

The officer on duty watched Traynor coming into headquarters. She had heard he was on compassionate leave. He looked tired. Adjusting the neckline of her uniform shirt, she leaned on the reception desk, appraising him as he came closer. She would have no problem showing him some compassion, plus a couple of other things, given half a chance. She arranged her face to warm-sympathetic. He walked past without a glance.

Inside Bernard's office, he went to the computer, entered the passcode, added search words followed by a quick key strike. He got a single response to his query: one death in Newton Heights in the last twelve months, that of Marion Cane. Jack Beresford's death had yet to be entered. He bowed his head. Was he on the wrong track? Straightening, he changed the search parameter from one to three years. A single response. A name unknown to the investigation to date. Pearson Fleming, sixty-seven-year-old male. Resident of Newton Heights. He read through details of the subsequent police involvement, printed all of it.

Getting out his phone, he made a brief phone call.

TWENTY-EIGHT

9.15 a.m.

Traynor drove past the turn for Newton Heights and continued for three-and-a-half miles, slowed down and took a left. He came to a residential area so small that within five minutes he had located the house he was looking for. He guided the Aston Martin between gates, on to an extensive open area and stopped, looked up at the rambling house. The front door opened and a woman appeared, her hand raised. Leaving his car, he approached her.

'Mrs Fleming?'

She smiled up at him. 'Come in, Doctor Traynor. I routinely warn visitors, particularly the tall ones, to watch their heads as they come inside. Some of our doorways are rather low, as you'll see. Follow me.' She led Traynor through the warm house to a sitting room where a man was already on his feet. On seeing Traynor, he approached, hand outstretched. 'Doctor Traynor, Conrad Fleming. You've met my wife, Angela. Would you like tea or coffee?'

'Thank you, no. I'd like to go straight to the reason for my visit.'

Conrad and his wife exchanged glances. He said, 'When you phoned to say that you were involved with a police investigation relating to Newton Heights and that you needed to talk to us about my brother, Pearson, we were very surprised and confused as to why a criminologist would be taking an interest. Pearson's death was the result of a tragic accident.'

'I apologize for any confusion or distress I may have caused you and your wife, but I need you to tell me what happened to your brother.'

Angela Fleming placed her hand on her husband's arm. 'A

little less than three years ago, Pearson was knocked down by a car which didn't stop.'

'I'm very sorry to hear that. Are you able to give me any details?'

Conrad nodded. 'We were living here, which isn't far from Newton, and we maintained regular contact with Pearson, mostly by phone. He was retired but still busy and not too keen on relatives just dropping by. By early January of that year, we were getting no response to our calls. We weren't unduly worried, but around the third day of failing to make contact with him, we drove over to his house. There was no response to our knocks and so forth and we had no key, so I rang the police in Longbridge, which is the nearest station to Newton Heights, and asked that they send somebody out. They said they would, but not until later that day, so we came back here. They eventually rang to confirm that he hadn't responded to them and that he hadn't been seen by neighbours. He was missing for two more days before police informed us that he had been found.'

'What did they tell you?'

'That he'd been involved in an accident on the Rednal Road. It's a narrow, curving stretch – you probably drove along it to get here. It's not well lit and there's no pavement for most of it. From what we pieced together it seems the police initially missed marks on the surface of the road. Once they did see them, they searched and found Pearson lying in a small hollow on open land to one side of the road.' This was similar to the information Traynor had obtained from his computer search. 'You identified him, Mr Fleming?'

'Yes, at the hospital where his post-mortem was done. Pearson had no identification on him. It confirmed that he'd been knocked down. The police concluded that a vehicle travelling at speed had misjudged the bend in the road and had struck him.'

'There were no witnesses?'

'No, none. It's just a country road, no houses and poorly lit. We were told that few people walk along it because of the potential risk.'

Traynor was thinking of Jack Beresford. 'Do you have any idea why your brother chose to do that?' He waited, saw them exchange glances.

'You need to tell him, Con,' said his wife.

He took a deep breath. 'My brother wasn't a well man, Doctor Traynor. He had some problems, but he didn't deserve to die like that.'

'I'm sure he didn't,' said Traynor quietly. 'Did your brother have a family of his own?'

'No. Pearson lived alone. I think he preferred it that way.'

'What was your view of the cause of your brother's death?'

'I was angry about it. I wanted the driver found and punished. When I realized that wasn't going to happen, I had to let it go.'

Traynor waited out the silence.

'It never made sense to me that Pearson would be walking there, or anywhere else, given his health, but obviously that's what happened.' He looked away.

'Are you able to give any details about your brother's health, the problems you mentioned just now?'

There was a brief pause. His wife responded. 'Pearson had been struggling with health issues for a while, but we didn't realize the . . . seriousness of his situation until police showed us photographs of the inside of his house. We were very shocked. He occasionally came here. Con would pick him up. The last time we actually went to his house, everything looked fine. It made no sense.'

'When was that?'

'I'd say it was about eight months before his death. Possibly a little more. As Con said, Pearson didn't encourage visitors. We did try.'

Her husband reached over, clasped her hand. 'My brother was a well-respected Cambridge academic. He'd retired from lecturing two years previously.' He paused. 'He seemed fine. He maintained contact with his university colleagues, but after his death we learned that he had let that slide. His college asked him on a couple of occasions to do some independent work for them, but – and we only found this out later – he refused. It's a common enough story, I suppose. All of Pearson's social contacts were part of the university. I suspect that after being retired for some time, he became increasingly insular. He refused all our invitations to come here. Shortly after the accident, a couple of police officers met us at his house.' He looked up at Traynor. 'We couldn't believe what we were seeing. Pearson had clearly been drinking excessively. I still have difficulty understanding what

we saw there. Wine bottles and glasses, everywhere just ...
chaotic. That's when we fully understood his reluctance to have
us visit.' He looked up at Traynor. 'All I can say is that the way
my brother was living prior to his accident was pitiful.'

Traynor was inside his car, rereading the post-mortem results
relating to Pearson Fleming. There was no reference to any
indication of problematic drinking.

11.23 a.m.

Traynor came into the office to find Watts on the phone.

Judd looked up, smiled. 'Hey, Will,' she whispered. 'He's in
a mood, trying to track down Jessop, the sol—'

The phone thumped the desk. '*Bloody* solicitors! Jones says
he's nowhere in the Heights, but I've told him to keep at it.'
Looking at Traynor, seeing dust on the sleeves of the usually
immaculate criminologist, Watts eyed the box he was placing on
the table. 'What's this?'

'Information from the basement about another death in Newton
Heights.'

Watts gave him a direct look. 'Just so you know, Will, I've got
enough on right now. I'm now working twelve-hour days, the
lads are knackered and Judd here should be at home by the look
of—'

'Leave it!'

'You need to add Pearson Fleming to the investigation,' said
Traynor.

Watts eyed him as he removed files from the box. 'Who's he?'

'A resident of Newton Heights until he disappeared about two
and a half years ago. This morning I spoke to his brother and
sister-in-law. They live in Hampton, a short drive from Newton.'
He opened one of the files, quickly turning pages. 'This confirms
the information I got from them. Days after Pearson Fleming
disappeared from his home, Longbridge police recovered his
body from land to one side of the Rednal Road. Evidence from
the scene indicated he was the victim of a hit-and-run accident,
neither vehicle nor driver identified.'

Glad as he was to see Traynor back in full-on work mode,
Watts wasn't about to be drawn in. 'There's nothing you've said

so far that's telling me this has any relevance to what we're dealing with right now.'

'Rednal Road, Sarge. *Walking*.'

'I heard. It's what people *do*. It's not enough.'

Traynor was now removing black-and-white photographs from a SOCO envelope. He placed them on the table, spread them out. 'These might change your mind,' he said quietly. 'Officers from Longbridge initially responded to Fleming's death as the disappearance of a vulnerable individual. You'll see why from these photographs. They were taken at his house approximately three days after he went missing. His brother, Conrad, told me that he was shocked when he viewed the house.'

They looked down at the photographs, their eyes moving over details of domestic chaos. Judd reached for one of a large sitting room, books and newspapers strewn about, used plates on the floor, wine bottles, one upright, the other lying on its side, what looked like a darkened area of carpet beneath it.

'It looks like this Fleming guy was losing it, big time.'

'All I'm seeing is a contributory factor to his accident,' said Watts.

Traynor looked down at the photographs. 'I've read all the police reports, the statements from his brother and sister-in-law. There's a reference to a man who was working in the area of Pearson Fleming's house, fairly close to the day of the accident. His brief statement indicates limited contact with Fleming, but what interests me is that he describes Fleming as "pleasant, somewhat confused and experiencing memory lapses".'

'That would be the drink.'

'No. Fleming's post-mortem makes no reference to alcohol.'

Traynor located the post-mortem report and handed it to Watts, who quickly read it, then reread it. 'This makes no sense. According to his hospital post-mortem, Pearson Fleming's remains showed zero indication of abuse of alcohol.'

'Exactly.'

'Why wasn't that anomaly picked up at the time?'

'My guess is that police focus was entirely on the accident as the cause of death.'

Watts frowned. 'What about this bloke who was working in the area where Fleming was living?'

'He's a Highways Department worker. He was repairing

paving close to Fleming's house at around the time he disappeared . . .'

Traynor's attention was now fixed on another photograph of the sitting-room floor inside Fleming's home, this one from a different angle, most of the detail obscured by lens flare. An unusual occurrence for a highly skilled SOCO photographer, one that would have been checked in situ and judged useless. Traynor searched the box, located a second photograph taken from the same position, this one minus flare. The various items on the floor of the dead man's house were all now clearly visible, light glinting off a specific area. He handed it to Watts, pointing at a specific detail. Watts looked at it, passed it to Judd.

'Is that what I think it is?'

'Glass.' Traynor nodded. 'Mirror glass, according to what I've read.'

Watts was studying the photograph again. He looked at Traynor. 'What else did you get from the family about this Fleming?'

Traynor chose his words. 'They were candid about what they saw of Fleming's domestic situation at the time he died, made no reference to his sexuality, but my impression from what they didn't say was that Pearson Fleming was possibly gay. If so, a man of his age and socially isolated might have been extremely vulnerable during those last months of his life.'

Judd stared at him. 'You're saying he was lonely, had kind of lost his way.' She looked to Watts. 'I'm seeing parallels here with Cane.'

Watts pointed at the detail captured inside Fleming's sitting room, then looked at Traynor. 'You're seeing a possible connection between these bits of glass on Fleming's carpet and the mirror recovered from Cane's house.'

'It needs consideration,' said Traynor. 'The inventory of items in Fleming's sitting room specifically confirms those pieces of glass as coming from a mirror.'

Watts went to the box, looked inside, removed two meagre files.

Traynor shook his head. 'What's inside those merely repeats what I've already said. Once he was identified as the victim of a road traffic accident, police interest in the inside of his house ceased.'

Watts paced. 'Get on to Longbridge, Judd. Find out who worked the case. Tell them we want more details.'

She reached for the phone. He transferred his gaze to Traynor. 'OK, Will, let's have it. Tell me what you're thinking.'

'I doubt this is coincidental. As Chloe said, there are similarities in terms of lifestyle and emotional presentation for both Cane and Pearson at the time of their deaths.'

'What else?'

Traynor took a folded sheet of paper from an inside pocket, opened it out on the table. Watts came and looked at it, watched Traynor's index finger move over the detail. 'There are also geographical links. Take a look.' He pointed. 'This is the Rednal Road and Jack Beresford lived *here*.' His finger moved on a short distance. 'According to Longbridge details, Fleming's body was found in *this* area, off that same road.' His finger moved further on. 'And here is the ravine where Jack's body was found.' He looked up at Watts. 'I don't understand the possible relevance of mirrors to the deaths of Marion Cane and Pearson Fleming, but they and these geographical links can't be ignored.'

Judd ended her call. 'Sarge? I've just spoken to one of the Longbridge officers who worked Fleming's death and requested what else they have. She says that everything they had relating to the Pearson case should be in that box.'

Watts frowned. 'She's right. It *should*, but it looks to me like it isn't.'

'That's what I said but, according to her, it's a closed case as far as Longbridge is concerned. I asked about other photos of the house. Apparently, there were a couple of external shots. She's sending them to my phone.'

Watts sat, his big hands clamped to his head. 'They saw "accident" all over Fleming's death because attending officers picked up what looked like problematic drinking. It looks like they *didn't* pick up on the results of his post-mortem, which showed that he wasn't a drinker.' He let his hands drop. 'This workman you mentioned, Will. You've got his details?'

'Yes.' He handed an A4 to Watts, who scanned it. A sharp *ping* had Judd reaching for her phone, her eyes fixing on its screen. She scrolled down to the second photograph, 'Oh, my—!' She held her phone towards them. 'You have to see this, Sarge. An external shot of Pearson Fleming's home at the time he died.'

She held her phone towards him. 'It's where the deacon and the church trainee live.'

Traynor said, 'Conrad Fleming confirmed to me that he inherited his brother's house and that he rents it to the church in Newton Heights. He thought his brother would have approved.'

TWENTY-NINE

2.15 p.m.

Stan Beech, Highways employee, was sitting opposite Watts, arms folded across his broad frontage. He had just confirmed that it was Pearson Fleming he had seen walking along the Rednal Road on the day under discussion. Watts eyed him in silence. 'How come you're so sure it was Fleming you saw?'

'Because, after some local complaints, my team spent two weeks repairing paving in Newton Heights, included some directly outside his house. I did that bit of the work.'

'Describe your contact with Fleming.'

'A nice chap, he was. A bit frail, like, but always up for a quick chat. Academic type. Knew a lot about history.'

'How did your contact with him come about?'

'He would come out and have a look at what I was doing.'

'What else did you get to know about him?'

Beech shrugged, his eyes drifting from Watts' gaze. 'He lived on his own.'

'And?'

'Put it like this: there was no woman in his life, if you get where I'm going.' He shrugged his big shoulders. 'Makes no difference to me. Each to their own, I say.'

'Did you ever see anybody at the house?'

'Only him.'

'Did he mention anybody in passing?'

'Never. He struck me as being on the lonely side.'

Traynor's words rushed through Watts' head. *Loneliness spelt vulnerability.* Marion Cane was lonely. Yet, he doubted Jack Beresford was. He searched for a word for Beresford. Came up with 'self-sufficient'. 'I'm interested in this sighting you say you had of Mr Fleming around the time he was believed to have gone missing.'

Beech's mild gaze was on Watts' face. 'I *did* see him. It was in the afternoon and I was on my way back to our depot in Longbridge. I was coming along the Rednal Road in the direction of Newton, and there he was, on my side of the road, walking in the opposite direction. I was surprised at how he'd changed since I'd seen him a few weeks before. Very thin looking, he was.'

Watts was getting a sinking feeling. 'Right. So, what makes you so certain it was Pearson Fleming?'

Beech looked nonplussed. 'Because it *was* him.'

'You were in your van?'

'Yes.'

'Dark, was it?'

Beech shrugged. 'Getting there.'

'So you're driving, it's getting dark, you pass a figure on foot who doesn't exactly fit your recall of the person you think it is, and you're moving along a road that requires some concentration.'

'That about covers it,' said Beech, unfazed.

Behind his face, Watts was well ahead of himself, a likely response from a Crown Prosecution lawyer inside his head: *DCI Watts, the 'evidence' you've provided for this 'sighting' of Pearson Fleming would be disposed of in seconds if it were presented to court . . .*

'The thing is, Mr Beech, eyewitness identification is *really* easy to criticize, raise doubts about, if you get my drift.'

Beech leaned forward. 'Mr Fleming recognized me, and probably my van.'

'You can't be sure of that—'

'Yes, I can. He raised his hand to me and I gave him a thumbs-up.'

Watts regarded him for several seconds. Beech looked placidly back at him. Clearly a phlegmatic type. Just as well if, as a sole witness, he was ever called to testify to what he had just said and had to face a roughing-up by a defence barrister. If this investigation ever got that far. 'Notice any other vehicles going past at that time?'

'No.'

'Nothing going at speed?'

'Like I said, there was nothing.'

Watts changed tack. 'Were you ever inside Mr Fleming's house?'

It got him a nod. 'He once let me use his house phone to call the office when mine was flat.'

'What did you see?'

'How'd you mean?'

Watts shifted on his chair, suppressing a quick surge of irritation. He enunciated each word. 'You were inside the house. Tell me what you noticed.'

'I was concentrating on my phone call—'

'How about when it finished?' he pressed, eking out fast-evaporating patience.

Beech shook his head. 'He'd disappeared along the hallway by then.'

Watts got a sudden urge to check what he had read in Fleming's file. 'Unsteady on his feet, was he?'

'Not at all.'

'What did *you* do?'

'I didn't want to just leave, so I called out to him. He never answered so I went in the direction he'd gone.'

Watts slow-nodded. 'Right. You're now in the house proper, as it were. I want all the details you remember.'

Beech thought about it. 'I was listening, like, and I could hear his voice coming from somewhere towards the back of the house. He was talking to somebody.'

'You're certain that one of them was Fleming's voice? That it wasn't a television or radio?'

'It was *his* voice. I followed it to a room at the back.'

'A sitting room?' asked Watts, not wanting to lead him but he could almost feel his hair growing.

'Suppose so.'

'OK, Mr Beech. I want to know every single thing you recall seeing in that room.'

Beech shrugged. 'It was a bit of a mess. That surprised me, him being on the posh side, a teacher at Cambridge, but my wife, she wasn't surprised. She says people like that, your middle class, they don't care what other people think—'

Watts held up his hand. 'Hang *on*. This room you're describing – who was there?'

Beech sent him a patient look, slowing his word rate, as if Watts was hard of hearing or thinking. Or both. 'Nobody. Just him.'

'Him, who?' asked Watts, dogged for clarity.

'Fleming.'

'So what about this person you say was with him? Where had he gone?'

Beech leaned forward. '*Nowhere*. It was just Fleming, standing there, facing a mirror on the wall and talking to himself.'

Watts stared. 'What was he saying?'

'He was really going at it, but I didn't catch all of it, except, "I'm finished!" Or "It's finished".'

'That it?'

'No. Then he says something like, "You don't worry me. I won't put up—" *No*, "I won't *stand* for it." He sounded like he was in a right mood, I can tell you.'

'Did he look or sound drunk?'

'Neither.'

Watts waited.

Beech gazed back at him. 'He ranted a bit more, but I couldn't make out what else he said. He was a bit excited, like.'

'How did you feel, seeing and hearing that?'

Beech shrugged. 'I was embarrassed to hear it and see him standing there. I'll tell you something. I never had him down as a drinker. I've worked close to some houses and I've seen one or two people totally—'

'Did you ever see him under the influence while you worked there?'

'Never.'

Watts went with a question to which he already had an answer. 'You didn't tell the police what you've just told me?'

'No. When I heard what had happened to him and that the police were involved, I didn't see the point.'

3.05 p.m.

Traynor walked inside the forensic lab. 'Afternoon, Adam. I just got your text.'

Adam stood, gestured to Traynor to follow.

'I've got some news on the eyedrops from Marion Cane's house. I've analysed their chemical content. Take a look at this.'

Traynor did, at a graph showing chemical analysis details, all of its columns registering little to no result, except for a single, raised spike.

Adam pointed to it. 'That indicates the presence of the chemical tetrahydrozoline.'

Traynor looked up at him. 'The eye drops were tampered with?'

'No, tetrahydrozoline is a common constituent of several over-the-counter eyedrops – entirely harmless if the drops are used according to instructions.'

'What are you saying, Adam?'

'I checked further. If tetrahydrozoline is introduced via the mouth, it causes severe headache, anxiety and confusion. In sufficient quantities, it affects the cardiovascular system, the gastrointestinal system, enters the blood and the central nervous system, causing coma and, in a number of cases, death.'

Traynor frowned down at the graph. 'Why so lethal?'

'It works systemically by slowing the breathing, the heartrate.'

'You're saying that Marion Cane bought eyedrops, *drank* them and—'

'She died.'

Traynor paced, turned to him. 'Why would she even think to do that?'

'I stay with what the science tells me, Will, but I think you might be on to something.'

Judd reached home feeling her last vestige of energy drain. Coming into the kitchen to loud greetings and leg-circling from the cat, she lugged the kettle to the sink, filled it, lugged it back again, switched it on and leaned against the work surface. She had always chosen to ignore the past. *Focus on the future, yay!* That future looked as if it might now be at risk. Giving in to the nonstop series of piercing miaows, she pushed herself away, gave Sassy her dinner, crouched beside her as she ate, stroking the soft fur, a lump forming in her throat. The future had always been her focus. Her default setting. A moving away from bad stuff when she was small to what she had hoped for, wanted and now more or less had. She hadn't planned on anything stopping it. Now it looked as though something might. She had to know.

There was a chemist's shop at the end of her road. It would still be open. She didn't move. A voice railed inside her head.

For God's sake, go and buy a bloody test!

THIRTY

Thursday, 28 November. 6 a.m.

The dog watched, whining as Traynor paced his study. 'Shush, Boy.' The information he had been given by Adam the previous day about the eyedrops Cane had used had thrown Traynor's thinking into the kind of chaos he found hard to tolerate. He turned, crossed the room for a sixth, seventh time, his chest in a vice. He forced himself to sit, got control of his breathing. In a semblance of calm, he reflected on the investigation to date, on the disintegrating lives of Marion Cane and Pearson Fleming and the information he now had from Adam. If he had known about tetrahydrozoline earlier . . .

Closing down that line of thought, he went instead with what he knew from research about those individuals whose weapon of choice is poison. The age range tended to be the mid-thirties to mid-forties. What else? Intelligent. Excellent planning ability. A marked capacity for patience. At ease with deceit. A high degree of cunning. Someone who used manipulation in preference to coercion. Yet this killer also had a capacity for violence, given that Jack Beresford was forced from his home and in all likelihood thrown into the ravine. A speeding vehicle for Pearson Fleming. And tetrahydrozoline for Marion Cane if it was present in the samples Connie Chong had taken from Cane's exhumed remains. There was an element of impatience, a need for a quick solution in the deaths of Beresford and Fleming. Was Marion viewed as easier to manage and control because she was a woman? Had whoever killed her placed flowers at her bedside? A greedy, exploitative individual. Greedy for what? Control? Money? Both? He began reviewing potential persons of interest. Bernard had spoken to Jessop, Cane's solicitor. He had described Jessop as a weak character with easy access to his clients' finances, yet the

signature on documentation he had produced had now been verified as Marion Cane's. *She* had moved her money, its current
location still unknown.

Traynor's focus moved to Ryan Bartlett. He had had access
to Cane's house and, in all likelihood, her bed. Bartlett was more
streetwise than intelligent, but with a capacity to relate to
someone needy, at least in the short term. And then there was
Devereaux, Newton Heights' GP, briefly Marion Cane's doctor.
There was no evidence that he had a similar role with Beresford,
but Traynor had found that the GP had a similar, brief role with
Fleming. His thinking moved to Partington, the vicar, whose
role defined him as a caring professional. A small yet significant
number of convicted poisoners had belonged to the caring professions. It gave them legitimate access to potential victims. In
some cases, their homes. The same could be said of Devereaux.
He was planning to talk to all three as part of the psychological
autopsy. With a staying motion to the dog, he went quietly
upstairs. In a spare room, he brushed his hair, eyed himself in
the mirror. He looked tense. More than that. He had that look
which had become familiar to him in the months and years
following what happened to Claire, was seeing again the configuration of fine facial lines of which he was unaware at times
when his psychological state was robust. Reaching for his jacket,
he pulled it on, turned to the door and stopped.

Jess was standing in the doorway, her robe loose over her
pyjamas. 'Where are you going, Will?'

He reached for his keys. 'I have work to do.'

'I want you to stay here with me.'

'I'm fine—'

'No, you're *not* fine!' Her voice shook. 'How many times have
you said that in the past, *knowing* you were struggling? *That's*
where you are now. Very far from "fine". If you continue like this—'

He walked towards her. 'I'm leaving to do my job.' They stood
facing each other in the doorway, he wanting nothing more than
to bury his face against her. 'I have to go, Jess. I have to do this.'

She stood to one side. He went past, down the stairs and out
of the front door. She stayed where she was, listened to the Aston
Martin's full-throated engine as it moved away and faded into
silence.

*   *   *

Traynor drove into Newton Heights and brought his car to a stop. There were lights on inside the house. Leaving his car, he walked to it, rang the bell. Inside, he could hear a morning radio programme, a woman's voice barely audible, followed by a male voice now approaching the door.

'I'm getting it!'

The door opened. Devereaux stood, his face registering surprise, his eyes darting to his watch. 'You should have rung. Mornings here are—'

'I need to talk to you.'

Devereaux looked to be considering a refusal. Moving aside, his eyes fixed on Traynor as he came into the house. He said, 'Second door on the left.'

Traynor went to it and inside what was evidently a home office, judging by two X-ray viewing boxes on one wall. Devereaux followed, closing the door with an insistent thud. 'I'm due at the practice in approximately ten minutes. What do you want?'

'Confirmation that you were Pearson Fleming's doctor.'

'I was, very briefly. What of it?'

'Were you ever aware that he was reliant on alcohol?'

Devereaux frowned. 'No, I wasn't.'

'Scene photographs taken of the interior of his house at the time he was missing strongly suggest that he was.'

'You're entitled to your opinion, but I have the advantage of being consulted by Mr Fleming on a couple of occasions during that last year of his life. I saw no signs of problematic drinking and he did not indicate such to me.'

'Can you confirm his reasons for consulting you?'

'No, not to you.'

'Do you have any observations on Marion Cane's personality?'

'I barely knew the woman.'

'During the time you had contact with her, can you recall anything specific about her behaviour?'

'She was a vague, confused and needy woman.'

'Did you experience any difficulties in understanding her or the way she interacted with you?'

Devereaux was on his feet. 'I don't know what you're getting at, but I don't like the tone of this conversation and—'

'Marion Cane was poisoned.'

Devereaux stared at him. 'That's *nonsense*.'

'It's a forensic fact, Doctor Devereaux.'

Traynor watched him regroup in a matter of seconds. 'I don't know where this "fact" originated or how, but as her doctor, I'm telling you that she died of natural causes which has been *confirmed* by examination of her exhumed remains.'

'The exhumation results may have been compromised due to Marion Cane's body having been embalmed following her death, but the police pathologist has agreed to conduct further tests on tissue samples—'

'Do you know what this sounds like to *me*? A police investigation determined to identify a death as murder—'

'What do you know about Marion Cane's use of eyedrops?'

Devereaux stared at him. 'I don't know what you're talking about. Now, if you'll excuse me—'

'As her doctor, surely you would want to know all you could about her death? When was the last time you spoke to Marion Cane face-to-face?'

Devereaux's face flushed. 'I'll tell you what I *want* right now! *You* out of my house!'

The door opened and a woman Traynor assumed was Devereaux's wife appeared, looking angry, her words little more than a whisper. 'What on earth is going *on*? The children are asking questions! You do realize that your voice can be heard all over the house?'

Devereaux pointed to Traynor, then to the door. '*He* is just leaving.'

Traynor walked from the room, their voices following him. 'What on *earth* has got into you, Guy? Doctor Traynor is working with the police—'

'Yes, and unfortunately for him, I know my rights. I don't have to answer his questions.'

Traynor turned to him. 'You seem very disturbed by my questions about Marion Cane, Doctor Devereaux. Why is that?'

Devereaux came into the hall, threw open the front door, glaring at Traynor. 'How *dare* you come into my home – *shut* up, Vanessa – inferring that there was something inappropriate about the death of one of my patients, based on what you say is forensic information. I don't know that and, for the record, I am not "disturbed", merely irritated that you've pushed your way in here at an inappropriately early hour—'

Traynor walked from the house, his departure punctuated by

the front door striking its frame. He walked to his car and sat inside. Devereaux had shown zero professional interest in what he had said about poison having caused Marion Cane's death. Like most professionals whose job it is to evaluate those who may have broken the law, Traynor had experienced verbal anger directed at him, had learned that much of it was due to one of two underlying, possibly linked, causes. Fear and guilt.

He was leaving Newton Heights when he received a text from Watts. He pulled over. Ryan Bartlett had been arrested early that morning in connection with Marion Cane's death, the specific grounds unstated. Traynor frowned at the frigid landscape beyond his windscreen. Bartlett had been the next call on his list. He decided to go to another house nearby to see if Eric Brook had returned. He reviewed what he had been told about the trainee's behaviour. Was he wrong in his view that this killer was likely to be in his late thirties, possibly more? Should he have factored in the possibility of mental health difficulties?

Traynor returned to Newton Heights, left his car, walked to the house and rang the bell. Its sound echoed inside. He rang a second time, then returned, frustrated, to the warmth of the car. Bartlett was no longer available and Matthew Redpath, a possible source of information on Brook, was not at home. He thought of Devereaux's outburst earlier. It had arrived without warning. He suspected it may have surprised even Devereaux himself. Fear and guilt. Fear of losing something? Guilt about something he had done? He stared out at cold and mist. Something was worrying the GP, and Traynor had an idea what it might be. He drove to the church, walked through the churchyard to the vicarage, rang the bell. The door was opened by a woman who gave him a startled look. 'Mrs Partington?'

'Yes?'

'My name is William Traynor. I'm part of the police investigation here and I would really appreciate a brief word with your husband, if possible.'

She stepped back and he went inside, followed her to the rear of the house where the vicar was sitting, busily writing. He looked up. 'Doctor Traynor! Come and sit down. Anna, could you bring more coffee—'

'Not for me, thank you, and I apologize for interrupting your work.'

'Not at all.' He indicated a chair.

Traynor remained standing.

'Is there something I can do for you, Doctor Traynor? I have to say that you look like someone who is rather low in spirits.'

His wife said, 'Leonard, I doubt those kinds of observations are helpful.' Her eyes met Traynor's. He saw a shadow deep within them.

'You're right, of course, dear, but is there anything I can do to help, Doctor Traynor?'

'You serve this community. Are you aware of anyone who harboured negative feelings towards Marion Cane sufficient to harm her?'

Partington stared up at him, mute.

'If so, you need to share it with me.'

'Our trainee—'

'*Leonard.*' His wife stared at him. 'You can't make accusations!'

'I'm not accusing anyone, but you know better than anyone the concerns I have for Eric, plus the stress he has caused Matthew. He needs to be found, although I'm convinced that any risk he might pose is to himself alone.'

'I've called at the house. He's not there. If you have an idea where he might be, I'd appreciate you telling me.'

Anna Partington turned to him. 'It's highly inappropriate of you to ask Leonard for such information. He takes his pastoral responsibilities to the trainees *very* seriously, and does so in a sensitive way.' She stopped, an angry flush slowly washing over the pale skin of her neck.

'It's my job to ask questions, Mrs Partington.'

She stared at him, then away. 'I just . . . I don't think it's right to involve Eric in a matter he can't possibly assist with. Neither he nor Matthew really knew Marion Cane.' She went quickly to the door and out. Partington watched her go.

'Sorry about that. Anna takes her role as my supporter very seriously and she does all she can to ensure that I'm not over-burdened.' He looked up at Traynor. 'Getting back to Eric, he's unlikely to go near the church because he knows that Matthew regularly checks that it's secure, and Eric doesn't have a key.'

He stood, and he and Traynor walked to the front door. 'Am I allowed to ask you about the progress of the current investigation?'

'Of course. What I can tell you is that it looks increasingly likely that Marion Cane's death was not due to natural causes.'

'Oh, dear,' whispered Partington. 'That *is* alarming. I'm sorry that I'm unable to assist.' Traynor watched him search for his next words. 'Ms Cane – Marion – never specifically sought me out, you know, although I have to say that my impression of her is that she very much gravitated to men.' He gave a tired smile, looked directly at Traynor. 'I obviously didn't make the grade, perhaps due to my calling, or perhaps a failing on my part to convey sufficient gravitas?'

Traynor left the house, still occupied by the shock that had registered on the vicar's face when he heard about the current view of Cane's death and the extreme concern that had registered on Anna Partington's when he asked about Eric Brook. Reaching the church doors, finding them locked, he continued in the direction of the trainees' house. It too was silent. He rang the bell, heard it reverberate inside. Partington was right to be concerned about this troubled young man, but as yet Traynor lacked sufficient details to guide him to an understanding of Brook's personality and his problematic behaviour following what appeared to be a relatively recent deterioration. He had no idea as to what Brook might be capable of doing. He got into his car and read through Chloe's notes of her conversation with Matthew Redpath, then drove out of Newton Heights and on to the city centre, yet another question occupying him. Why was Anna Partington so fearful?

THIRTY-ONE

9.45 a.m.

Traynor crossed Chamberlain Square, went quickly up the steep steps to the main doors of the huge Victorian building and inside its echoing entrance hall. A uniformed security officer behind a sturdy counter sent him a smile. 'Welcome to the City of Birmingham Art Gallery, sir. Would you like some help?'

Traynor showed his university ID. 'I need to speak to one of your art restorers—'

'Conservation work comes under the museum, which is next door, sir, but I'll give them a quick ring and see if I can get somebody down here.'

Traynor paced, listened to the security officer talk into the phone. Hearing it go down, he went back to him. 'They're sending somebody now. There's a bit of a rush on over there. Some of the paintings due to go on display need a bit of seeing to.' He gave Traynor a proud smile. 'Did you know that this city is home to a major collection of Pre-Raphaelite paintings? We've got 'em all here, you know: Burne-Jones, Millais— Oh, here's Dom. He'll take you where you need to go. This place is a rabbit warren. I still get lost after fifteen years here . . .'

Traynor turned at the approach of a shortish, smiling man coming towards him. 'This way, Doctor Traynor.' As they walked, he said, 'Our staff here, particularly Jim whom you just met, are rightly proud of our art gallery and museum, although I don't think we've ever had an official visit from a criminologist.'

'I'm assisting West Midlands Police with an investigation. I believe a member of your staff might be able to help us. My understanding is that she restores paintings here.'

'We have several. Do you have a name?'

'Yes. Milly Adams.'

He nodded. 'You're in luck. Milly divides her time between our different sites, but she's here today.' He took out his phone. 'Excuse me. I'll check that she is able to speak to you.' Traynor paced. Call ended, he led Traynor along quiet corridors, up marble stairs, through a wide door and into a high-ceilinged room. 'Your visitor, Milly! Doctor William Traynor of West Midlands Police.'

Dom departed and the young woman sitting in a pool of light looked up at Traynor, removing magnifying equipment and rubbing her forehead. She smiled at him. 'Conservation work is impossible without an Opti-visor, but it's always a relief to take it off. Now I'm trying to work out how I might be of assistance to West Midlands Police.'

'I'm not an officer, Ms Adams. I'm a criminologist assisting on a case. You're familiar with a place called Newton Heights?'

He watched surprise register.

'Of course. My boyfriend, Matt, lives there.'

'Is the name Eric Brook familiar?' He watched a subtle change in her face.

'Yes. Matt shares a house with him in Newton. Actually, I don't know Eric that well— Please, have a seat.'

He took the chair opposite her, waited as she carefully replaced the cap on a tube of paint, smiled up at him. 'This is about the death of an elderly man there, and also a woman? Matt mentioned it. I hope you're not expecting me to know much more than that. I used to go over to Newton at weekends, but now Matt comes to me here in Birmingham.'

'You're aware of recent events there?'

'That the police are investigating, yes. Matt has told me a little about it and he's obviously concerned. It's unbelievable in such a lovely place.' A smile replaced her frown. 'You've probably seen the church. Matt and I are getting married there next summer. We're really excited about it, and we're both hoping that whatever is happening there is sorted out as quickly as possible.'

Seeing the young woman's evident happiness, he smiled. 'Congratulations, if it's not too soon.' He paused. 'You've said that you don't know Eric Brook well, but is there anything you're able to tell me about him?' He watched her face change. She reached for tubes of paint, carefully replaced them in specific places inside a large box.

'Actually, Eric is the reason I don't stay in Newton. Initially, he was making occasional visits there, which mostly didn't coincide with mine, so there wasn't a problem. It became one when he began sharing the house with Matt.' Still not looking at Traynor, she turned her attention to a nearby oil painting secured on an easel.

'Ms Adams, I need whatever information you have, although I appreciate it might be difficult for you to give it to me.'

'I'm sorry. I know you have a job to do and, for the entirely selfish reason I've just given you, I do want the police to sort out whatever has happened, but Eric Brook has caused so much disruption and added stress to our lives, particularly Matt's. He's always been so sympathetic to him. Matt has worked hard to support Eric. Leonard – he's the vicar there – isn't very worldly, and I think he made a wrong choice with Eric. You should know that as well as his immaturity, Eric obviously has other problems, but I don't want to make his situation there even more difficult.'

'It might help us if you're able to be more explicit.'

Her face reddened. 'I was staying there regularly with Matt during the weekends. It was really good for us to have that time together. We both have busy lives. But then Eric came to live at the house full-time. It wasn't long before I started feeling very uncomfortable when he was around. There were times when Matt would have to leave the house early on church business. I didn't like him going because Eric was there and . . . there wasn't a lock on the door of our room.'

'Are you saying that you were fearful of him?'

'I don't want to sound melodramatic, and there was nothing I can specifically point to, but, yes, I suppose in a way I was. I think most women sense when something isn't right. That's how I felt about Eric. After a month or so, I told Matt I wasn't going to stay over at the house anymore and I didn't. That was several months ago. Obviously, Matt wasn't happy about it.' She looked up at Traynor. 'We both love our weekends together, so we changed our arrangement. Now he comes to me, but Leonard wasn't happy about Eric being there alone, so Matt had to reduce the time he spends with me to just Saturday evenings.'

Her colour high now, she said, 'It's not the same, Doctor Traynor. All relationships need time and that's what we don't have enough of at the moment.' She looked up at him. 'I'm sorry. You don't know me; you're wanting facts, and I'm getting into really personal, emotional matters you haven't asked for.'

'It's not a problem,' he said quietly. 'I understand what you're saying. It's always good to hear about the positive relationships people have, even if there are difficulties. I don't tend to experience much of that kind of positivity in the work I do.' There was a short silence. 'Are you able to describe the nature of Eric Brook's problems as you saw them?'

'Of course.' She pushed back her hair. 'Where to start? After the first week or so of Eric being at the house full time, he started playing his music really loud, like a teenager, yet he has to be in his early thirties. It was really odd. Matt is a mild kind of person. I don't know if you're aware, but his father is a vicar in Essex, so Matt is very motivated to do well in Newton. He didn't want to cause problems for Eric, so he dealt with the music issue himself, but Matt's still shouldering the responsibility for Eric's behaviour. I probably shouldn't say this, but that suits Leonard. I don't know if you've met him? He's very nice but, as I said, not worldly at all, and I think he's relieved to have Matt there, doing a lot of the work. Sorry. I'm going on, aren't I? The times I did stay over while Eric was there, he hardly seemed to sleep, always moving around the house. When Matt left in the mornings, I felt really . . . well, vulnerable, hearing Eric wandering around, so I made sure I was up and dressed. I would go downstairs and say "Hi" to him, but he tended to leave the room without speaking. There was one time he didn't leave. I made myself some coffee, but I felt so uncomfortable that I went back upstairs to our room. That's when he followed me, so quietly I didn't hear him. As I turned to close the door, he was just *there*, with his hand on the door, *looking* at me.'

'Did he speak to you at all?'

'Yes, but I couldn't make out most of what he was saying – something about wanting me to help him with some demon inside him or after him—' She shook her head. 'I was *so* frightened, and that's when I heard the front door open and I pushed past him and ran downstairs to Matt. He didn't know what the hell was going on and I didn't tell him, but later, when Eric was out – he would do that a lot, just disappear – I told Matt. That was around the time we agreed that he would come to my place.' She shook her head. 'It makes me feel so tired just talking about all of it, and it's still there, the anxiety, because *he's* still there, causing Matt stress. He says it's good experience for when he has a parish of his own. I'm afraid I'm not so accommodating about it.'

Seeing her discomfort, Traynor changed the direction of his questions. 'During the time you stayed over at Newton Heights, did you get to know anyone living there?'

'Not really. By the time I finished work, drove there and had dinner with Matt, it was often late and we'd just chill because he was tired, too, so I didn't get to meet anyone— Oh, wait, I did. Eric had leapt over a wall or something and hurt his foot. The local GP came to the house because Eric was making a real fuss about it. It didn't look that bad to me. Then the vicar's wife arrived to bring some medication – painkillers, I think.' She smiled. '*That* probably rates as a party in the Heights. I'm just hoping that what's happening there at the moment will be sorted quickly. To be honest with you, I really want the situation with Eric sorted, because the vicar has been discussing Matt having a future there. Apparently, the local population is steadily increasing and there's sufficient demand for two—' She stopped. 'Doctor Traynor, it feels like I've talked nonstop since you arrived. It's just that Matt and I are both rather stressed with the situation right now.'

She reached down on her side of the table, then straightened, an envelope in one hand. 'I'm not sure if this is any use to you, but I've got a photograph of Eric Brook.'

She slid the envelope across to Traynor. He opened it, brought out the photograph. She pointed. 'That's him in the background, there.'

Traynor looked down at Brook who appeared unshaven, sullen; at Milly's face pressed close to that of a bearded Matthew, both smiling. Two people in love. Traynor thought of Jess. He should not have left the house the way he had. 'Might I borrow this? I'll keep it safe and return it to you as soon as possible.'

'Of course.' She opened a drawer, brought out a stiff, more robust envelope. 'Put it in this.'

Traynor took it. She saw the slight shaking of his hands as he attempted to slide the photograph inside.

'Here, I'll do it,' she said quietly, taking envelope and photograph from him. 'It's tricky, isn't it?' She slid the photograph inside the envelope and handed it to him. 'Are you OK, Doctor Traynor?'

'I'm fine. Thank you.'

THIRTY-TWO

11.09 a.m.

Traynor was outside the building, pulling cold air into his chest. It was the impact of seeing the photograph, the physical closeness, the happiness, that had triggered a sudden rush of anxiety about Jess. Back inside his car, he took out his phone. 'Bernard, you need every officer you can spare searching for Eric Brook.'

'Purpose, Will?'

'Safety and protection of the public and Brook himself. He doesn't have transport, so I suspect he's still in the Newton area. I'm going there to see if I can find him.'

'Will, I've got officers still in the area. I want you to leave it to them—' He ended the call. He made another. 'Where are you, Jones?'

'Just coming into Newton, Sarge.'

'As soon as you see Will Traynor there, let me know.' He ended the call.

Traynor reached Newton Heights after a forty-five-minute drive in heavy traffic. Leaving the Aston Martin in the pub car park, he had walked just a few yards when he heard someone call his name. Matthew Redpath was some way off, coming towards him. Reaching Traynor, he said, 'I'm looking for Eric Brook. Have you noticed anyone tall and thin, probably wearing red jeans?'

'No.'

Redpath sighed. 'I've been to all of the places he knows, the area around the church and Marion Cane's house. He must know by now that his time as a trainee here is finished, that he can't stay. I'm really fearful of its impact on him and his behaviour.'

'Are you saying you believe he poses a risk to others?'

'From what I've heard, that's your line of work rather than mine. My worry is that if there's a formal search and he realizes that the police are looking for him, he might become *really* disturbed. If that happens, I wouldn't want to predict what his response might be.'

'When did you first suspect that he might have a serious problem?' asked Traynor.

Redpath frowned. 'It's been a gradual realization. Funnily enough, when I talked to you about Eric's fascination with Marion Cane, that's when it hit home for me. Up until then, it was a general unease and even that wasn't consistent. Once I got him to turn his music down, I found him to be mostly OK.' He gazed around. 'I'm wondering if he has a problem with women in general. My girlfriend, Milly, got really tense when she stayed over and he was around. It got to the point where she didn't want me to leave her alone in the house when he was there.'

'Did you report your concerns to the vicar?'

Redpath shook his head. 'I'm afraid I didn't – at least, not the true extent. I should have, but the truth is I felt sorry for Eric. To be honest with you, once the police began their investigation here, I did wonder if it might have anything to do with him.'

'He's been here for a considerable time?'

'Yes, and visiting regularly for quite a while before that, to familiarize himself with the place and the people.'

'This morning I talked to Milly, your girlfriend, about him.' Traynor watched surprise register on Redpath's face. 'She said very much what you've just told me. She's clearly anxious for you.'

Redpath nodded. 'She told you of our plans?'

'Yes.'

'We're really happy about living here, which is why I want this business with Eric over and done with.'

'Where will you live?'

'Right here, where I live now. Leonard has taken the decision not to seek future trainees. There will be no need as I'm staying.'

'You enjoy your work here.'

'Very much. My role is largely pastoral, which has increased my insight into people and relationships. Why they endure. Why they fail. It's a big part of what I want to do here, to counsel and support people who are going through relationship breakups or bereavement. Leonard is happy to avoid that kind of thing. Between you and me, he struggles when people get emotional. I've already started that role in a very limited way. I listen when parishioners voluntarily raise such issues and, where possible, I encourage a change of thinking. I draw on my own experience, you see. Three years after my mother died, my father married again. I was happy for him and, some years on, it's given weight to my personal theory about relationships, that an optimal period for recovery from bereavement or marriage breakdown is around three years. Although they might not realize it, by then most people are actually ready to move on.' Traynor was still processing this when Redpath said, 'I think I read somewhere that your wife died. I'm really sorry. When did it happen?'

Traynor's head and chest tightened. 'Eleven years and ten months ago.'

Redpath shook his head. 'I'm sorry. It's a sad thing to happen to anyone, but what I would say is that you're way beyond the three-year period of adjustment.'

Traynor glanced at his watch. 'It's time I left; let you get on with your day.'

'It was a pleasure. We have a lot in common, Doctor Traynor. We both have work which requires an understanding of people. Getting back to Eric, if the police learn anything of his where-abouts, I trust they'll let me know?'

'They would probably inform the vicar.'

'Yes. Of course.'

Traynor watched him walk away, thinking over his words about loss. *Not the careless optimism of youth for someone in his mid-thirties.*

He returned to his car, drove a short distance and parked again. Leaving it, he took an indirect route to the church, then detoured to a wooded, undulating area of land. He had seen it previously and was now considering the possibility that, emotionally disturbed as Eric Brook appeared to be from what he had heard, it might be viewed by him as a place of peace where he could avoid people. He went slowly down the sloping land, the surrounding trees gradually blocking much of the available light, his training and knowledge of mental health difficulties keeping him alert for the slightest hint that he might not be alone here. If Brook was here, the last thing he wished to do was startle, upset or antagonize him. After walking for a couple of minutes, he suddenly stopped, listened, picking up low rustling noises to his left, which then diverted to his right. It sounded like someone was forcing a way through the heavy undergrowth and tree cover. He scanned the immediate area to the right, seeing foliage move in the absence of any breeze. It suddenly parted. A tall, thin figure appeared in red jeans, arms flailing wildly at branches, his face agitated. Seeing Traynor, he stopped.

The criminologist stood perfectly still, arms relaxed at his sides, hands fully visible, his voice low. 'Hello, Eric.'

'Get *away*! Come any closer and . . . I'll *hurt* you!'

Traynor remained where he was, absorbing the detail of the

young man's clothing, the torn padded jacket, jeans muddied to the knees, and one hand clutching a small knife.

'Who *are* you? Who *sent* you?' He looked around, his eyes wild, a sob in his voice. 'I told you! Leave me *alone. Don't* come closer!'

Looking beyond him, Traynor caught sight of Jones and Reynolds now standing some distance beyond Brook. Aware of the impact this might have on Brook's already stressed state, he kept his voice quiet but firm.

'I've been looking for you, Eric. I'm here to help you. I'm not a police officer.' He got no response beyond an implacable stare. 'If you feel uncomfortable here in Newton, or you believe you might be in danger, I think you should come with me.'

Brook continued to stare at him.

'Can you do that, Eric? For your own safety?'

Brook wavered, then raised his right hand, pointed the knife, light piercing a break in the trees, glinting off it. 'You're trying to *trick* me. Stay away!'

'I mean you no harm, Eric, I promise you.' He watched the young man's eyes moving constantly from side to side.

'How do you know my name? Who *are* you?'

'My name is Will Traynor,' he said, his voice still low.

The knife wavered. 'I've heard that name . . . don't know where . . .' He hung his head. 'I'm tired . . . cold. I'm . . . lost.'

'We can talk about that, Eric, but first you need to put down the knife.'

Brook looked at it as if he had forgotten he had it. He opened his hand. Let it drop.

'Now, come to me.'

Traynor remained where he was as he came down the slope and started walking slowly towards him, his arms folded, pressed against his head. He looked exhausted. He was less than three feet away, crying now.

'I did something really bad. At a house. Got inside. Stole some bread.'

'Did you hurt anyone, Eric?'

'No.'

Eric came slowly to him. Letting his arms drop, he looked directly into Traynor's face, then rested his head against his shoulder.

'It's OK, Eric,' whispered Traynor, as Jones and Reynolds slowly approached. 'You're safe now.'

Watts listened as Jones and Reynolds described the scene they had witnessed earlier. 'You should have been there, Sarge. It was un-bloody-believable! There's this young guy with a knife, acting out and threatening, and there's Will just standing there, talking to him, calm as you like. I tell you, that takes some balls. More than I've got.'

'It takes training, but I get where you're coming from. You started telling me about the theatre on Broad Street.'

'We went there to check for any CCTV they might have of Marion Cane. There was nothing, but we've found the cab driver who picked her up from there and drove her home. One of the other cabbies there tipped us off.'

'Where's the driver?'

'He's here and he's not very happy.'

'That makes two of us, but I'm hoping my mood's about to improve. Where's Judd?'

'Don't know, Sarge.'

He stood. 'Both of you, with me.'

They followed him one floor up to one of the interview rooms. Inside, Watts activated camera equipment. The man in the next room came into view. 'What's his name?'

'Dave Seeley.'

'Has he got form?' He took the sheet Jones was offering and read it. 'Cautioned for drink driving, three years back. One conviction for purse theft a year after, nine months, suspended.'

The door swung open and Judd came in. They studied Seeley onscreen, coat off, mouth set, sending disparaging looks to the young officer standing next to the door, another to the machine-made coffee in its plastic cup on the table in front of him.

'Ready, Judd? You two, stay there and observe.'

Reaching the interview room door, index finger to his lips, Watts stood, then gave the door a sudden, brisk push, his voice loud. 'Mr Seeley!'

'*Shit!*'

Seeley was half standing, clutching a dripping cup, the table in front of him awash. Watts signalled to the officer by the door, who went to a dispenser, tugged squares of paper and dropped them in front of Seeley, who started dabbing. 'I've got coffee all over my bloody trousers! I've been waiting here for half an hour and I want to know why I'm here at all!'

'We're about to get into that, Mr Seeley. I'm Detective Chief Inspector Bernard Watts. This is Constable Chloe Judd. Your memory for an event six months back might see you out of here in under an hour.'

'What "event"?' snapped Seeley, still irate. 'I'm starting to think I should have somebody here before I say a word—'

'Got a phone number, have you? Feel free to ring it while you think about your loss of earnings as you wait for somebody who can be bothered to turn up in the next couple of hours. Your choice.'

Seeley's eyes narrowed on cameras in two corners of the room. 'Is all this being recorded?'

'Only if it turns formal. Let's see how we get on.'

Uncertain, Seeley's eyes moved quickly between him and Judd. 'What would I have to tell the police? I'm a cabbie, not some lowlife on the rob.'

'Don't sell yourself short, Mr Seeley.'

Leaving Seeley to pick through the few words for a slur, Watts turned to the officer at the door. 'Nip down and get Mr Seeley some more coffee in a proper cup.' Then back to Seeley. 'Milk? Sugar? What's your preference?'

'Getting back to bloody work! What's this about?'

'Forget the coffee.' Watts studied him. 'Marion Cane.'

'Never heard of her.'

'Follow the news, do you?'

'Only the football.'

'Back in January this year, you had an altercation with another cab driver outside the Rep Theatre in Broad Street which led to *you* driving Marion Cane to Newton Heights.' Watts saw a ghost of dawning comprehension. He nodded. 'I knew you'd remember her.'

'I *don't.*'

Watts glanced at Judd. 'Strange that, isn't it? Stan Wyatt, the other cab driver, was very clear about the to-and-fro he had with Mr Seeley about Ms Cane.'

Judd nodded, going along with it. 'He was, sir.'

Seeley's lips compressed. 'What's that lying bastard said about me?'

'Mr Wyatt was very helpful. He told us how keen you are on your work. The way he tells it, he was parked outside the theatre that evening, first cab in line, about to accept Marion Cane as a fare to Newton Heights when *you* took advantage of some nearby kerfuffle to get her into your taxi instead.' He glanced at Judd. 'That about the size of it?'

'Bang on, sir.'

'What I'm waiting to hear is why the keenness to get her into your cab?'

'I don't have a clue what you're on about.'

They both sat, their eyes fixed on Seeley. After a twitchy minute or so, he shrugged. 'Look, Wyatt's blown what happened out of proportion—'

'If you're thinking this is about you hijacking a fare, think again. It's the woman herself that's got our interest.'

Seeley's legs were now moving in small, sequential bounces. 'I've just remembered. It was late. My last job that night.'

'You need to tell us about it. All of it.'

Seeley looked at him, then away, closed-faced. 'What's to tell? She got in my cab. I put her address into the GPS, some place beyond Longbridge. Drove her there. She got out, end of.'

Watts' eyes narrowed. 'You're saying that you never spoke to her, and she never spoke to you?'

'Right. I don't encourage conversation from fares, and if she's told you different, she's a liar—'

'She had to speak for you to know where to take her—'

'That's all she said!'

'Following which, you would have spoken to her again when you arrived.' He leaned forward again. 'Mr Seeley, PC Judd here will tell you that I'm not known for my patience. Quite the reverse, in fact.' His eyes fixed on Seeley's. 'Did you drive yourself here?'

'Yeah, so? A couple of your Gestapo told me to follow 'em, which I did.' A short pause. 'To be helpful.'

'Much appreciated. When did you last have an alcoholic drink?'

Seeley's eyes flicked away, then back to Watts. 'Last night, after my shift.'

'Let's get back to Marion Cane. See if you can improve on your recall of her. What she said to you, what you said to her. I want it all.'

Seeley's eyes moved to the wall clock. 'I've just realized what you're on about. There was a bit of a mix-up at the rank and—'

'We're past that. Marion Cane. What do you remember?'

'Nothing, except what I've said!'

'What did she look like?'

'How the hell . . . This is months ago!' Seeing Watts' eyes fixed on him, he sighed, looking put-upon. 'Fifties. Blonde. Well dressed. That's it.'

Judd slid a photograph across the table towards him. He looked at it.

'Does she look familiar?' asked Watts.

'Could be. It looks a bit like her. Apart from giving me her address, she never spoke the whole journey. Not that I cared. I prefer it to people yacking. I took her to Longbridge, then on a couple of miles to this right posh area.'

'Had you been there before?'

'Never.'

'What's the area called?'

'New-something-or-other.'

'Carry on.'

Seeley sighed. 'I drove her to her house.'

'The houses in that area are spread out. Not easy to locate.'

'She told me where it was, pointed it out.'

'So, she talked to you again.'

'If you call that talking.'

'Let's have the rest.'

'There is no "rest"! This is ages back—' Seeing Watts' face change, he said, 'Just give me a minute . . . I parked at the house. Waited for her to get out. She didn't. Just sat there. That's when I really started regretting picking her up. It was like she didn't want to move. Didn't want to leave my cab and go into the house. I had to get out and sort of encourage her. Eventually, she did, and I left her there.'

Watts sighed, rotated his big shoulders. 'Talking to people, getting information out of them when they'd rather not give you anything is very tedious. Isn't that right, Officer Judd?'

'Yes, sir.' They both stared at Seeley.

Watts said, 'If you're planning on going back to work today, don't waste any more of my time. What else?' Seeley was now looking edgy as well as put-upon.

'I need to *think*.' After a brief pause, he said, 'She was a weird one, all right. Like I said, she just sat there, saying nothing. It crossed my mind she might be a psychiatric case, or on some kind of medication, but obviously well-off from her clothes, the house. Eventually, she gets out, and what does she do? She just stands there, in the bloody rain, and now I'm well into wanting rid of her.'

'I guessed you're the sympathetic type.'

'*Listen*, in my game, you meet all sorts. Some you wouldn't want to meet. She wasn't my responsibility. I'd done my part of the bargain by getting her home. If you want my opinion, she shouldn't have been out on her own! Whoever was inside that house waiting for her should have been looking after her.'

They stared at him. 'How did you know there was somebody waiting?' asked Watts. Seeley rolled his eyes. 'I happened to glance up at the house, didn't I? Saw somebody moving behind one of the upstairs blinds. As I started the cab, she was still standing there, facing the house. Last thing I saw was some bloke opening the door to her.'

'Describe him.'

'I dunno! Dark hair. Taller than her. Bit of a beard. It was too far to see any more.'

'Yeah? Where were you?'

Seeley fidgeted. 'I stopped the cab a few yards away. Call of nature. I could still see the house.'

Watts slid an enlargement of a photograph Traynor had sent. 'Is this him?'

Seeley reached for it, leaned back, squinted at it. 'Not sure. Could be.' He looked up as Watts stood. 'Mr Seeley, my colleague PC Judd will take a statement from you about what you've just told us. She'll be expecting detail. A lot of *describing* words!'

'There's hardly anything else to say, and I'm losing money hanging about here!'

Placing his big hands on the table, Watts looked down at him. 'What I'm thinking, Mr Seeley, is that as soon as you laid eyes on Marion Cane that night, you wanted her in your cab because you summed her up as a likely source of a *big*, *fat tip*. Where've you parked?'

Seeley looked up at him. 'I got lucky. Found a place on the road outside here.'

'I'm about to make your day even luckier. When you're finished here, you leave your taxi where it is and hop on a bus.'

Seeley stared up at him. 'You're *joking*.'

'Deadly serious. Either that or I get somebody up here to breathalyse you. What's your choice?'

'Bus.'

'Good. Now, let's see how well you do on that statement.'

An hour later, Watts was in his office, seeing the first smile on Traynor's face in days.

'I watched the interview, Bernard. It was textbook.'

Judd came in, looking upbeat, waving a statement. 'You've still got it, Sarge.'

He took it from her, read it, shook his head. 'It's circumstantial, and I wouldn't call anything Seeley's said a lead.' He pointed to his own face. 'Beards are common enough and they can disappear in ten minutes.'

He eyed her across the table. 'Thanks for assisting with the interview. Now I want you to go home.'

'What? *Why?*'

'Because you've got dark shadows under your eyes and I don't want any argument.'

Following a brief detour to the chemist's shop, Judd let herself into her house. Dropping her bag and coat on the stairs, she fetched a paper cup from the kitchen. Reaching for the small package inside her handbag, she looked down at it lying across her palm, panic rising in her chest, making her heart race. The fact that she had bought it said that she had a problem. She closed her eyes. She couldn't carry on like this, wondering, worrying, feeling exhausted. Package in one hand, cup in the other, she went upstairs to the bathroom, Sassy in pursuit, and did what she had to do. She looked at her reflection in the mirror. Sarge was right. She looked rubbish. Perched on the side of the bath, she waited, watching the display countdown. One minute. Two. Three . . .

She looked down at the result. Had to read it twice before she made sense of it. A gasped laugh of sheer relief burst from her mouth, which changed to a sob.

A couple of hours later, she was lying on the sofa, her head splitting. She had been thinking what her life would have been like if the result had been different. She would now be facing the prospect of twenty-four-hour sole responsibility in a role for which she had no model. Hearing the doorbell, a lump rising in her throat, she fingered away tears, not moving, waiting for whoever it was to go away. It rang again. Forcing herself from the sofa, now aware of a familiar low, dull ache, she went into the hall, checked the caller and opened the door.

'Hey, Chlo. I thought I'd drop in on my way home.' Jones followed her into the sitting room where she lay down on the sofa, the kitten climbing on to her stomach. 'You OK? You look . . . off.'

'Thanks.'

'Have you been crying?'

Getting no response, he put both hands in his jacket pockets and brought out two cans of premixed Bacardi and Coke. '*Ta-da!* What d'you say?'

She looked up at him and laughed. It morphed into more tears. She wiped them away. 'I can't think of a single reason why not.'

Giving her a long look, he left the room, returned with two full glasses, ice cubes clinking. 'Here you go.'

She took one of them, swallowed a mouthful, eyes closed.

He sat opposite. 'I've been watching you these last couple of weeks, Chlo.'

'That sounds reportable.'

'I'm serious. You haven't been yourself. You've looked worried, tired and, just . . . narky.'

'Sarge will tell you that narky is my default setting.'

He eyed her, knowing she had a temper. He pressed on. 'I've been wondering why an early twenties, single woman with a job she loves and works hard at, that pays well, might be looking so worried. The answer I got made me think twice about the Bacardi—'

'Park it right there, Detective.'

Lifting the kitten off her stomach and on to the floor, she gave him a direct look. 'Let's say that a problem I thought I had has proved to be non-existent, I overreacted and I'm now waiting for the Bacardi to kick in and ease some very welcome stomach cramps.'

He nodded. 'Good. That's . . . good.' He paused. 'If it wasn't sorted, what would you have done?'

'There was never anything to sort, and if I'd taken the iron tablets I got from the doctor a couple of months back, I wouldn't have gone through a load of pointless aggravation.' She gave him a direct look. 'I don't want to hear any of what I've just said repeated at headquarters—'

'You won't. We're mates, but, if it had been . . . something else—'

'It never was, Ade, so just leave it, yes?' She raised her glass. He did the same.

THIRTY-THREE

Friday, 29 November. 6 a.m.

About to leave home for headquarters, Watts got an email confirming that Eric Brook had had a quiet night following a check-up by a police medic and was sleeping. A second email arrived in response to a question Watts had raised. Brook's admission to Traynor that he had broken into a dwelling close to Newton Heights and stolen food had been confirmed by Officers Reynolds and Kumar, who had visited the house the previous evening and spoken to a George Landis, the elderly homeowner who had confirmed the break-in. Asked about a visible bump on his head, he had responded, 'Nothing to do with the break-in. Fell over the bloody dog, didn't I?'

An hour later, Watts rang Traynor. 'I've just received confirmation. Brook did break into a property, but the injury that occurred to the homeowner was accidental. All I have to do is decide what happens to Brook now. I prefer your advice on that issue over anybody else's. Where are you?'

'I've just arrived at the university. I'm planning to go through everything I have on the Newton Heights investigation. I'll talk to you later about Brook.'

Having reached his office, Traynor closed the door and leaned against it, his chest pounding. He had just run a gamut of well-meaning colleagues wanting to commiserate with him about his 'situation'. They meant Claire. He couldn't handle it. He would be out of here after one more check through his notes, when he hoped everyone else was occupied with lectures or tutorials.

Taking his notes from his backpack, he placed them on his desk, sat and began a meticulous read-through of all of them. An hour later, he had the detail inside his head. He now knew the type of killer they were looking for. A patient individual, willing to play a long game. Someone capable of violence when it served a specific purpose. A poisoner and a persuasive thief whom he suspected of trying to manipulate Marion Cane into moving her money so that it was accessible to him. All three million pounds of it. Someone with a glib mouth and a superficial charm. Devereaux entered Traynor's thinking because of his defensiveness, his anger. Observations within his home indicated that Devereaux enjoyed a lifestyle which cost. He was also a smooth character with an ability to charm, a characteristic he didn't appear to waste on his own wife. Marion Cane had been his patient. Traynor strongly suspected that Devereaux's defensiveness was due to his knowing Marion Cane intimately and his fear that if his wife knew about it, he could risk losing everything.

Ryan Bartlett also demanded consideration. It was highly likely that the relationship between him and Cane was sexual. Now that he was in custody, his associates could be followed up, including any who had connections to illicit drugs. The vicar's wife had also appeared defensive. She was some years younger than her husband. While he was not old, his general presentation was one of a genial man who lacked energy, who left much of his church duties to Matthew Redpath, the young trainee. Was it possible that the vicar's wife was involved with someone else?

One feature of this case kept emerging with marked regularity. Sex. Traynor reflected on all he had learned about Marion Cane, what those who had known her had said about her, the impressionistic sketch on the wall above her bed, which Bernard had dismissed due to its vagueness. Traynor had seen its subtle colours, its shadings and recognized its intimate meaning. During the investigation, Marion Cane had often been presented as a woman who craved sex. Having revisited all of the available information, he now felt profound sympathy for her. Marion Cane had been terrified during those last few months of her life.

She had known she was in danger and was searching for someone who might protect her. Traynor stared ahead. How was control of Marion achieved? And by whom?

Jess came into the sitting room where Boy was lying in his basket. He looked up at her. She crouched next to him, stroked him, looked at her watch. She would take him to the open land beyond the park, let him run.

'Don't look so sad, Boy. Will's coming home soon.'

The words were reassurance for herself as well as the dog. During the time she and Will had been together, there had been times when his mental health had impacted their relationship, but never like this. He was unreachable. The news he had now, after more than a decade, was the worst, bringing with it grief and anger and, yes, guilt that he wasn't able to stop what happened. That he had made another life for himself. Knowing all of this did nothing to ease her emotional and physical ache for him. She briskly rubbed the soft, black fur between the dog's ears, smiled. 'Want *walk*, Boy? Yes? Boy want walk?'

Hearing her phone, she went quickly to the kitchen, wanting it to be Will, needing to hear his voice. She reached for it. 'Hi.'

'Hello, I'm sorry to bother you, but is Doctor Traynor there, please? This is Officer Jones. I'm part of the current investigation and I need to speak to him very urgently.'

'I'm sorry, he's not here. Have you tried his phone?'

'Yes. He didn't respond. I left a message but he hasn't come back to me.'

'That doesn't sound like Will—'

'I'm sorry to put this on you, but we urgently need some investigative information which Doctor Traynor said he would bring here this morning. I'm wondering if he might have forgotten about it. I'm sure you're busy, but would you mind checking if he's left anything?'

'Of course. It's not like Will to forget something like that.'

She did a quick search of the kitchen. 'I can't see anything, but he left quite early so I've no idea what his plans are for the day. Wait. He mostly keeps work-related information in his study. I'll have a look to see if there's anything there. It'll take only a minute or so.'

Carrying her phone, she went along the hall to the room at

the front of the house, eyes moving over the tidy desk. 'I'm in his study now, but I can't see anything here. Just a minute, I'll look inside the briefcase he sometimes uses.'

'I'm really sorry to trouble you.'

'It's no trouble.'

She lifted the briefcase on to a chair, opened it, looked inside and raised the phone. 'There are some papers here. If you could give me an idea of what I'm looking for?'

'Some printed sheets.'

'There's a buff-coloured envelope here and . . . inside it, some sheets—'

'That's it! I know this is an imposition, but right now we're at a critical point in our investigation – is it possible for you to bring it to us? I'd send somebody to get it, but we're really overstretched here—'

'Yes, of course. Where are you exactly?'

'We're a mile or so past Newton Heights, off the Rednal Road.'

'Will has described the place to me, that it's off the road. I can park and walk, yes?'

Boy's ears shot up. He barked.

'*Shush*, Boy!' And to Jones, 'If somebody could look out for me, I'll be in a cream-and-black Mini. I should be with you in about half an hour.'

'That's really good of you, Mrs Traynor. Somebody will be waiting for you. We're not accepting incoming calls because the investigation is now upgraded to Highly Confidential. Oh, and don't bring the dog. We've got the K9 team here.'

'I'm on my way.'

She drove to the city boundary and on, along increasingly rural roads, the buff envelope on the passenger seat beside her. It wasn't like Will to forget things he said he would do, but he had been under enormous strain these past few days. She took some deep breaths. She was waiting for the right moment to suggest that he go back to therapy. She glanced at the envelope lying beside her. From what Officer Jones had told her, it sounded like there had been a sudden, big development. She hoped so. She wanted an end to the investigation so that Will could get some rest.

Focusing on the increasingly rural road ahead, she drove on, following its curve. Seeing movement some way ahead, she reduced her speed. A figure was standing on the opposite side of the road, both hands raised, arms waving.

She slowed, opening her window as she got closer. Seeing him point to a narrow track between two fields, she nodded, made a right turn into it, and drove slowly along, getting a signal from her rear-view mirror to continue straight on. She did so. He followed. Reaching the end of the track she stopped. He was now at her door, opening it. She reached for the envelope and got out. 'Officer Jones?'

He nodded, his voice low. 'We're very grateful for your help, Mrs Traynor. Our investigative team is a short walk in that direction and Will has just arrived.'

At the mention of his name, the anxiety she had felt during the drive dissipated. She smiled at Jones, held out the envelope. He shook his head. 'It's best you give it to Will, directly. I think he might benefit from seeing you.'

Her anxiety returning, she followed Jones along the narrow path to where the land ahead appeared to be sloping downwards. He turned to her. 'It's not too steep but it can be slippery so I'll lead the way. Take care and stay close to me.'

She did as he said and they continued, trees pressing close on either side, daylight fading, the faint, occasional sounds of traffic now gone. Stepping carefully, she listened for sounds coming from somewhere ahead. They reached the bottom of the slope. She gazed around then at Jones. 'Where is everyone? Where's Will?'

He put his index finger to his lips. 'He's just along here,' he whispered, pointing directly ahead. 'We're brought in some high-tech equipment. Everyone's under silent orders.'

She nodded, walked on, the ground flattening out now and less slippery, Jones following. A breakthrough in the case was what she had been hoping for. She might suggest to Will that they have a few days away, somewhere warm where they could both relax. Somewhere he would be beyond the reach of his work. She would encourage him to switch off his phone. That thought brought a small smile to her face, knowing how unlikely it was. Except for this morning. She walked on, details of Jones' phone call back inside her head. *Officer Jones. Mrs Traynor. Don't bring the—* She slowed. Something wasn't— She flinched at a sudden, sharp sensation on the back of her neck. She touched it, looked down at her hand and the tiny smear of blood on her finger.

'Insect bite,' said Jones. 'Nearly there.'

The ground under her feet was uncertain now, the path itself moving, rippling. *Insect bite . . . in November?* She felt something grip her upper arm. She looked down at his hand, disoriented, trying to recall what she was doing here, struggling to form a name. '*W–i–i–ll.*'

'He's waiting for you,' he whispered, releasing her arm and watching her drop, senseless, to the ground.

THIRTY-FOUR

4.10 p.m.

Jones came into Watts' office, followed by Reynolds with Boy on a lead. They had gone to Traynor's home at his request, following his several failed attempts to contact Jess during the day. Now, seeing Traynor, the dog gave a series of ecstatic barks. He took the dog's lead, knelt down and stroked him, then looked up at Jones.

'You went over the whole house?'

Jones nodded. 'She's not there, Will. Neither is her car.'

'She had no plans to go out, as far as I know, and she prefers to avoid driving when it's dark. Anything inside the house to suggest—?'

Jones shook his head. 'Everything in place and normal as far as we could see, right, Tobes?'

Reynolds nodded. 'All neat, except for a briefcase and a few loose papers in the kitchen.'

Traynor stared up at him, looked at Watts, then shook his head. 'I didn't leave anything in the kitchen. Everything relating to my work is kept in my study, so there's no chance of it being seen by Jess or my daughter.' He got out his phone. 'I'll ring again.' He stood, paced, shook his head. 'That was my eighth call.' And to Watts, 'I want Adam on this.'

Traynor came into the forensic office, Watts following. Seeing their faces, Adam got to his feet. Traynor said. 'I can't reach Jess on her phone. I need you to track it, *now.*'

'No problem, Will. It's a smartphone?'

'Yes.

'Give me the number.'

Traynor gave it, then paced as Adam tapped computer keys. They waited. It felt like an eternity. 'It's switched on and I've got its GPS pinpoint.' They came to him, looked to where he was pointing to map details and a tiny flag.

'Give me a second to zoom in.' Traynor waited, forcing himself to breathe, his eyes fixed on the screen's details. Adam pointed again. 'Yep. That's where it is.' He zoomed further in, the on-screen information no longer a tight complex of indecipherable features, his finger tracing an indistinct line snaking its way across the screen. He looked up at Traynor, with a glance at Watts. 'It's somewhere in the ravine where Jack Beresford was found.'

Seeing Traynor's face drain, Watts touched his arm. 'That site's been closed this last day or so. Any reason you can think of why Jess's phone would be there?' Beyond words, Traynor stared at the screen and shook his head.

They were inside Heritage's office, Heritage waiting on the phone, Traynor moving back and forth.

'Sit down, Will.'

Traynor held out his hand to Watts. 'I want my car keys, *now.*'

Watts shook his head. 'You're in no state to drive—' He braced himself on a split-second's anticipation that Traynor might try to take them from him, then watched him sink on to a chair. Heritage put down the phone.

'Officers arrived at the scene several minutes ago and they're anticipating specialist search equipment arriving very soon.'

Traynor was on his feet again, heading for the door, Watts following. Nothing was said between them from the time Watts drove out of headquarters. They passed the Newton Heights turnoff. Watts drove on, made a right on to the narrow track between two fields, followed it to its end and came to a stop. He switched off the ignition.

'I know it's asking a lot, but I need you to hold it together—'

Traynor was out of the vehicle, Watts following him in the direction of the ravine. They reached the downward approach, picking up sounds some way ahead. Watts grasped Traynor's arm. It felt hard, unyielding. Watts avoided a direct look at him. '*Easy*, yeah?'

They went down into the ravine. It was full of officers, several searching a small area encircled by blue-white tape, another four removing thermal imaging equipment from its packaging. Watts risked a glance at Traynor. His face was parchment, his eyes heavily shadowed. He looked as though he might fall any minute—

'*Here!*'

All eyes went to Jones, on his knees, his arm raised. Traynor's response was immediate. Watts went after him. Reaching Jones, they looked down to where he was pointing. Traynor gave an almost imperceptible nod. 'Jess's phone,' he whispered.

A second shout went up. 'Everybody! Move over to *here*, *now*!'

They did, as four SOCOs, each with a hand-held imaging device, moved forward, then separated to specific areas of the ravine. Watts tracked their steady progress, one following the old railway track. After a couple of minutes, he glanced at Traynor, his eyes fixed on the search, his hands at his mouth. Minutes ticked by. So focused were they that a sudden shout and arm-waving from the SOCO at the track startled both of them.

'I've got a very faint reading!' He pointed ahead. 'It's coming from *that*.'

Watts looked at a small, rectangular structure he barely recalled from previous visits here. He and Traynor moved quickly to the SOCO. They looked down at the device's screen, at the mix of colours from yellow to orange signifying heat, plus purple and black for cold areas. Watts was seeing a predominance of purple. The SOCO pointed to the small structure.

'It's an old coal store from back when this was a working railway. The only reason we're picking up anything is because of the thinness of the metal.'

Officers were converging on it. Watts turned to Traynor, whose face was empty of colour and expression, wondering how he was still on his feet. He looked up, saw Heritage coming down into the ravine. Reaching them, Heritage took Traynor by his arm.

'Come over here, Will, while they do their jobs.'

Two of the officers were kneeling before the structure, each grasping a bolt. Both bolts slid smoothly. Together, they lowered the flimsy metal sheet. In the sudden silence, Watts took a few steps closer, trying to make sense of what he was seeing. Somebody rushed forward, shone a light. It fell on to a mass of gold curls and lit them like fire.

'*No!*'

Before anybody could respond, Traynor had reached her. He and the two officers gently brought her out and on to the grass. Two foil blankets arrived. The officers stepped back, others watching in silence as Traynor secured them around her, followed by his arms and his upper body, sharing his heat with her, his mouth moving, his words inaudible.

Within five minutes, Chong arrived and went directly to Watts. 'Has she spoken at all?'

He shook his head. The pathologist went quickly to Traynor, her gloved hands reaching out. 'I need to look at her, Will.'

Like an automaton, he moved aside, eyes still fixed on Jess. After ten long minutes, there was a sudden shout. 'Paramedics have arrived!'

Hi-viz jackets were moving down into the ravine, coming towards them.

Connie was on her feet.

'What's the situation here?' asked one.

'I'm the police pathologist. She's deeply unconscious. Cold. Her breathing is shallow, BP low, pupils dilated. No gross injuries identified but I haven't moved her since she was brought out of that.' She pointed to the coal store. 'She needs to be tested for sedative or muscle relaxant: GHB, temazepam, ketamine and so on.'

Watts signalled to officers nearby, who joined the paramedics kneeling on either side of Jess. 'Help them move her up there.' He looked up at Traynor, his eyes fixed on Jess as she was moved.

'Come on, Will,' Connie said softly, taking his arm. 'Let's give them some space.'

Saturday, 30 November. 7.10 a.m.

Watts walked the long, bright hospital corridor to a small, quiet area where Traynor was sitting, his head bowed. 'Will?' Traynor looked up, his face chalk-white.

'What have you been told?'

'Only that they've located an injection site at the back of her neck. They're running tests, trying to identify what it is. They wanted me to leave. I wouldn't. They let me see her for a couple of minutes, but that was' – his head dropped forward – 'I don't know when. She's drifting in and out of consciousness.'

'Has she said anything about why she was there?' asked Watts.

'Something about a phone call—' He was on his feet as a nurse appeared and beckoned to him, saying a few quiet words. He looked at Watts. 'I can go in and see her for a couple of minutes, but they're insisting that I then leave. They've promised to ring me if anything changes. As soon as they do, I'll be back here— Who's this?'

Watts turned to the big, uniformed officer pounding the corridor towards them. 'That's Javid. He does martial arts, probably chews nails as a snack. He'll be posted outside Jess's room. I'll keep in touch with the hospital. Try to get some rest, mate, yeah?'

He drove directly to headquarters, finding Judd in his office. She looked up at him. 'How's Jess? Where's Will?'

'She's still in the hospital. They suspect drugs. Will's been there all night.' He glanced at her. 'You look like your old self.'

'I'm too young to have an "old self". How is it that whenever I'm not around, stuff kicks off?'

'I'd call it luck. How did you hear about Jess?'

'Ade rang me. He's mega-pissed off about his name being used as a decoy. He's also told me about Will finding Eric Brook. I went down to the custody suite earlier to see him, but he was still sleeping, so nobody could tell me anything. What's your thinking about Jess?'

'That whoever abducted her has more than a passing familiarity with our Newton investigation.'

'Like, an inside job?'

'Or somebody who's making it his business to follow what we're doing.'

'What happens now?'

'We find who it is.'

She followed him to the whiteboard, watched as he reached for a marker. 'Good idea. Get all potential persons of interest listed. I've got a name. The GP, Devereaux. He's got access to all kinds of drugs, knows how to administer them, and he's already on my list for Cane.' She paused. 'What about Solange from the pub? She'll know a lot about what goes on in Newton and I bet she has more than a passing familiarity with drugs.' She looked up at him. 'Ryan Bartlett?'

'I interviewed him in the early hours. He's been charged with drug offences unrelated to our investigation and sex with a minor.'

'Solange?'

He nodded. 'She's just shy of her fifteenth birthday.'

'Bastard!' She watched as he wrote, then stepped away from the whiteboard, read the names aloud. 'Marion Cane. Jack Beresford. Pearson Fleming.' She frowned, looked at him. 'What's your point?'

'See any links between these three people?'

'They're all dead.'

'According to Will, Marion Cane wasn't sex mad. That was her sister's view of her. I think Will's right. Cane was scared witless of somebody who had control over her. That same somebody who knew that Jack Beresford tipped us off about her death, which meant *he* had to be silenced.'

'But Pearson Fleming *never* even knew Cane. He died ages before she arrived in Newton.'

'Yes, but he and Cane had a lot in common. Both were well-off and both developed problems while they lived there. Cane was slowly sinking into vagueness and confusion, and the same for Fleming. In his case, it seemed linked to booze. Except that it wasn't.'

Judd shook her head. 'I still don't get it.'

'Will can explain. He says Cane and Fleming were both victims.'

'We already know that.'

'He means while they were still *alive*.'

'How? *Why?*'

'The "why" is about getting hold of what they had. Cane's sister is going to inherit her house, but not her money. Even when she was losing her grip, Cane was still savvy enough to move it.'

Judd said, 'Fleming didn't leave a lot of money. What he had was probably stolen, but his brother got his house which he now rents to the church.' She stared at Watts. '*He* benefitted from his brother's death because he still owns it. Is he the killer? What else has Will said?'

'Given his current situation, not too much, but he's described this killer as playing a waiting game. He's in no hurry. He'll kill again when he sees the time is right.' He went closer to the whiteboard, his eyes moving over the three names. 'According to Will, he regards what he does as an investment business.' He saw her eyes widen. 'It's been done. Cast your mind back to a GP up north who had a similar line of thinking, but for a lot less reward.'

She stared back at him.

'Possibly before your time, Judd.'

'Are you saying you suspect Devereaux?'

'I'm talking about how some killers have a role which helps them fit in, operate below the radar for years, doing what they do, then moving on.'

'That won't happen! We *know* too much about this case.' He looked at her.

'What exactly do we know about him, Judd?'

'He kills for gain . . . he blends right in . . . knows Newton Heights.'

He watched her thinking, saw sudden recognition in her eyes.

'Conrad Fleming owns his brother's house. Get him in!'

'Because?'

'How about he killed his own brother, then realized, "This is a nice earner".'

Watts shook his head. 'Pearson was a *victim*, just waiting to happen. That's patience, Judd. Whoever he is, this killer has a lot of patience. It's the MO that's still bugging me. I'm waiting to talk to Will.'

The door opened. It was Reynolds. 'Sarge! Just had a phone call that there's a small car, a Mini, on fire a couple of miles on from the ravine. It sounds like it's gutted. SOCOs say it's arson.'

THIRTY-FIVE

7.45 a.m.

Traynor went into his study, Boy following. He looked down at the hundreds of words he had written, turned away, paced, his fingers pressed to his mouth. This was personal now. Images of Jess flooded his head: the blue of her eyes, her wide smile, her laughter, the glorious hair, her body which he adored. *I cannot lose Jess, I love her, I need her, I cannot lose her.*

A broiling, overwhelming mix of anger, grief and longing washed over him. He seized all of his notes in both hands, crushed them, hurled them at the wastebasket as Boy peered at him, ears down, from the doorway. Half of them missed their mark. Fell to the floor. Traynor turned his back on them. On another rush of fury, he whirled, kicked the wastebasket, sending it flying into the air, then rolling across the floor, scattering wads of paper as it went. Fear adding to his anger and grief, he leaned against the desk, his chest pounding.

Hearing the click of claws on wood, he looked down, saw Boy looking up at him. He crouched, put his arms around him. 'Hey, Boy. It's OK, yes? All OK here.' The dog whined. Traynor stroked him. 'Sshh . . . Jess is coming home soon.'

He started gathering the scattered A4s. Dropping them on to his desk, his breathing ragged, his eyes moved to Jess smiling at him from her photograph. His movements mechanical, he smoothed the sheets, reading the lines of words. He reached down for his backpack. It prompted another whine. 'It's OK, Boy. I'm not leaving.' He took out his iPad. The dog came quietly to him, sat at his feet, its eyes fixed on Traynor's face. Stroking the soft fur between its ears, he brought his psychological autopsy notes on to the small screen, seeing words and phrases he had gathered about Marion Cane from those who had known her, a woman increasingly aware of her own vagueness, confusion and forgetfulness to a point where she had probably begun to doubt her mental state. Pearson Fleming's thoughts were unknown. All the signs within his home indicated that he was very troubled. But not alcoholic. Of the people he had talked to about Marion Cane, Traynor fully trusted one. Theresa Yates. She had described Marion as troubled yet still able to maintain control of her life to a degree. His eyes moved over words on the small screen. *Mirror. Confusion. Dizziness. Drugs.* Cane had done all she could, despite the increasing impact on her ability to stay mentally sharp, despite her distrust of her own judgement, memory and possibly her sanity. She had not craved sex. She had wanted someone to *be* with her.

Someone she could trust to protect her. Her reluctance to take the Valium was an indication that she had had some awareness that she was in danger. Was she at all aware that her killer's patience was dissipating? That he was now ready for another murderous act? He reached for his phone, located a number, waited.

'Post-mortem suite.'

'Igor, is Connie there?'

'She is. Hang on.' He waited.

'Will?'

'Hello, Connie. Have you tested Marion Cane's tissue samples for the tetrahydrozoline Adam identified in the eyedrops found in her house?'

'I'm doing it now. Of the ten-plus samples I took, I haven't found it. I'm down to the last three.'

Traynor closed his eyes. 'How would anybody know about the lethal aspect of eyedrops?'

'That's been my thinking, so I checked online. The answer looks to be just about anybody who's curious and types in the right question.'

Call ended, Traynor was now seeing how late he was to recognize the coldness, the stealth of this killer who sent Jack Beresford to his death in the ravine, who ran down Pearson Fleming with a speeding vehicle, both he and Cane victims of a slow, insidious dismantling of them both as individuals. He was seeing the cruelty, the callousness behind all of it, yet still could not connect it to a name. His head filled with rage. The attack on Jess was merely collateral. Intended to confuse, distract and discourage the investigation.

His phone clamoured. He reached for it. The hospital. Jess was not responding as well to treatment as doctors had anticipated. She remained unconscious. Would he come? He moved in a frenzy of worry and self-blame for his jacket, his keys. His work had placed Jess in jeopardy. His phone rang again. It was Adam.

'Sorry to ring you, Will, but I can't reach Bernard. I've got some info—'

'Adam, you'll have to try Bernard again. Sorry.' He cut the call.

*   *   *

Watts listened to Adam giving him what he had. 'It's DNA.'

'At last! Whose?'

'It's complicated, Bernard.'

'Keep it basic.'

Adam pointed to the rug. 'What I've got from this is a DNA mix.'

'You mean, more than one sample? I wish I'd known. I've just spent fifteen difficult minutes with John Heritage who's wanting progress, but now we've *got* it. Who's in the mix?'

'It's not that simple. Analysing DNA mixtures is time consuming. It often produces ambiguous results. What I can tell you is that one of the contributors was Marion Cane.'

'Right. Who else?'

'Two other individuals.'

'Sounds like a bit of a party.'

Adam shook his head. 'Not necessarily. The DNA could have been left at different times.'

Watts waited. 'OK. Who are they? Where's the problem?'

'It's in the DNA technology itself. It's so sensitive now. DNA mixtures always existed but we didn't know about them. If we ever picked them up, we steered well clear of analysing them.'

'I'm still at "complicated".'

Adam chose his words. 'You know that we don't analyse entire genetic sequences. We look at short segments of DNA.' The door opened and Judd came inside. 'Those short segments vary with each individual. The variations are called alleles.'

'I've heard of them!' Judd said. Watts looked at her. 'Remember that course you sent me on a few months back? It's possible to chart alleles. What you get is spikes showing they're there in the sample and you're on your way to a DNA profile.'

Adam nodded. 'You're right. Except that that's where the problem arises. Alleles from different individuals can match.'

'Hang on. What Judd said about charting these . . . things. You can do that, right?'

'I've already started doing exactly that. Some of the spikes are so small, they're almost invisible, plus they're on the same chart so it's difficult to know who they belong to—'

'Don't tell me that that's "end of story".'

'Not quite. Once the chart is finished, we've got software that might give us a probability as to who contributed to the DNA—

'So, now we're on our way to an identification of both?'

'Yes, if the individuals are already on the DNA database and, like I said, we're talking *probabilities* here, not straight identification.'

Watts headed for the door. 'Thanks, Adam. No offence, mate, but I'm sick to death of ifs and maybes.'

At home, Traynor came into his study. He had stayed with Jess, talking to her, holding her hand, until one of the doctors insisted that he leave on the promise of a phone call if there was any change, no matter when. At his desk, he reached for the envelope Milly Adams had given him. Removing the photograph, he looked down at the configuration of the three people in it. Milly blissfully smiling, a smiling Matthew standing close behind her, gazing over her shoulder at their photographer, she resting against him, their faces touching, their pose a testament to the intimacy between them, while Eric Brook frowned behind them. Traynor looked up, seeing his own reflection in his study window.

At last, he knew. *Reflection and control. It was there all the time. I should have seen it, but I didn't—*

His phone rang. He seized it. It was the hospital. He listened to what was being said, ended the call, grabbed his jacket and keys and rushed from the house to his car. Inside, his hands-free phone lit up. Bernard.

'I'm on my way to the hospital right now, but you need to know. Marion Cane's death was about control, Bernard. The same for Pearson Fleming. Their killer's presence was constant. Inescapable. That's how he took complete control of them.' He navigated the Aston around a vast island. 'Mirrors and messages. This case was always about—'

'Will, you're dropping out! Say again! *Repeat*, Will!'

Traynor's voice returned, strong now. 'They endured months of psychological abuse by a consistent process of gaslighting. Talk to Eric Brook—'

The call ended. Judd was staring at Watts, her eyes wide. He repeated what Traynor had said, watched her absorb it.

'It all makes sense,' she whispered.

'Heard anything from downstairs about Brook?'

'An hour ago, the duty officer rang to say he was demanding to be released.'

'Yesterday he was grateful to be here. Let's hear what he's got to say.'

Eric Brook was looking agitated. 'I'm waiting for my solicitor to ring to say she's found me a hospital place.'

'You think you need that?'

'*Yes.* I have to feel *safe.*'

Watts studied him, knowing that he couldn't remain at headquarters. 'What's on your mind, Eric?'

'*Nothing.* I feel better than when I came here but I need to leave! *Now.*'

'Tell us why you're so nervous—'

'You should be asking that GP questions, not me!'

They left him, Judd's face incredulous. 'Why aren't you keeping at him? He *knows* something!'

'Can't be done. He's classed as psychologically vulnerable.'

He took out his phone, tapped a number, got a response. Judd listened to the brief exchange. 'Yeah. I hear what you're saying. Eight fifteen, here at headquarters.' He ended the call. 'Devereaux has agreed to come in tomorrow after telling me how impossible it is for him to fit it in today.'

Judd looked at him. 'Sounds to me like he wants some thinking time.'

THIRTY-SIX

Sunday, 1 December. 8.15 a.m.

Judd seized the clamouring desk phone as Watts came into the office. 'Thanks. I'll tell him.' She ended the call. 'He's here and, I quote, "gobbing off, demanding to be seen".'

'You surprise me.'

Watts reached for the notes he had made during his previous day's phone conversation with Traynor, leisurely patted his pockets, removed his West Midlands Police lanyard from one of them and dropped it over his head, identification details visible.

'You're preparing to make this formal,' she observed, 'and enjoying the situation.'

'Can't fool you, Judd.'

Leaving the office, they walked the corridor, an increasingly strident voice now coming to them. Devereaux was at the reception desk, in full ego-throttle. 'Now, *you* listen to me! DCI Watts has requested that I come here for *God* knows what reason, which he didn't specify. I have plans for today and I object to being told to wait around amid this—'

Coming into Reception, seeing the waiting clientele, Watts silently completed the GP's sentence: *rabble*. Pointing upwards for Judd to continue upstairs, he approached the desk, getting grins of recognition from several individuals in tracksuits and peak-to-back baseball caps, avidly watching the action at the desk.

'Thanks for coming in, Doctor Devereaux.'

At sounds of suppressed mirth and a single 'Ooh-*er*!', Devereaux turned to Watts. 'Whatever this is about, I want it over and I want it done! Aspects of my professional work intrude on my weekends and I've had to reschedule my day's plans to be here.'

'I get where you're coming from. Work-related stress. It's a killer—'

'I am *not* stressed, merely impressing on *you* that some of us belong to professions that come with significant expectation. Whatever this is about, I'll be leaving within ten minutes.'

Watts led the way upstairs and into an interview room, where Judd was waiting. Devereaux sent her a quick glance, then took the chair Watts was indicating. He sat, head high, not making eye contact with either of them.

Watts said, 'This is Police Constable Judd. She'll start the interview.'

Devereaux flicked her a brief, disparaging look. 'When you say interview—'

'Don't let that worry you,' said Judd.

'I'm *not* worried.'

'I have some questions to ask you about Marion Cane, Pearson Fleming and Jack Beresford. I'll start with Jack Beresford.'

'I never knew him. He wasn't a patient.'

'You probably knew him well enough to recognize him by sight.'

Devereaux sighed. 'So?'

'Tell us what else you know about him.'

'Elderly. Local family. That's it.'

'What about Pearson Fleming?' She watched some speedy thinking start up.

'I was called out to him once. It sometimes happens because I live in Newton Heights. My response is always to prioritize patients' needs over my—'

'What was Mr Fleming's problem?'

Devereaux looked irritated at being cut off. 'He was very unwell, unsteady on his feet. A relative was there and I wrote out a prescription.'

'What did you prescribe?'

'Excuse me?'

'It's OK if you don't remember—'

'Young woman, I remember perfectly well. It was fluoxetine, but I don't see that as relevant.'

Watts eyed him, happy to let Devereaux create more trouble for himself.

Judd said, 'Tell us about Marion Cane.' They watched him grow still.

'I don't know what you mean.' He glanced at Watts. 'I already told you about my professional contact with Ms Cane.'

'We're interested in the non-professional contact you had with her,' said Watts.

'There was none.'

'You're saying that *all* of your contact with Marion Cane took place at the health centre?'

'That's exactly what I'm telling you.'

'You never visited Marion Cane at her home?' Watts was picking up the beginnings of tension around Devereaux's eyes and mouth. 'I did not.'

'You may be unaware of specific items of Ms Cane's property that we've removed from her house. The forensic department here at headquarters is busy examining them. I'll describe them to you. One mirror with an ornate wooden frame, a total of twelve Valium tablets recovered from her bedroom and' – Watts' eyes were on Devereaux, seeing no change in his facial expression – 'also, from her sitting room, one large wool rug patterned in red, blue and—'

Devereaux was on his feet, looking as though a plug had been pulled on the colour in his face. 'I want my lawyer.'

It had taken a while for Devereaux's lawyer to put in an appearance. When he finally did, he and Devereaux had a brief conversation, the upshot of which was the lawyer advising him to make whatever he knew about Marion Cane available to the interviewing officers. The interview, now formal, recommenced, Watts indicating that it was being recorded. Devereaux said nothing. He looked unwell.

'Doctor Devereaux, thirty minutes ago I referred to a rug which was part of the furnishing of Marion Cane's sitting room. If that rug has any personal relevance to you, I'm advising you to say so, now.' He and Judd waited.

The GP glanced at his lawyer. Getting no immediate help there, he folded his arms and addressed the floor. 'It's . . . This was a while ago. I just happened to be passing her house one evening and she came out and . . . she indicated that she wished to speak to me. So, as her GP, I followed her inside and—'

'Date?'

'It was last year, October time – the twenty-eighth, twenty-ninth, possibly the thirtieth. My wife was carving pumpkins for the children and I decided to take a short walk around the Heights, a purely spur-of-the-moment thing—'

'You went to Marion Cane's house,' prompted Watts.

'I just happened to find myself . . . There was nothing clandestine about it. I also happened to see Marion's brother-in-law and we acknowledged each other, as one does. You can check with him.' Devereaux's face regained some colour.

'We would if we could. What did Ms Cane want to talk to you about?'

'She invited me into her house, said she was feeling very anxious and unwell. She asked if I would provide another prescription to ease her anxiety.'

'The same fluoxetine medication you had prescribed previously, which she never collected?'

'Yes.'

'Did she collect this one?'

'I assume so.'

Watts nodded. 'Your practice will probably be able to confirm it, including the date?' He saw Devereaux's colour seep away again. 'Actually, what I just said about a prescription. I'm no sure now that I did provide one. I write so many—'

'So, there you are, inside Marion Cane's house, and she's describing her symptoms to you.'

Devereaux's lawyer touched his arm, whispered to him. Afte a long pause, Devereaux nodded. The lawyer looked across a Watts.

'My client is prepared to provide brief details of what tran-spired, after which he intends to leave.'

Watts' eyes moved to Devereaux. 'That will depend on wha your client tells us.'

They came into Watts' office. He switched on the kettle, added teabags to two mugs. Bringing them to the table, he set one down in front of Judd. 'In the morning, I'll watch the recording of what Devereaux said. Right now, I'll settle for you reading through the notes you made. They're probably as good.'

'Pretty short and sweet, Sarge. According to Devereaux while he "just happened to be passing" Cane's house, she comes out, invites him inside. She offers him a drink. He chooses whisky. She goes to the kitchen to get some crackers, "nibbles" according to him, and when she returns to the sitting room, the shirt she is wearing is unbuttoned, exposing her breasts—'

'And Devereaux is like a rat up a drainpipe,' snapped Watts.

'Across the rug, more like. Sex occurred on said rug. He left the house with some difficulty, according to him, because she pleaded with him to stay. On his way home, he referred to seeing the church trainee, whom he described as "bloody odd" but refused to say more. He went directly home to enthuse over his kids' pumpkins, the *pathetic* bastard—'

'Facts, Judd.'

'That *is* one. He avoids his wife because, according to him, he'd started a guilt trip, my words, about having sex with Cane, after which he says it never happened again, denied any contact with her via phone, email, text, Twitter, Facebook, Morse code, smoke signal, blah blah. On that score, he denied having his phone with him today. Said he'd drop it in here.' She looked at Watts. 'You know what I think.'

'Yep.' He took a mouthful of tea, swallowed. 'He went back for more. I've sent Reynolds to collect his phone.'

'What do you think of Devereaux as her killer?'

'My jury's still out. Yes, his job means he can lay his hands on meds and there are aspects about him that sound like the narcissism Will has told us about during other investigations, *but* I can't see him drawing attention to himself by supplying her with Valium, a now out-of-favour drug.'

'His job could easily have cued him into this tetrahydro-stuff in the eye drops.'

'Possible.'

'What?' She nudged.

'When Devereaux arrived here, he was a good fit for what I was expecting for this killer. Arrogance. The big I-Am. But once the interview was really underway and it was obvious to him that his explanation was going—'

'Tits up—'

'*Judd*—'

'I'm ahead of you. I remember Will saying once that people with problematic personalities are basically consistent in their presentation because the personality is what they *are*. It's *them*. They can't conceal it. OK, they can do a bit of superficial faking, but I don't think Devereaux was faking. Once he could see it was falling apart for him, he gave it up.'

'We've got a voluntary DNA sample from him, so now we wait and hope that Adam sorts out the rest of the mix from that rug.'

When Traynor arrived at the hospital, he was taken to one side and told that Jess wasn't responding to treatment and was still unconscious. They had allowed him to stay with her, encouraged him to talk to her. It was now early evening.

A nurse came into the room carrying a tray.

'Here we are. One coffee and some nice biscuits.'

He didn't look up. She glanced at his partner lying there, unmoving. 'She's in good hands, you know, but you just want her well and home with you, don't you?'

He nodded, still not looking at her.

'Right, I'll leave you to it.'

She went to the door and out, quietly closing it, recalling the day his partner was first admitted. He was that stressed he initially refused to leave when asked to do so. Later, once he was allowed to see her in private, she had walked in on him sitting by her bed, his head down, quietly breaking his heart. She sighed. A bit of emotion was nice in a man. She had heard that he was something to do with the police. He was tall, so it fitted. They made a handsome couple. Not privy to any medical details, she just hoped it turned out well for them.

THIRTY-SEVEN

Monday, 2 December. 6.38 a.m.

Watts' office door opened and the custody sergeant leaned inside, his face tense. 'Sarge? Brook is getting very agitated, asking for Doctor Traynor.'

'I'll come down.'

Watts came into the custody suite to find the custody sergeant booking in a swaying, scruffy-looking individual. 'I'll just finish processing this one—'

'You wha'?' demanded the drunk. 'How 'bout some respect f'*me* as a taxpayer!'

The duty sergeant glanced at him.

'Cyril, you've never had a job that was legit in all the years I've known you, *and*' – he pointed to himself – 'it'll be *my* tax that pays for you to sleep it off. Sit down over there. Go on!'

They watched the drunk shamble away from the counter, an officer holding him by his arm.

The duty sergeant looked at Watts. 'The good news is your lad's gone quiet.' He jerked his head in the direction of the holding area, and Watts followed him along the corridor, waited as he unlocked a door and stood back. Eric Brook was sitting in a corner of the narrow bed, his legs drawn up to his chest, arms wrapped around them. He looked up at Watts.

'I want to see Doctor Traynor!'

'He's not available. How're you doing, Eric?'

After a lapse of some seconds, Brook said, 'I don't like the noise here, the doors, the shouting . . . I have to see Doctor Traynor, tell him I didn't hurt anybody in that house I broke into.'

'We know you didn't.'

Relief flooded Brook's face. 'That's something I wouldn't do. I did steal something, though. Some bread. I was hungry and upset and confused and . . .' He lowered his head to his knees.

Watts left the room, returned with a chair and sat down, looking at him, seeing for the first time how frail he was. 'You need to talk to me, Eric.'

'What about?'

'Marion Cane.'

Brook's head shot up. '*No!* I don't know her. I *never* saw her, never said anything to her—'

'You visited her house.'

'*No*. That was a *mistake*. Matthew came. He told me I shouldn't have gone there.'

'Why did you go there, Eric?'

'She was kind to me.'

'Marion talked to you?'

His hands pulling at his clothes, he stared at Watts. 'Sometimes. She talked to me when she was at the church. Told me the names of the flowers she'd brought.'

'What was she like?'

'Nice . . . I liked her.'

'Was that a long time ago, Eric?'

'I don't know. It was before I came to live in Newton. I was just visiting . . . I didn't know anybody. I was lonely. She seemed to know how I was feeling without me telling her. Once I was actually living there' – he looked away – 'I was so unhappy and upset and lonely . . .'

'Why was that, Eric?'

Brook avoided eye contact. 'Don't know. That time I just told you about, I'd been to her house before, but nobody knew about it.'

'What happened that time, Eric?'

'It was the way I was feeling that day. I was pent-up. She let me in. Gave me a drink. I thought she was a nice, kind person.'

Watts' thinking was moving fast. This conversation was shaping up to be something he needed to formalize, but he knew he had to avoid any sudden change to the current situation. 'Go back to how you were feeling that day, Eric. Tell me about it.'

Brook looked away again, his face tightening. 'Unwell. Really frightened. I needed somebody to talk to. Somebody I could trust not to repeat it.'

'Repeat what, exactly?'

Eric's arms encircled his knees again. His head bowed. 'You wouldn't believe me.' He glanced up at Watts. 'Marion *did*. She believed me. She *said* she did. But that next time I went there, Leonard, the vicar, was just leaving and she told him she didn't want me inside her house again. That she wanted me to go.'

Watts saw more tears.

'Did something happen when you were at that house which upset her?'

'No, *no*.' He looked frantic. 'I swear! It wasn't me. Don't send me back to Newton, *please*. I hate it there. If you send me back, I'll—' Out of words, he bowed his head again and wept.

Watts left him and went to update the duty sergeant. 'There's been no official charge so far because of the state he was in when he arrived here. The old guy who owns the house he broke into isn't keen to have him charged, but what I've just heard is making me wonder if he had some kind of involvement in Cane's death. He's not fit for a formal interview. He needs to go somewhere for psychiatric evaluation. I'll see if I can contact Will Traynor for his advice.'

He left the custody suite and headed to reception, preoccupied with his suspicions of Brook and his own limited insight as to what was going on with him.

'Bernard?'

He looked up to see Traynor coming into the building. Watts went to him, relieved to see him, shocked by the exhaustion on his face. 'What's happening, Will?'

'It took a while, but Jess is slowly rallying. I'm on my way home for a shower, then back to the hospital.'

'That is good news.' Watts paused. 'There's something I need to tell you – I'm really concerned about Eric Brook.'

Traynor listened to Watts' description of Brook's behaviour.
It's possible he's experiencing some degree of paranoid ideation.
doubt he has a serious psychiatric problem, but what you've
ust told me suggests he's hugely anxious, possibly frightened.
He won't divulge everything until he feels safe. I'll ask Anton,
my psychiatrist, if he can help.' He sent a quick text and received
a response within a minute. 'Anton has agreed to accept Eric as
a patient and he's attached contact details, which,' he tapped his
phone, 'I've just forwarded to you—'

Traynor's phone pinged. It was the hospital. Jess was fully
conscious and asking for him.

THIRTY-EIGHT

Tuesday, 3 December. Mid-afternoon

Traynor was moving restlessly from room to room, re-
positioning flowers he had bought, waiting for a call from
the hospital to say that he could collect Jess and bring her
home. His phone rang.

'Will, it's Anton. I've completed a preliminary evaluation of
Brook and I'd appreciate it if you'd tell me about your direct
experience of him.'

'I found him after he briefly disappeared. Since then I've just
had one conversation with him. He presented as somewhat paranoid, very confused, possibly fearful. I'm consulting on three
homicides there and I thought it possible he was somehow
involved in them.'

'He's referred several times to a Marion Cane. Who is she?'

'One of the victims.' Traynor waited. 'Did you get anything
from him about his feelings or attitude towards her?'

'Yes. He feels very badly let down by her. I wanted to ask if
you have any thoughts about how Eric views himself?'

'I'm sorry, Anton, I don't. He was too distressed for any kind
of personal introspection. DCI Bernard Watts, who's leading the
investigation, asked him a few questions about Marion Cane and
what had happened to her. I understand he said, "It wasn't me."

Bernard wasn't able to get more from him.' There was a pause. 'What's your opinion of Brook?'

'An angry and extremely distraught young man.'

'Any ideas as to a specific cause?'

'As I said, he feels he's been badly used, misunderstood and blamed in some way. Those feelings relate directly to this Marion Cane. Does that sound at all logical to you, Will?'

'Yes, in the sense that during the police investigation there were reports of his odd behaviour around her. That's when he briefly disappeared from where he was living.'

'Are you aware of anyone in the area who was concerned for Eric prior to his problems reaching a head?'

'Yes. The local vicar, his deacon and the deacon's girlfriend. The deacon was attempting to support him emotionally.'

'I think Brook's current condition is a direct result of his enduring a significant degree of stress and fear for some considerable time.'

Traynor absorbed the words.

'Will?'

'I heard what you said, Anton.' He paused. 'I think I need to come and see you on my own behalf sometime soon. Restart my therapy.'

'No problem. It happens with PTSD. How about I pull some possible dates together, email them to you?'

'Thank you, Anton.'

He ended the call, then paced, thinking of all that had been said over the last few minutes about Eric Brook. He searched his desk, located the photograph Milly had given him. He stared down at the smiling young couple and the troubled Brook. 'How could I have been so *obtuse*? This was *telling* me what happened to Marion Cane and Pearson Fleming and *how* it was done, but I never connected it to *him*.'

His phone rang. It was the hospital. Jess was due to be discharged in the next half hour.

7.35 p.m.

Judd stared out at Newton Heights as Watts parked the BMW. 'Why *now*? Couldn't it have waited until tomorrow morning?'

'In my experience, the early evening is a good time to find people at home.'

'Do you want to share the visits between us?'

'No. We go to each house together—'

'Hang on. What if something's said and somebody else doesn't like it?'

'Credit me with *some* sensitivity. Each house we go to, we see them separately. Got the list?'

She nodded.

'It shouldn't take long. People generally don't go into detail about what we're after.'

'Let me see the list again.' She took it from him. 'Want me to suggest the order we see them in?'

'Go on.'

'First, Devereaux because we've already got an admission from him. Then his wife. After that, Partington, followed by his wife, followed by Matthew Redpath.' She looked up. 'Why's he on the list, and why Jessop?'

'For completeness. Let's get it done.'

It took longer than expected. Almost two hours later, they left Newton Heights with no words exchanged during the journey which ended at Judd's house.

'Come on in.'

'I'd better get off—'

'No.' She opened the passenger door, looked at him. 'It's now half ten and that was some of *the* most invasive questioning I've been a part of. *You're* my senior officer. I need a debrief. *Now.*'

'All right, calm down. Get the kettle on.'

He followed her to her house and inside, where they were ambushed by a famished cat. 'You see to her and stop her racket.'

He searched kitchen cupboards, found bread, then into the fridge for cheese, organized plates, made tea, good and strong, found a large tray, loaded it and carried it into the sitting room where Judd was sitting, staring straight ahead, the cat occupying itself with an extensive wash and brush up.

She glanced at the tray. 'I'm not hungry.'

'Here.'

She took the plate, swallowed a mouthful of tea, took a bite of cheese, then another. 'Don't tell me it's all part of the job because I know. We hear all sorts of stuff and we just go with it.' She turned to him. 'What we were just part of – I can see a couple of those relationships hitting a wall.'

'That's up to them. Would they have told us a quarter of what we got if we'd brought them into headquarters on zero grounds? Or maybe you'd prefer to do it that way and be facing official complaints? It's what happens when people won't be open what they've been up to. We had to do it. Bring stuff into the open. Challenge 'em. Hear what they had to say. It's basic police work—'

'I *know* that. It's the fact that it was one after another!' She ate, drank tea. He did the same.

She got up. 'I'm still hungry. How about you?'

'Go on, then.'

In ten minutes, she was back with another loaded tray. 'Rolls, ham, guacamole – *don't* turn your nose up – more cheese.'

They ate in silence.

'This guacka-stuff is all right.' He took a mouthful of tea. 'Right. Let's see what we've got.'

He brought out his notebook. She took her notes from her bag. 'Devereaux admitted to having sex with Marion Cane on a total of six separate occasions. According to him, it stopped because his wife found out. According to his wife when we spoke to her, he had insisted it was once only, but she followed him, saw him go into Cane's house several times—'

'Which is when she got the full drift and lost it big time, threatening him with divorce.'

Watts consulted his notes. 'Leonard Partington denied having sex with anybody. When we spoke to his wife, she stated that he's impotent and has been for the last three years or so—'

'Bloody embarrassing,' muttered Judd.

'She's also admitted to having a sexual relationship with somebody but refused to name him.'

'So, what happens to her for non-compliance?'

'Nothing, as yet. Depends how desperate we get. One thing's for certain. Newton Heights is a hotbed for sex. Figure that out.'

'Probably to do with it being countryside,' said Judd absently. 'Loads of animals around the place.' She referred back to her notes. 'Matthew Redpath and his girlfriend talked to us together. He was the only one who was at all sympathetic towards Marion Cane, describing her as an unhappy woman. Both referred to Eric Brook's problematic behaviour around Cane, but neither mentioned anybody, resident or otherwise, whom they suspected of having known Marion Cane intimately.'

Judd looked at him. 'They're both young, and the girlfriend doesn't live there, so I'm not surprised they don't know any of the gossip.' She paused. 'I wonder what will happen when it all hits the fan at the vicarage? How about Anna Partington, who seems a nice woman, leaves the Rev for whoever she's having it off with and— Hey, *there's* a benefit to Matthew Redpath. He'll get the job!'

Watts frowned at her. 'It doesn't work like that. There are bishops and others who have a say. This isn't Cluedo. It's people's lives.' He chose his words. 'Have you considered that Leonard Partington knew she was having a sexual relationship with somebody?'

'No, but now you've said it, remember what I heard inside the church? I bumped into him outside. He was very red in the face, and when we arrived at the vicarage, *she* was looking a bit stressed. Guess what I'm thinking.'

'That he knew what was going on and he condoned it.'

'It's possible. Neither of them would identify the involved male. *She* refused, point-blank.'

'She might have to, eventually.'

Watts quickly wrote, then flipped his notebook closed. 'Jessop the accountant had nothing to tell us. He's not likeable, but in his case, there was no sex.'

'Apart from what he was having with Gymkhana, who he's been involved with for the last five years,' said Judd. 'He's divorced and she's single, so who cares?'

Watts nodded.

'We also know there was no fraud. While she was alive, Marian Cane took steps to protect her own finances. Why? She knew her killer *really* well.' He looked at Judd. 'Is that enough of a debrief?'

She looked up at him. 'Any of them you want to move from person-of-interest to suspect?'

'I need to think about it.'

She walked with him to the door, turned to him, suddenly shy. 'Sarge? I just wanted to say thanks.'

'For what?'

'For being concerned when I wasn't well.'

'You're welcome.' He looked down at her. 'Nothing serious?'

'No, nothing serious.'

She watched him walk away, keeping her voice low. 'See you tomorrow, Sarge.'

'You will.'

Halfway home, Watts changed his mind and diverted to headquarters. The young officer on duty raised his hand. 'Sarge? Got something for you here.'

Watts took the large internal envelope from him. Opening it, he took out an item wrapped in clear plastic.

'A bit of old scrap metal,' observed the youth.

Watts looked inside the envelope, removed a single A4 sheet bearing his name. He read what was on it and took all of it to his office, where he laid it on the table. He reread it, his thoughts drifting back to the dark evening he spent at Jack Beresford's house. When the two inexperienced young officers arrived from Longbridge, he had ordered them to search the immediate area outside. He looked at the 'scrap metal'. It was a number plate they had recovered during their search, taken back with them to Longbridge and logged it there instead of sending it to headquarters. Looking at the numbers and letters, he took it to the computer terminal, switched it on. He entered the registration details and got a result. It belonged to a hire car, plus details of the company that owned it. Watts got out his phone, thinking that the odds of finding anybody there at this hour were zero. His call was picked up.

'Apologies for the lateness. This is West Midlands Police. We're interested in a car owned by your hire company.' He gave the registration and got quick confirmation. 'What exactly happened to it?'

'The customer who hired it on a two-day rental was local—'

'Local to?'

'Colchester, Essex. According to him, he ran into a wall, but I wasn't convinced, given the dents on it and the mileage, which didn't tally with what he was telling us.'

'Where's the car now?'

'Scrapped. It wasn't worth getting the dents knocked out and paint job done. It was no loss. Done a lot of miles overall. Want me to email you the details?'

'If you would. You're working late.'

'Somebody has to keep our records up to date. I'm glad of the break. I tell you one thing that surprised me. Him lying like that, given who he was.'

Watts listened, thanked him again and ended the call, looked up as his office door opened.

'You're *just* the person I wanted to see, Will.'

'I thought I'd drop by, saw the BMW.'

'How's Jess?'

'She's recovering well.' He gave a tired smile. 'Better than I am. I can't seem to step back from her, which isn't helping. My daughter is at the house, so I thought I'd give her some space, come and see you.' He shrugged, ran his hand over his hair. 'It took me a long time to see it, but I know who killed them, Bernard.'

'So do I.' He passed the A4 sheet to him, watched him read, saw his confirming nod.

Watts looked down at the number plate. 'Job done, Will. Except that I have to be certain before I look him in the eye. I want to see Jess tomorrow. I need to show her two photographs. Is she up for that, do you think?'

THIRTY-NINE

Wednesday, 4 December. 12.35 p.m.

A young woman opened the door. 'Hi. Come in. It's Bernard, Dad! Go straight through. I've got a lecture in half an hour so I'll leave you to it.'

Watts followed the long hallway to where quiet music was playing, Traynor waiting.

'Keep the tone, the pace gentle, yes?'

Watts followed him into the room where Jess was sitting, looking flushed and well.

'Hi, Bernard! Come on in. Sorry about the heat in here. It's the one hangover from what happened. I'm still feeling cold.'

Seeing Traynor hovering around her, Watts asked, 'Do you feel up to me bringing you something to do, Jess?'

'Are you serious?'

Traynor took her hand. 'It might be challenging.'

'I know, but I want to do it. I need to do it.'

They sat, Watts reaching inside his heavy jacket, bringing out an envelope. He placed it on a low table, pointed to it. 'I've brought two photographs to show you. The first is of one person. The second shows three people. I want you to look at both, then tell me if you recognize any of them, yes?'

'I understand.'

Traynor said, 'Are you sure you're ready for this, Jess? If you do recognize anybody, it could be upsetting—'

'I have to do it, Will.'

Watts brought out both photographs. Keeping one of them back, he placed the other in front of her, one he had taken earlier that day. 'Do you recognize this person as the individual who attacked you?'

She looked down at it, then up. 'No. That's not him.'

Removing Ade Jones' ID photograph, he replaced it with the second. 'I want you to look at all three people in this one.'

She looked down at it.

'Is there anyone in this photo you recognize?'

She gazed down at it, slowly bringing her hands to her mouth.

'Jess?'

'I'm OK, Will. It's just that I haven't been able to bring his face to mind at all since it happened, but now—' She looked at Watts, then pointed. 'It's *him*.'

Watts asked, 'How certain are you?'

She looked up at him. 'Is one hundred per cent enough?'

FORTY

Watts had spent several hours with Judd planning the interview. His inclination had been to include everything they knew, but knowing that there would be a further opportunity, he had finally reduced it to what he considered the main issues. His phone rang. It was Connie. 'I've been testing Marion Cane's tissue samples for traces of tetrahydrozoline. I've found it.'

'What does that tell us?'

'That she was poisoned by person or persons unknown administering eyedrops, possibly concealed in a drink of some kind. I have something else for you. I've identified the drugs used on Jess. A mix of ketamine and gamma-hydroxybutyric acid – GHB for short. It could have killed her.'

Five minutes later, the phone rang again. Their interviewee had arrived with legal representation.

Forty minutes into the actual interview, Watts' face was relaxed, his whole demeanour open to the man sitting opposite them. Behind his face, his tension was approaching the stratosphere. He had got him talking, had listened to his brief, bland responses, each of them a flat denial of all knowledge. Traynor's view had been that what they needed from him was unlikely to come easily, if at all. 'I doubt he will take responsibility for any of it, no matter what we have on him.' So far, he was right on the money.

Watts glanced at the wall clock, looked at the young face opposite. Open, yet devoid of emotion, his posture suggesting a willingness to participate. Watts had seen occasional glimmers of surprise – for example, when he had asked for his opinion about the three deaths. Nothing of evidentiary value had been forthcoming. He had remained passive, his general stance relaxed. Knowing his guilt, Watts wondered how he was managing to maintain it. He had read somewhere that if a suspect attended a polygraph test with a small object such as a stone in his shoe, that tiny, physical distraction was sufficient to maintain calm and beat the test. Aware that it was irrelevant to the situation here, he still sent a glance beneath the table to feet casually crossed at the ankle. In any event, Traynor had dismissed such tricks as ineffective. Watts glanced at Judd. She had said little so far. Had left it to him to lead. He could see frustration behind her careful facial expression. Their interviewee looked much as he had when he arrived. Amiable. Somewhat quizzical. A little aloof.

Time to ramp up the action. Aware of Traynor watching remotely, Watts reached for the single evidence bag they had brought in with them, opened it and brought out the item, his eyes on the face opposite. Watts laid it on the table.

'One number plate. Badly damaged, but still legible.' Still the same blandness, yet with a tinge of something that suggested sudden, intense thinking.

Watts pointed. 'That damage occurred when the vehicle to which it was attached left the road and ploughed straight into Pearson Fleming, a sixty-seven-year-old man, a retired academic who had worked all his life to do his best for his students and who never hurt anybody.' He moved his finger over the plate. 'Mr Fleming's DNA was found right *there*. The driver had no grudge against Mr Fleming. No huge dislike. He was simply impatient. He had spent months grooming Pearson Fleming, loosening his grip on reality, and had decided that now was the time to separate him from what was the real objective: the property he owned. What do you think of that? Who goes to those lengths to do *that*?'

'I'm not thinking anything,' the man responded. 'I have no idea.'

'Somebody with a *lot* of patience, is who. He didn't get his hands on it, because Fleming had a will, leaving his property to his brother.'

'DCI Watts, I'm no expert on criminal behaviour, but, in your place, any suspicions I might have would be circling around that brother.'

Watts leaned forward. 'I see your thinking, but, like I said, this murderer is playing a *long* game. He was always prepared to kill Conrad Fleming in the fullness of time. When he dust settled, so to speak.' He studied the face opposite. Still amiable. Nothing to suggest there was anything much going' on behind it. 'Because he's somebody who thinks no more of killing somebody than he might swatting a fly. Can you imagine that?'

'I cannot. It sounds inhuman.'

'You're right,' said Watts. 'That's exactly what it is.' He had rehearsed Traynor's explanation and was now ready to deliver it. 'How about I give you a bit of context to this killer's way of thinking and operating? Jack Beresford's death was straightforward violence. Why? Because Jack had a lot of *time* to spare. He spent much of it walking around the area where he lived. Jack was your observant type. Ex-police officer, but you probably know that.'

'I do not.'

'Whatever he saw or knew got him killed at ninety-two. Doesn't bear thinking about, does it?'

'It's unpleasant, certainly.'

'Pearson Fleming died because his killer got impatient. It was a similar picture for Marion Cane, although minus the violence.'

'I still don't have any idea what you're talking about.'

'We know what happened to Doctor Traynor's partner, the date-rape drugs you used on her—'

'This is madness.'

'You're right.' Watts leaned forward. 'That's not all we know. Marion Cane and Pearson Fleming were both victims of a particular type of psychological assault. *Gaslighting.*'

The man opposite gazed at him. 'I have no idea what that means.'

'I'll enlighten you. The individual who killed them slowly, persistently manipulated them to the point where they doubted their perceptions of themselves, their lives and their self-worth. They were both systematically put down and lied to in order to erode their belief and confidence in themselves until their grip on reality began to fail them.'

'That's impossible.'

'You'd think so, wouldn't you? Usually, it's done by an individual who's living with the victim. But this gaslighter was inventive. He had refined the process. When he wasn't actually face-to-face with Fleming or Cane, he still exerted his presence. Can you see where this is going?'

'No, I cannot.'

'Both Marion Cane and Pearson Fleming had mirrors in their sitting rooms. It was how their killer exerted control over these two isolated victims from a distance, by leaving small messages stuck to those mirrors to reinforce his continuing influence. And when he was actually present? He was standing behind them, drip-feeding his influence directly via their reflections, his eyes fixed on theirs, being sympathetic and encouraging initially, offering friendship and, in Marion Cane's case, love, until they were both psychologically dependent on him. That's when the tone probably changed. He became abusive, demanding money, a change of will. I suspect he jeered at Marion's need for him, mocked Pearson Fleming's sexuality—' Watts saw his face contort. 'Did I touch a nerve there, Mr Redpath?'

'I have no idea what you're talking about. I came here at your request to assist your investigation. I've answered your questions to the best of my ability. I can't help you any further because I don't know what you want from me. What you've just said sounds like speculation—'

'We'll be examining your finances.' He watched the face opposite his harden. 'Marion Cane moved her money because she knew you'd got your hands on some of it, and the same for Pearson Fleming.'

Judd started as Watts' hand shot out, his finger pointing at the number plate. 'This is solid evidence! Your father hired the car to which *that* plate was attached and you used it to run down Fleming on the Rednal Road. We also have a witness who has identified *you* as responsible for an attack on her at the same ravine where Jack Beresford was found dead.' The phone rang. Watts stared at it. He had ordered a block on all calls for the duration of the interview. He reached for it, listened, finished the call, his eyes locked on to Redpath again.

'In case you haven't realized the bad situation you're in right now, that call has just made it even worse.' Getting zero response, he said, 'We've got your DNA on an item from Marion Cane's house.'

'I would remind you that I have acknowledged being inside that house—'

'So you have. Got any guesses as to where your DNA was
ound?'

There was a brief pause. 'A door handle, perhaps?'

'Think again! Marion Cane's sitting room. A place you know
xtremely well.'

'I do not.'

'A well-furnished room where *you* had sex with Marion
'ane.' Watts stood, his eyes fixed on the face opposite his. 'On
er *rug.*'

A mix of shock and surprise on the face opposite was extin-
uished as quickly as it arrived.

'Matthew Redpath, I'm arresting you for the murder of
Iarion Cane, the murder of Jack Beresford and the murder
f Pearson Fleming—' The officer stationed at the door moved
loser.

Redpath spoke. 'I categorically deny involvement in any of
10se deaths. All three accusations are laughable. I never knew
1is Beresford. My only connection to Mr Fleming and Ms Cane
/as one of helping and supporting them. My life to date, my
alling, is a testament to my support of others in need. If you're
lanning another interview, I shall not engage.'

Watts turned his back on him. 'Get him out of here.'

'hey left the interview room, Judd thinking about the first time
he met Redpath and how impressed she had been with his
incerity. 'I'm a useless judge of character.'

'No, you're not. Remember when you went to the church that
me and heard two people . . . at it? That turned out to be one
f the key moments in this investigation—'

Judd's head shot up. 'It was Redpath! And the vicar's *wife.*'

Traynor came into Watts' office, having watched the whole
iterview. 'Good work, Bernard.'

'I'm not anticipating getting any acknowledgement of respon-
ibility from him. I don't know how I managed to keep it together
1 there. The whole time, I felt like punching his lights out.'
Vatts turned to Adam, his big hand clapping him on the back.
'You're a star for getting that DNA evidence.' He shook his head.
I feel like I've run a marathon and he sat there as if every word
said to him meant nothing.' He shrugged. 'Not that it matters,
vith what we have on him.'

Traynor said, 'I'm anticipating he'll submit a plea of "N
Guilty".'

Watts stared. 'Never!'

Several days later

Connie Chong came into Watts' office. 'Ready to go?'

He looked up at her. 'Where?'

'You promised me dinner and G and Ts.'

'I did?'

Her brows lowered.

'I remember.' He patted his pockets, looking for his keys.

'You didn't book a table, did you? Which is OK, because I did

'Where?'

'My favourite starred restaurant.' She watched more pattin
of pockets. 'Now what?'

'Just wondering if you've got some money— Just kidding, n
need for violence.' He reached for the phone. 'I'll just ca
Traynor's mate, the psychiatrist, about Eric Brook. He's hopef
that by the time of the trial, and away from the influence and thre
from Redpath, Brook will be capable of giving evidence. I nee
to hear him confirm it.'

'Do it. It's the last time you talk shop this evening.'

That evening Judd opened her door to Ade Jones. 'Right on tim
I've got a heavy-duty casserole ready.'

'You *cooked*?'

'Less of the amazement! I do have *some* skills in that are
Come on, I've got drinks waiting.'

He followed her, plus some inviting aromas coming from th
direction of the kitchen. He grinned down at the little cat. 'Givin
yourself a manicure, Sass? I've got something for you.' H
opened the Amazon package and brought out an item, removin
the plastic bag around it. Sassy watched, her paws resting o
his leg.

Judd grinned. 'A fish toy, Sass! Yay!'

'More than that, Chlo! *This* is Floppy Fish. Hang on—'

He gave it a small thump and dropped it on the floor wher

t flip-flopped across the tiles. The cat took off, disappearing under a chair where she crouched, staring at it.

'*Sassy.*' Judd laughed. 'Where's your courage, *girl!*'

Late February

On arrival for the first day of the hearing, Watts was taken to one side by the prosecution barrister. 'As of this morning, he's still pleading Not Guilty to all charges.'

Watts nodded. 'It's not over yet.'

By four p.m. that afternoon, it was. Redpath had been found guilty of murdering Marion Cane and Pearson Fleming, the abduction of Jess, the jury unable to reach a decision on Jack Beresford's death. Watts was now inside his vehicle, entering the Queensway underpass, phone reception dropping like a brick. He had just managed to give Connie the gist of the outcome. It was part of what made the job difficult. People who beat the system and often got away with some or all of it. He regretted the verdict on Jack. His death would remain open, theoretically, although the judge in his careful summation had conveyed his view of Jack's death. After the verdicts, Watts had hung around inside the building, avoiding waiting journalists and questions as to whether the police really knew what they were doing, whether they had done all they could, were they worth taxpayers' money, and so on.

Leaving the underpass, he drove on, soon slowing at congestion at the traffic island ahead and waiting, people scurrying between vehicles. On a light change, he moved off, choosing a left-hand turn rather than face another island hold-up ahead, listening to the quiet hum of the BMW. Later, he and Connie would be eating out at the best curry restaurant in the city in his estimation. He would stop off on his way home and buy champagne. He and his team had got a result. An indeterminate sentence for Redpath. He felt himself starting to relax. Never ask for or expect perfection from anything. As-good-as-it-gets is enough.

*   *   *

Traynor came into his quiet house. Jess still hadn't replaced her car so he listened for sounds that she was here. He called her name heard noise from upstairs. She was still unsettled and he didn' want to startle her. He called again.

'Jess?'

'I'm coming.'

He stood, looking up as she came into view and walked down the stairs towards him.

'How did it go?'

He told her. 'At least he'll never be free.'

She walked away from him, looked out at the garden. 'I've arranged to go and stay with my mother for a few days.' She turned to look at him. 'I have to go, Will.'

'Is she ill?'

'No. I need some time to think.'

He went to her, put his arms around her. 'What happened to you, what he did, is difficult to handle—'

She disengaged from him. 'It's not about that, Will. It's about us.'

'I know my stress causes us problems, but working with Antor these last few weeks is making a real difference, Jess. I promise you I'll keep on top of it from now on. I'm sorry that the work I do put you in danger.'

She came to him. 'I don't blame you for that and I'm really pleased that you're in therapy again. The truth is we're both hostages to whatever news arrives relating to Claire. We've been so happy together—'

'We have. We *are*.'

'But I've suddenly realized that our life together, how happy we are, is determined by one single factor: Claire. It's true, Will and you know it.'

'I'm sorry,' he whispered.

'It's not your fault. It isn't anybody's fault. It's how it *is* and I can't see it changing—' Seeing tears fall, he went to her, put his arms around her.

'It will change. It already has.'

'Yes. Because there's been no news, no more developments in Oxford.' She pulled away from him. 'What's going to happen, Will, if next week, next month, there *is* some news? A small piece of evidence, a sudden breakthrough? I can tell you what will happen. It will take you over. You'll go there. You'll want to *know* everything the police know. You'll follow it up—'

'*No*—'

'You will! I understand. She was your wife and you loved her, and what happened to her and to you is the worst that could happen to anyone. I *get* it, but I don't think I can *live* it, waiting for the next time, watching you exhaust yourself because she's back with us. Between us. I'm sorry for what happened to her and to you, I truly am, but I never knew her, so I don't love her. I love *you* and I can't live like this, waiting for the next—' She covered her face with her hands and sobbed.

He went to her, held her close. 'I love you Jess and I understand and I'm sorry. Stay with me, please. Don't give up on us.'

They remained locked together, something he had been thinking about for a while coming into his head. 'Let's get married.'

She pulled away from him. 'How would that change what I've said? Nothing is going to change between us because Claire is dead and you won't rest until you know what happened to her. Until you do, she's with you, in your head and in your heart, and it feels like sometimes there's no room for *me*. I won't share you, Will.' She walked away from him. 'I'm going to phone my mother to let her know that I'll see her tomorrow.'

The following morning, he drove her to the station, found a temporary parking space. 'You'll phone to let me know when you're coming back?'

'Yes.'

They got out of the car. He fetched her holdall from the boot. 'I'll carry this inside—'

She took it from him, kissed him and walked to the concourse entrance.

'*Jess.*'

She turned as he came to her, threw his arms around her. After a minute or so, they separated. He watched her walk away until she merged into the vast, crowded concourse.

Arriving home, he listened to the silence, picking up the sounds of the dog coming towards him. 'How do you feel about a *long* walk, Boy?' The dog barked. Traynor watched him run to the front door, turn and look at him.

'Let's walk until we're too tired to think.'

ACKNOWLEDGEMENTS

This is my opportunity to express my gratitude to everyone who has helped and supported me during the writing of this book: my agents, Jade Kavanagh and Camilla Bolton, Kate Lyall-Grant and Joanne Grant, publishers at Severn House, and Sara Porter, my editor, for her unflagging patience and kindness.

Once more, I am indebted to Dr Colin L. Graham, Honorary Lecturer in Analytical Chemistry at the University of Birmingham, for his keenness and flair in respect of chemical 'weapons'. Thank you, Colin.

Thank you, all.

Ingram Content Group UK Ltd.
Milton Keynes UK
UKHW012013250723
425770UK00007B/348

9 781448 3080